# LIGHTS
# OUT

BAYNARD KENDRICK

# LIGHTS OUT

**WILDSIDE PRESS**

To

LIEUTENANT LLOYD GREENWOOD, U.S.A.A.F.
who has vision.

# Acknowledgment

*Lights Out* would not have been possible without the unending help and co-operation of the Surgeon General's Office, the staff and patients of Valley Forge General Hospital, and of Old Farms Convalescent Hospital (Sp.) and the enthusiastic interest of the boys who have sacrificed their sight so that the people of the world might have another chance to see.

B. H. K.

# Contents

BOOK ONE

# Overseas

# 1. THE WALL

THE truck slewed sideways over a hidden obstruction in the packed-down snow. Sergeant Larry Nevin twisted the wheel with frost-numbed hands. The muscles of his arms tightened and went into a fixed routine. His right leg straightened to touch a pedal with booted toe. The truck lumbered back into slimy wet ruts and bounced along.

"Those tires are slicker than a baby's behind," said Larry.

Beside him, P.F.C. Jimsey shifted his rifle to a more comfortable position across his knees and said, "Nuts, Sarge! You can't drive with your eyes shut tight. You've been asleep again. Let me take it."

"You don't know where we're going." Larry pulled a knit khaki muffler up tighter across his mouth. His lips were chapped and split, and talking caused him pain.

"Neither do you when you're sleeping."

"Why not?" asked Larry wearily. "I've made this haul so many times in the last forty-eight hours, I can drive it blindfold."

"Like hell," said Jimsey. "There we go again!" The wheels had dropped hard in an invisible hole. Larry Nevin set his teeth and swore as the rear end banged down on the axle and the overloaded body creaked a noisy protest.

The ruts leveled out. After a while, Larry and Jimsey began to talk again.

Jimsey asked, "What's the idea of driving forty-eight hours without a rest? Are you the only G.I. in France who can drive a truck, or are you personally trying to win the war?"

3

"I'm a sucker," said Larry. "I was born that way and can't help it. The engineers are bridging a river, and need stuff faster than the Krauts can blow it away."

"They're always building something for us to cross," Jimsey complained. "When I get back I'm going downtown to Brooklyn Bridge and look at it every day, but I'm never going across it."

Larry turned briefly and looked at the boy beside him. A growth of beard was thick on Jimsey's mud-daubed face. Beneath the rim of his helmet, his red eyes were sunk over cavernous cheeks. A filthy, nondescript uniform bulked large under part of a camouflaged parachute that Jimsey had salvaged somewhere and turned into a shawl.

"Christ!" said Larry. "Do I look as dirty as you?"

A grin touched Jimsey's mud-caked lips. "They'd throw you out of a fancy-dress ball." He peered through the shattered windshield. "Maybe you're right about me driving. I wish this stinking fog would let up. You can't see anything and neither can our fliers."

"We're running into the valley." Larry passed a map to Jimsey. "Take a look."

"I'd like to look at something with skirts on," said Jimsey.

"Or off," said Larry. "There was a girl down home—"

"Where's that?"

"Florida."

"I've been to Miami."

"So has everybody, including the Air Corps. This is a little town upstate—Palatka. It's on the St. Johns River."

"I don't know it."

"You wouldn't, Jimsey. It has a lumber mill, a furniture plant, and a lot of wholesale houses. That's about all. In the spring—"

"You were talking about a dame."

"Yeah. Chris is her name. She likes trout fishing, and I do too."

"Pretty?"

"Yeah. Pretty."

Larry checked himself; the road turned off somewhere soon. Chris had hair like honey and blue eyes that looked through you. Her dancing was something. She was cool and sweet, a bit bossy, maybe, from teaching kids in school, but cool and sweet like a Florida spring. You never got very close to Chris, but who ever got too close to a girl he was go'ng to marry?

A guy with any brains chose his future wife with care, adding up her points as one might buy a mule. After all, women fell definitely into one of two classes—those who did, and those who didn't. A girl in the first class was fun, but you never married one. She was something to take out with a bottle of whiskey, and investigate in the back seat of a car.

Larry Nevin wasn't a dope. He knew he was tall, dark and good-looking. God knows enough dames, including his mother, had taken pains to tell him so. Then why not pick the best? Chris was not only pretty; her father owned a barrel factory and lots of good potato land. Might as well have a father-in-law with dough.

Yessir! Landing Chris Paterson was a nice piece of business that lifted the Nevin family several rungs up the social scale. Of course, Larry's two years at the University of Florida placed him a shade above most of the boys in Palatka, but his status was lowered by working in a filling station during the summer.

Still he was a pretty smart apple, ready to take his place in the scheme of things after the war. He'd fit into Mr. Paterson's barrel factory nicely and help the old man handle things the way they should be handled. No foolishness from labor and uppity Negroes. That was one of the main troubles with the country—the Negroes were getting too damned independent. He'd heard his mother say so time after time. Now he was hooked firmly into the Army. Once he got home, he and a lot of other fellows would show them. The United States was never made to be run by the Negroes and the Jews.

The truck bounced on. Jimsey settled down, pulling the

tattered parachute tighter around him, either lost in thoughts of his own or respecting Larry's silence.

Larry flexed his fingers, seeking lost circulation. God in heaven! Once he'd bopped the Negro boy at the filling station for looking at Chris when she was wearing her yellow sweater. It had made him quite a hero in the eyes of everyone in town. The war had done something to him. Strange that, looking back, his heroism seemed a little silly.

He didn't hold much with religion, but some things he'd heard from the Bible stuck with him. Maybe because he thought they were dirty. There was a passage somewhere about lusting after a dame.

The Bible was full of those things, rising up to plague a guy when he thought he might die in the morning. Silly things like "Thou shalt not kill!" Things he'd have to fight out alone. He damn sure wasn't going to the minister, that smug Dr. Bannerman, if he ever got home, and ask for advice. That would be a picture!

"Well, well, God bless you, Larry, my boy. You've done a noble work for your country. Shall we kneel together and thank the Divine Providence that you're safely home again?"

"Tell me, Dr. Bannerman, should I tell Chris that I've mentally ripped her clothes off a dozen times while I was away? Should I ask her to forgive me for talking about her to other fellows? Actually she never seemed real to me while guys I knew were dying in bunches. My mind was full of marriage, but most of the marriage took place in bed. Is that what the Bible calls 'lusting' after a dame?"

"There's an M.P. ahead," said Jimsey, shifting his gun.

Larry braked the truck to a rattling stop, and the M.P. came up beside it.

"Where ya headed?" The leggings and armband on him, contrasted with his uniform, looked clean.

"Bridge at Co-ordinate forty-five and twenty-two."

"Road's out," he said tersely.

"I came through last night." Larry flapped his arms across his chest.

"You and Von Runsted," the M.P. said. "Go three miles down and take Thirteen."

"Mines?"

"If there are, you'll find them, won't you? It's supposed to be clean." He waved them on.

"A wise guy," said Jimsey. "I bet his sister went up on the roof with Polacks before she was sixteen."

"Can't you get your mind off women?" asked Larry.

"Sure," said Jimsey. "Let's talk about that Red Cross dame we met last spring in the London canteen."

The road grew worse. The snow-laden hedges thinned, and trees loomed out of the yellow mist pointing skyward with shattered branches. Litter, pushed to the roadside, lay shapeless and dead, remnants of tanks and German trucks; an ack-ack tilted sideways, silenced forever; beside a hedge, a formless thing that once was part of the Nazi fighting machine.

Larry slowed as they turned on Road Thirteen. Another M.P. appeared and waved them on. The road must be clean. Larry leaned from the cab and asked.

The M.P. came back with the standard question, "Where ya going?"

"Bridge at forty-five and twenty-two."

"You'll hit what's left of a village six miles from here. Ask there. It may be you can't get through."

"That would slay me," said Jimsey.

The truck moved on.

"What's the time?" asked Larry.

"Somewhere around eight." Jimsey shuddered. "Every day since this fog set in, I've hoped it would get warmed by noon. It never does. It's always the same at night or dawn. Listen!"

"Eighty-eights," said Larry. "Jesus! They're throwing everything in but Hitler's boy friend. One clear day, and our bombers could stop that."

"Sure," said Jimsey. "And the war'll be over by Christmas—next Christmas. Or will it? Maybe I'm wrong."

"I used to go hunting on Christmas Day," said Larry. "I had the best pointer in Florida. A dog called Tip. Sometimes Chris would come along. We'd leave home early in the morning. There'd be frost on the ground, and sometimes a mist on the roads. It wasn't filthy fog like this. It was white and clean, like cotton. I'd run the car into it and it would roll up into balls like powder puffs and bounce along. Then suddenly the sun would come up and all the fog would be gone. By noon we'd come home with ten or twelve quail. Mother would cook them for supper the day after Christmas."

Jimsey said, "I never went hunting. The only thing you could hunt in the Bronx is another bar. Watch where you're heading!"

"I guess I'm really sleepy as hell," said Larry. "What's that ahead to the right, Jimsey, a tank or part of a wall?"

"Maybe we've hit the village. Let's stop and have a look. I don't like it, Larry. Are you sure we're right?"

"We took Road Thirteen, if that's what you mean."

Larry cut the engine. If they were near a village held by Yanks, there should be men around—men and guns, jeeps and tanks.

The eighty-eights sounded closer. He could hear the drone of a single plane prowling about in the clouds overhead. Around the truck there was nothing but sickly yellow fog, dead as the things they had passed on the road.

It cleared a bit with a touch of breeze. Now he could see that the grayish bulk through the swirling fog was part of a ruined wall.

The guns ahead doubled. To the left of the road a mortar coughed, and as though by signal an American battery not far away opened with a fury that tore the fog to tatters. Smoke drifted in from somewhere, stinging Larry's eyes and nostrils.

He'd been through the whole damned thing before—so many times it was nothing but a bore. The shells would get closer, pinging into the back of the truck, maybe even shattering part of the already shattered windshield.

He started the engine. The chances were he'd have to drive from the road. He and Jimsey might find better shelter lying down close to the ruined wall. After too long a stretch of seeing guys dying around you, the war became impersonal. Death became impersonal. Fear was probably in you, but it became impersonal too. Nothing could really ever hit you. Somehow you *knew*.

A rifle cracked, slicing the deafening artillery with a sharper sound from close at hand.

Larry peered through the windshield to get a better view of the wall.

It was eight feet high at one corner, and snow had clung to its grayish stones that looked rotten with age. A large bare spot was near the top, and on it the lichens had made a pattern in greenish-gray. The pattern descended in ripples and rills to disappear behind the snow. It reminded Larry of some evil waterfall cascading down on a winter's day.

The stones that made up the wall were square and heavy, mortared tightly together. At the lowest end, an icicle had formed. It was glinting even in the dullish light of the foggy morning.

"That's a hell of a funny-looking wall," Larry said to Jimsey. "It must have been part of a church before it was shot away."

"There's a bastard—" Jimsey's voice sounded most peculiar.

Larry turned to look at him. He was slumped down strangely, plucking at the parachute that served him as a shawl.

"Jesus!" said Larry.

Jimsey was hit. It had happened again. Nobody ever got Nevin. He could fight like hell, drink like hell, and swear like hell, and nothing ever touched him. Shells and rockets and land mines blasted thousands around him, but he lived in a vacuum in the middle of the God-damned war.

"I'm in bed," said Jimsey feebly.

"Try to sit up, Jimsey. I've got to get you the hell out of here."

"I'm in bed now with a nice warm babe." Jimsey slumped down farther.

"Try to sit up, Jimsey. I have to drive like a bat out of hell. If you sit limp like that you'll fall." The last M.P. they'd passed could get Jimsey to the nearest medics. Larry tried to think back. The crossroads couldn't be very far.

Jimsey muttered, "There's a sniper—"

"Try to sit up, Jimsey. Let me help you."

"Keep away, Larry. I'm in bed now with a nice warm babe—"

Larry leaned forward to release the brake. There wasn't any time to argue. He'd have to drive on anyhow. His hand was on the lever when something pinged and hit his forehead with no more shock than a blown pea.

Jimsey and the parachute vanished. Everything vanished. It was utterly ridiculous. He'd be okay in a second, for nothing ever got Nevin.

He'd rest a moment and pull himself together. Right now the only thing in his head was a picture of the wall.


## 2 . JIMSEY

IT WAS very dark and the guns were very loud. Somehow they had blended all together, German and American, until the noise had become a ball, and the ball in turn had grown into a sphere the size of a planet. The individuality of each weapon was lost entirely. One blast melted into another. Life might go on forever like that, and Larry rather liked it. In such a world there was no necessity for thinking. Death was triumphant, lending a touch of grandeur to the whole silly performance.

The trouble was that the sound had set up vibrations, and the vibrations had given Larry a headache. It was a purple headache, full of little rills and ripples, something like the waterfall of lichens on the wall. It was a headache of entity and being, a major pain bearing an authority of its own.

It was strange that the headache was similar to the guns, a formation of individual pains, each as distinguishable as the separate drops of the waterfall, yet each indistinguishable because the drops were one.

Undoubtedly, he was suffering from an illusion. The Army was full of illusions, creeping on you to disturb your restless sleeping. Rarely were illusions good. The majority had to do with heat and cold; marked discomfort, such as toothaches, and vivid warnings of coming death and danger. Sometimes, sleeping curled up in the truck, there were illusions that the truck was moving, running wild for the German lines. Occasionally, just to make the others worse, came an illusion that Chris was sleeping beside you, or that you were safely tucked in your bed at home.

Now it was a headache. He could turn over and easily dispel it, but the effort was a hell of a lot of trouble. Maybe the easiest course was to brush it away with his hand. The pain was bound to vanish once he plunged his fingers into the dreamy waterfall.

He found he couldn't move his arm and decided to wait. The Army was full of waiting. Wars were full of waiting—damn little fighting, just waiting. Waiting for A,B,C,D, and V Day. Wait long enough and, like death, things finally come along. After a while the headache would vanish, probably when the truck quit jouncing him up and down.

"Jimsey!" His own voice sounded muffled.

"Take it easy, Sergeant." A hand touched his shoulder. "Cigarette?"

"Yes." That's what he wanted—a cigarette. Funny he hadn't noticed it before. A smoke would be ideal; might even stop the bouncing. It wasn't a truck after all. The entire world was bouncing. How the hell could it be a truck, when he and Jimsey were lying on the ground?

"It's lit. Just drag."

A cigarette went between his lips, hurting the spot that
was chapped and cracked. He dragged deep, thinking about
the voice that wasn't Jimsey's, thinking about the darkness
and his headache, thinking about the warmth of his eyes and
the uselessness of his arm.

"You're not Jimsey." He trickled out smoke and inhaled
again. Who had said tobacco smoke didn't taste when you
couldn't see it?

"No." The cigarette vanished, wafted off by some disem-
bodied hand. The voice and the hand had some connection
with each other. One motivated the other, or vice versa. Maybe
he was a prisoner of war. Nazis who spoke English had filtered
inside the American lines. If he was a prisoner, he'd be blindfolded. Sergeant Larry Nevin, missing in action, prisoner of
war. His head hurt worse with the effort to understand.

The cigarette came back again. "Just drag."

"Who are you?"

"Reynolds. A medic."

"Where's Jimsey?"

"Jimsey?"

"The guy who was with me." His mind was clearer now,
but he wasn't going to let them know. Prisoners were always
questioned. The fog was still thick and damp around him,
though it felt much warmer. He might say something he didn't
intend to say if he let himself go. Some people talked on
awakening, when thoughts were part of a murky dawn.

"Oh. Jimsey's okay." The cigarette vanished. Reynolds was
good, whoever he was. He understood about cigarettes, had a
feeling for them. A cigarette choked you if you kept it in
your mouth too long.

Reynolds wasn't going to fool Larry with his skillful kind-
ness. That was a Nazi trick. Be kind. Then when you find the
guy won't talk, quit being kind.

Larry decided to use a trick of his own. He'd ask the voice
some questions. If it answered, he'd play dumb.

"Is Jimsey a prisoner of war?"

"A prisoner? What makes you think that, Sergeant?" Reynolds sounded funny.

"I thought maybe—"

"Why don't you try to sleep now, Sergeant?"

"I thought maybe you'd captured him too."

"What do you mean—'too'?"

"Like me. A prisoner of war."

"For cripe's sake, you're not a prisoner! You're in an American ambulance."

"What's the blindfold for?"

"That's a head dressing, not a blindfold."

"Why can't I see?"

"It's over your eyes. You got a nasty head wound, but you're okay now."

"You mean—?" A finger of ice touched the base of Larry's spine. He didn't know what he meant.

"They bandaged your head at the battalion aid station," Reynolds explained. "Now you're on your way to the collecting station. Don't you remember?"

"No," said Larry. "I must have drawn a blank somewhere. I remember Jimsey and a wall. Where's Jimsey?"

"He's okay. Now try to sleep."

"This damn thing bounces."

"They've been shelling the road. They're giving it another dose right now."

"Why can't I see?"

"It's over your eyes. The bandage."

"What for?"

"Sulfa packs."

"On my eyes?"

"On your forehead. Does it hurt you?"

"My head aches."

"You'll be okay."

"Why can't I use my arms?"

"You're wrapped in a blanket."

"Will they take off the packs at the station?"

"Maybe. We're getting there now."

The annoying jouncing slacked and after a time stopped altogether. Doors opened. Voices spoke, most of them subdued with caution. Larry caught a phrase about Diffenbachles-Hellimer. He began to move, sliding along feet foremost, blankets tight around him. He felt himself lowered gently and jogging along. He had it now. He was lying on a litter. His cheeks stung in a sudden contact with icy air.

Then he was warm again. The jogging stopped as the litter was set down. Men were around him, some groaning softly, some just breathing. The smell of medicaments was heavy. Blankets slid from around him, scratching slightly, until his right arm was bare.

"How are you feeling, son?" A warm hand touched his wrist and stayed there, pressing with a professional finger.

"I'm okay, sir." He recognized the surety of an officer's tone. "My head aches."

"We'll soon fix that."

A needle stung his arm. He tried to raise it to touch his head, but the blankets returned to pinion him. He relaxed, taking refuge behind a screen of pinkish dots that were making designs on a background of swimming yellow—colors that had come from nowhere.

"Are my eyes okay?" He asked the question without entirely caring. The dots were thick and comforting, but the thought of his eyes was on his mind and the question provided something to say.

"Sure thing, son," the officer said.

"I can't see with this bandage on."

"You stopped one with your head, son. I'm afraid for a while the bandage will have to stay." A hand rested lightly on his shoulder. "Good luck, son."

The dots whirled swiftly. Larry drifted away.

An ambulance was moving again, but he didn't mind it.

The road felt smooth, the speed was slow, and the dancing dots were full of comfort.

Hazily, the rolling stopped and the litter went through space again. Blankets moved. Voices spoke. A needle stung his thigh.

"Drink this, bud."

A tube went between his tender lips. Larry sucked on it gently and coffee trickled down his throat, dreamlike coffee that warmed and thrilled him. A washcloth laved his mud-caked face. Under its touch he slept again.

He was being lifted from a third Army ambulance when the pleasant mist of morphine narcosis began to disperse. A familiar sound was missing—the rumble of artillery. Larry stirred on the litter.

"How ya coming?" The litter was lowered.

"Where am I now?"

"Nancy."

Larry thought that over. He wanted to sleep, to drop back into the wonderful world of whirling dots where there were no headaches, no thoughts that he dared not voice to himself, no icy fingers to touch his spine.

"What's at Nancy?" he forced himself to say.

"Evacuation hospital."

"Hospital?"

"Yes."

"Hospital? How long do I stay?"

A paper rustled against his blanket. "That depends. You're lucky. You may be leaving for home now any day. Here. Hold this under your tongue."

A thermometer slid into his mouth, and suddenly he realized he was wounded. Larry Nevin, casualty. He remembered Jimsey, remembered the wall. It must have been a year ago. The Army was slow. He'd go on forever, jolting, stopping and riding, always in darkness. The pain in his head would never stop. What was the use of going home?

The thermometer was taken out. The litter moved, was

rearranged, and moved again. "We're giving you a little shot of plasma, Sergeant. Lie quite still."

Another needle, this time finding a vein.

Footsteps passing. Voices speaking, always low. Damn it all, did everyone have to mutter? They were keeping something from him, holding back the terrible truth, all of them scared he would hear what they had to say.

He asked quite loudly, "Are my eyes all right?"

A voice said, "Sure," and the casualness calmed him. "You were hit in the head."

"They told me that. How long ago was it?"

"Just a few hours."

"Like hell it was. I've been traveling weeks."

"You were hit this morning. The medics found you on Road Thirteen. It's only three in the afternoon. Easy now." Larry felt the needle leave his arm. The voice went on. "We can tell you more about your head wound after we make an x-ray."

"Is Jimsey here?"

"Who's Jimsey?"

"The guy who was with me. I was trying to help him when that goddam sniper got me."

"I'll have to find out. You guys keep pouring in. I'll let you know." The litter moved. "Steady now. Can you turn your head? That's the boy. We're going to shoot an x-ray."

Electricity buzzed and crackled.

Larry dozed again, and after a while he was slid off onto a table. There were many people standing around. The air was pungent with ether.

He felt very ill, and his forehead hurt, and the bandage was tighter across his eyes. He moved a little and said, "I'm thirsty."

A girl's voice answered. "Good morning, Sergeant." She hadn't been there a minute before. Her fingers were cool as they touched his cheek. It might have been Chris. She slipped some ice into his parched, dry mouth, and it tasted good.

"Why is it dark if it's morning?" asked Larry. "I thought it was only three o'clock. That guy was nuts."

"Your eyes are bandaged." She gave him more ice. "You've slept all night. This is another day."

"How long will I be here?"

"If you feel all right, they may fly you to England tomorrow. Do you want more ice?"

"No. Are my eyes okay?" She would tell him the truth.

"Don't worry, Sergeant. Try to sleep some more. Your eyes are okay." She touched his cheek with her fingers and left.

He started to call her to ask about Jimsey, but decided not to. Somehow this morning he knew about Jimsey. Guys you met in a fighting army came and went away.

# BOOK TWO

# Valley Forge General Hospital

# 3. THE WHISTLE

SOMEONE was whistling.

The whistle had been going on for quite a while, beating against Larry Nevin's ears with a scratching persistence that he found most irritating. It was a casual whistle, varying from a few soft notes pushed between somebody's pursed-up lips to an equally soft staccato obbligato from between the teeth, blending into the noise of footsteps and the clank of dishes.

Forty-eight hours before, he had been hoisted into the cabin of an A.T.C.'s four-engine Douglas C-54. That was in Paris, France. At least, that's what had been told him. For seven days, since the sniper's bullet struck him, he had seen absolutely nothing. For a whole week he had found himself dependent on information received from others by word of mouth.

In the same length of time, he had learned to distrust that information. Doctors and nurses had been evasive. His bandages had been removed and dressings changed. Night, they had told him, yet he'd always been able to see at night. Wounds, they had told him—something about a plastic job on one of his eyes, a necessity of avoiding strong lights, and proceeding with lots of caution.

"Just lie quiet, Sergeant, and take it easy. Your eyes are going to be all right."

"How long?"

"Those things take time."

"How long?" Five days of absolute blackness. What did they know about time?

"Colonel Green at Valley Forge is an absolute wizard," they'd told him in France. "He can tell you more than we can. That's why we're flying you home."

So now he was home, or at least in the U.S.A. Thirty hours in a thrumming transport plane and he was home. Boy, this was what he had dreamed about in Africa, in Italy, in England and in France.

This was it, no kidding! This was driving down Palatka's main street—Lemon Street—but the name wasn't funny to Larry Nevin. There was sun on the red brick sidewalks, cokes in the drug store, and the bar next to the James Hotel.

There was sun on the St. Johns River, and hyacinths choking the waterway, and a clear space by the drawbridge where a freight boat had just plowed through.

There was cornbread for supper, grits and gravy for breakfast, and greens from the garden cooked with pork for dinner.

There was Chris by his side looking happy and proud, a greeting from the Mayor, a kiss from his mother, a handclasp from Dad, and the smell of drying cypress in the air.

Millions of feet of cypress lumber stacked along the river. Just about dusk the bats came out of the lumber piles. God knows how many bats. For fifteen minutes they'd stream up into the sky, making a filmy cloud between earth and the shining sunset. He liked the bats. They caught mosquitoes and frightened Chris, who pressed up closer against him.

What had made him think of the bats? Like hell he was home!

Even in the short time he'd been at Valley Forge he'd heard about the mural. George Washington sitting, chin in hand, staring out at the endless plains.

What was the difference then or now? A hundred brick buildings, crammed to the hilt with wounded men? Valley Forge Hospital or Valley Forge, what was the difference? 1777 or 1945? The endless plains were still covered with snow. The air was still icy with biting chill. Americans were still suffering. There wasn't any difference, except that the Americans were a little warmer now, and Sergeant Larry Nevin was among them.

Damn the man who was whistling! He was whistling like a little boy, whistling like a fisherman waiting for a cork to bob, whistling like a nitwit full of idiotic happiness. He couldn't even carry the simplest tune.

Didn't he know that Larry Nevin's eyes were bandaged, that Larry Nevin might never be able to see?

Or would he?

He began to listen to sound in the ward. Already, in just a few hours, he had learned to recognize the nurse's footsteps, lighter than those of the men about him.

Her voice had been nice, but had showed no trace of sympathy. She'd have been very sorry to know that Larry couldn't see. In seven days his mind had grown keener, searching for clues, seeking an answer, suspicious of voices. Surely if the nurse had thought that his eyes were injured she'd have betrayed herself by showing him sympathy.

"Don't you want any supper, Sergeant?"

"No." Larry realized that a tray had lain untouched across his knees for quite a long time. How did the idiots think he could eat with his eyes bandaged tight?

The man who was speaking laughed softly. "I offered to feed you, but you snapped my head off. Would you like some help now?"

"No, goddam it!" said Larry. "I'm not hungry, I tell you." He wanted to hurt people, kick them and bruise them. They were all such fools.

The tray was lifted. The man said, "Have it your way."

"I want to see the doctor," said Larry. "I have a right to see him, haven't I?" He felt ugly and surly. "I'm not in here with chickenpox. I just got back from overseas."

"Sit tight, Sergeant. Captain Phelan's very busy. There're a couple of other fellows in Ward One, in case you don't know it. And more in Ward Fourteen. Have a little patience and the captain will be along." The man went off with the tray.

The whistler stopped. Larry heard voices, and after a moment laughter. He turned over in bed and covered his ears. They were talking about Larry Nevin. He knew it, felt it, was certain. If he listened closely, he might hear it all, but he didn't want to. He wanted to die, not go through life an object of people's pity, a subject for their talk and laughter.

All day men had come near and spoken, fellows who sounded friendly. Each time, he had refused to answer, and each time they had gone away. He was glad of it now. He'd make his way through life alone. Palatka would never see him, for he'd never see Palatka. He'd find a city where no one knew him, and live a life alone and friendless. A dog, perhaps, but no one else, no one who could laugh and mock him.

The plaintive whistle started again, beating through the guard of his covered ears. In a flash, he realized that he was being very silly.

He didn't know. He hadn't yet talked to the doctor. The men in Ward One were walking around, not stumbling and falling. They had come to visit, offered him smokes, been introduced by a sergeant. They were laughing and singing. One of them persisted in everlastingly whistling.

Three of the men in beds quite near him had gone out to bowl that afternoon, and were talking about a dance in town in the evening. Some were even going to a picture show. If his eyes were injured he wouldn't be in with men like that. Without his eyes, he was scared to move, couldn't even eat, had stayed in bed all day.

He pushed himself up from the pillow, and dropped back again. The nurse's feet were crossing the ward accompanied by another pair. Inside of Larry, a great light flamed. Captain Phelan was finally coming to tell him his eyes were okay.

They stopped by his bed and he gave them a grin. A paper rustled.

Captain Phelan said, "I'm glad to see you're feeling better,

Larry. Is something wrong with the feed in here? You haven't eaten a bite all day."

Larry liked the sound of the tired voice, the voice of a man who had seen a lot. He'd know the truth, and no kidding now; how soon he could see, how long the interminable blackness would last, how many operations. This man would know and tell him before he left him.

"I haven't been hungry, Captain."

"He's had his trays," the nurse put in, "and sent them away untouched."

The captain laughed. "What you need is exercise, Larry. You should have been up and taken a walk around Valley Forge. It's cold outside, but it's been a beautiful day. Anyhow, our corridors are warm."

Larry didn't reply. Skillful fingers were touching his bandage. Scissors snipped.

"Turn your head this way," the captain said. "I'm going to remove the packs from your eyes and shine in a light. It won't hurt at all, Larry."

"I'm not afraid of its hurting, sir." Larry's tongue felt dry. "I'm afraid of—" He faltered and added, "—not seeing. I want to know if my eyes will be okay."

"This is a test for refraction."

Larry didn't ask what refraction meant. There was only one test for the human eye—could it see?

The packs came off and the world was dark, dark and very quiet. Even the plaintive whistle had ceased. Larry felt metal touch his cheek, and his nose was grazed by a finger. The metal moved to his other cheek.

"Is the light on, Captain?"

"Yes, Larry. It's on."

"You're sure it's on?"

"Certain, Larry." The voice was very tired.

"Now turn it out."

"It's out now, Larry."

"It doesn't make any difference, Captain. Are the lights on now, in the ward, I mean?"

"They're on, and it's still quite light outside. It's only six."

"Six in the evening?"

"Yes, Larry."

"There's nothing over my eyes right now?"

"Nothing."

"What about the test, Captain, the—"

"The refraction?"

"Yes."

"It's not so good."

"But you said there was nothing over my eyes. Why can't I see, Captain Phelan? Why can't I see if the lights are on and it's still only six, almost day?"

"Your right eye was hit with a bullet, Larry. It's badly damaged."

"You mean it's gone?"

"Not gone entirely, but badly damaged. I think Colonel Waters—"

"Can save it?"

"He's the plastic surgeon, Larry. He can make it look much better."

"And Colonel Green can save it?"

"You'll have to ask him tomorrow. I wouldn't want to say."

"But, Captain—"

"Yes, Larry?"

"The left eye's okay? Colonel Green can operate. They told me in England that Colonel Green is a wizard. The colonel can do anything. That's the truth, isn't it, Captain Phelan?"

"Ask him tomorrow, Larry." The captain turned and spoke to the nurse.

"Captain!" Larry stretched out a hand in the darkness. The captain's strong fingers closed about it. "Tell me the truth. I can't wait until tomorrow. I've waited too long in blackness now."

"Can you take it, Larry?"

"I asked you."

"That bullet destroyed your optic nerves."

"And Colonel Green—"

"He's not God, Larry."

"You mean I'm—" There was still a word he'd never be able to say. "You mean it's lights out forever, Captain? I'll never see?"

"I'm afraid so, Larry."

He lay for a long time clinging fast to the captain's hand. When the captain unloosed his fingers to replace the bandage, Larry started to cry gently.

His mind was full of sunshine, dappling the St. Johns River, making shadows under the pine trees, running riot in Chris's bright hair.

The nurse and the captain went away, and after a time the nurse came back and touched his arm.

"Drink this, Sergeant. You've had no food and there's something in it to help you sleep."

Larry sat up and drank it. He was one of the bats in the lumber pile, buried forever in darkness. He'd drink anything, eat anything, try anything—except living. For living he didn't care.

Yet he'd have to go on. The sniper had played him the dirtiest trick of all—or maybe it was the medics who had saved him—the medics and the meddling doctors, proud as hell of their sulfa and their plasma. Jesus Christ, once in a war you couldn't even decently die!

Thumbs up, Nevin! "V"—for Victory! Atta baby, big boy, carry on! Carry your little tin cup and get yourself some pencils. Listen close and hear the pennies fall!

You can't see the women shrink away in horror. You can't see the people pass with a smile of pity. You can't see the tears on the cheeks of your weeping mother. You can't see a thing in the whole damned world. What in the name of God are you worrying for?

Maybe the nurse is giving you poison. Drink it quick, for

everything is ended. You're just another sightless man, and a man without eyes is nothing. Here's a toast to nothing—a toast to darkness! A good stiff toast in poison—the eyeless man's only joy!

The whistle started across the ward. He lowered the glass from his lips and yelled, "Quit it, goddam it, quit it! My eyes are gone. Do you hear me, you fool? My eyes are gone. I can't tell night from day."

"He doesn't hear you, Sergeant." The nurse took the glass from his fingers. "That's Corporal Bruce. He's deaf and blind and minus an arm. When he's feeling tops, he whistles. None of us mind."

"Blind. Blind. Blind. Blind!" The nurse had said it—come right out flat-footedly with the word he'd been avoiding—the only word that could make him weak with fear. Corporal Bruce was deaf and *blind*. What the hell did deafness matter? What the hell was losing an arm?

Larry Nevin was blind. Just keep on repeating it. Say it over a million times. Burn it into your feeble brain.

"Blind as a bat—blind—blind—blind."

Maybe if you say it enough you'll be able to say it right out loud someday!

## 4. THE LETTER

IT MUST be morning.

In this strange world, the factor of time had become a major problem. All your life you woke from sleep and opened your eyes. If it was light outside, you looked at the clock. In ten or fifteen minutes the hands would creep around to seven, the alarm would go off, and you'd have to get up or be late for school. If it wasn't light outside, you gave a sigh and settled down to sleep some more.

Sometimes you remembered it was Saturday. Then you

turned over, dug deeper in the covers, and waited for your
mother to call, "Larry!"

For a while you pretended you didn't hear. Outside the sun
was bright, already climbing high. In back of the house, Tip
was barking at the neighbor's chickens. That was a fake. He
was letting you know he was ready for an afternoon of hunting. He always barked when he heard your mother call.

Then a bullet came . . .

It must be morning.

A smell of food was in the air. Miss Bailey, the nurse, was
talking to someone across the ward. Her voice was cheery.
Dishes clanked on trays. A fellow was singing:

> "I landed at the beach in Anzio.
> Along came an .88; got to go.
> I got the .88 blues."

That was a hell of a serenade for early in the morning. The
German .88 was a blinder, filling the air with a million lancet-
sharp slivers of steel. If those slivers ever hit a man's face—

> "—got to go.
> I got the .88 blues."

Anger surged through Larry. He really had to go. God, it
was worse than being a kid again. At least a baby had diapers.
Did they expect him to lie there in blackness all morning and
wet the bed? Maybe he was just supposed to scream.

He swung his legs over the side of the bed and pushed down
the covers. The anger gave way to self-pity as he reached down
with a probing toe to touch the floor.

What now? Grope around and shove his hands in some
fellow's face, or ask Miss Bailey? He'd be damned if he would!
He'd use the bedpost first. No woman was going to take him
by the hand and lead him to the latrine.

"Are you Sergeant Larry Nevin?"

"Yes." It was a man's voice, at any rate. That was something.

"I'm Corporal Flagg—Jim Flagg. I'm glad to see you're up."

A hand touched his. Larry set his teeth and shook it. "It'll be my job to show you around until you get the hang of things," Flagg went on. "Here are your slippers and a dressing gown."

Larry put them on. It seemed a tiny triumph, and he was grateful to Flagg for not helping.

"Do you want to wash up before breakfast?"

"My back teeth are floating," said Larry.

Flagg laughed. "Why didn't you say so? Here, take my arm with your left hand. Lightly. That's it. You'll learn never to let anybody push or propel you."

Larry found himself following Flagg with growing confidence.

"Feel the right edge of the mat with your foot," Flagg told him after the first few steps. "You'll be on to it after a couple of tries and follow it right from your bed in to the latrine."

They went through a door. Flagg closed it behind them and touched Larry's hand to the edge of a toilet seat. "There you are, Larry. Go to it."

He felt much better. He was twenty-three years old, and up until the time he was hit in France life had plodded on for him in a most ordinary routine. A small Southern town, parents of very moderate means, a memory of a depression, a haphazard education with a couple of years at the University of Florida, and then the war.

He had sensed an almost complete retrogression during his three years in the Army, a return to some bestial state of civilization which he found it difficult to comprehend.

The sniper's bullet had temporarily blacked out not only sight, but thinking. The captain's words the night before had closed a door. Now, performing a simple bodily function had given Larry a rebirth into a startling new existence. It was frightening, but palliating the fright was an interesting challenge, the challenge to live and learn things in a brand-new world, the challenge of life that is felt by a growing girl or boy.

Under Jim Flagg's guidance, he began to explore the latrine, mastering the layout by sense of touch: the height and depth of the bathtub, the lid and flushing of the closet, the hot and cold spigots of tub and basin. It was amazing how many confusing things were compressed inside of a bathroom: the location of soap and toilet paper, steam pipes that could burn the hands, elusive stoppers dangling on a chain.

As they left the latrine, Flagg instructed him how to use his arm, either left or right, and warned against groping. "Hold your arm straight out in front, Larry, parallel to the floor. Good. Now bend your forearm across your chest at right angles to your upper arm."

Larry tried it.

"No, not so low," Flagg corrected. "Your forearm also should be parallel to the floor. Good! Now extend and relax your fingers. They'll protect the far side of your body. Your extended arm protects your face. Here, try it and see." He demonstrated on the open door. "Can you find your bed without my help?"

"I can try," said Larry. "I'll follow the edge of the mat with my foot, same as I came in."

"Keep your arm up," Flagg cautioned.

Larry turned from the mat when he thought he was right, took two steps and struck his arm against a wall. The disappointment was crushing. He had built up hopes and now they were gone. He'd never find his way around, never be good for anything at all.

"Swell!" Flagg chuckled. "That's as good a first try as I've ever seen."

"I'm lost," said Larry.

"You're never lost. Put out your right hand and feel," said Flagg.

Larry's fingers touched cold round metal. He moved them downward and felt a pillow. He was safe back home. The head of his bed was up against the wall.

"Your tray's on the bed," Flagg told him. "I'll get a chair. You can use your bed for a table."

Larry listened as the chair was moved. He'd never listened to chairs before.

Flagg said, "You'll soon be eating in the mess hall," as Larry sat down.

"There's cereal in a package, cream and sugar, coffee, toast and butter, and two hard-boiled eggs on your tray," Flagg told him. "Shall I fix them for you?"

"No." Larry reached out tentative fingers. He was facing this the rest of his life, this reaching into nothing for unfamiliar objects to be put in his mouth and swallowed.

Two peculiar round things were in a china dish. He moved them slightly. He never knew that eggs felt like that. He could tell they were eggs from their queer lopsided roll. A box was snug in its binding of waxed paper. He fumbled with it, turning it over and over, seeking an opening. One hand slipped and struck a cup. Hot liquid spilled.

Flagg said nothing as Larry swore.

Larry wiped his fingers on the dressing gown and went at the box again. At last he found an opening, shoved in a finger and grinned as the paper tore. He pried open a pasteboard top, located the bowl, and tested the cornflakes with his finger to make sure they were going to pour. When the dish was full he added cream from the pitcher.

The sugar was a problem. He wished that Flagg wasn't watching. He felt like a fool.

"I'll show you a trick," said Flagg. "Spread your fingers wide over the bowl, palm down, and sprinkle the sugar through. You can use it for salt and pepper too."

It worked. He didn't object when Flagg showed him how to peel the eggs. It was sort of a game. A hell of a game. A game with a single player. Larry Nevin learning to eat without slopping himself at the age of twenty-three. Well, by God, he'd learned once. Give him time, and he'd show them what he could do.

After breakfast he learned to shave.

Strangely it brought home more clearly than eating the fact that every phase of life would have to be mastered anew. Yet he realized that with the new he would cling to the old and familiar. In the latrine, with his shaving brush ready, he located the mirror and stood before it. There were habits that couldn't be broken, habits you didn't want to break. Men used a mirror for shaving. It was the sensible thing to do.

The lather went on by a sense of feel. Flagg warned him about the razor blades. They must be handled with care and disposed of with caution, positively never left around. The familiar blades were objects of danger to men who couldn't see.

Again Flagg showed him a trick or two. You kept sideburns of equal length by putting an arm across your head, feeling the sideburn and shaving up to your fingers. Some fellows kept dark glasses on and shaved up to the rims, but Flagg considered the technique poor.

Shaved and dressed, he went to talk to Lieutenant Bob Atkins, who received him in a little room.

"Hello, Larry." The lieutenant shook hands across a desk. "I'm glad to see you're up and around so soon. Cigarette?"

"Thanks," said Larry. He reached out and after a second or two a cigarette touched his hand.

"Have you matches?"

"Yes, sir," said Larry.

"Try laying one flat along the cigarette with the head of the match near the tip and striking them both at the same time. Then hold the match right there and puff until you get a light."

Larry found it worked. "That's neat, sir."

"Yes," said Atkins. "There's a chair behind you. Make yourself comfortable, Larry. We have a lot of talking to do. It's my job here to answer questions, tell you something of Valley Forge—the doctors you'll see, and the instructors. I can also tell you about the Veterans' Bureau. They'll look after your pension when you're discharged. You'll have a couple of hundred a month coming to you."

"When can I go home?" Larry asked him.

"I was waiting for that." The lieutenant laughed softly. "I've talked to a couple of hundred of you fellows and that's never missed as question number one. The answer is—it depends entirely on you."

"I'd leave today," said Larry quickly.

"I don't doubt it." Atkins laughed again. "The only thing is that when you do get home we want you to feel at home. We want to make sure you can walk around your house and your own home town, that you can eat with ease, dress yourself, take care of your clothes, and ride a bus. We're going to teach you something of Braille, a little workshop, and the right technique of using a cane. When you can pass a test showing us that you're good enough, you'll get a month's furlough."

"How long will that take me, Lieutenant? To learn to pass that test, I mean."

"Six weeks, possibly. You're pretty quick from what Corporal Flagg has told me. Maybe you can do it in less. It's pretty easy."

Larry stiffened in his chair. He found an ashtray on the desk and disposed of his smoke. How the devil could a man with vision know what was pretty easy? How could he know about hard-boiled eggs, a cereal box, and the long, long road between bed and latrine? How could he dream of pants and shirt that hid themselves, of a million things that Larry Nevin had learned in a day?

"There'll be a lot of tests right now," the lieutenant was saying. "Psychiatric, neurological, x-rays, and all that sort of thing. Then you'll have classes in Braille and typing."

"I had some typing in high school."

"That's fine. It will help you on your way. Flagg will help you in orientation and travel, and also Lieutenants Harkness and Conklin. You'll meet them today. I understand you have a minor plastic job. Colonel Waters is working overtime.

There are a couple of thousand men in here. You'll have to sit tight until your turn comes along." He suddenly paused, then asked, "Have you written home, Larry?"

"How the hell—" Larry checked himself. "No, sir. I haven't."

"Why not?"

"I guess I didn't want to. Maybe I didn't know what to say."

"Why don't you write a letter right now?"

"Myself, you mean?"

"Sure. Your folks will like it, in your own handwriting. Here's a fiberboard, some paper and a pencil. Take them."

Larry reached out and found a heavy piece of corrugated cardboard, the ridges spaced apart about the width of a tablet line. Clipped to its surface was a sheet of paper.

"Use the index finger of your left hand to mark the line you're writing on," the lieutenant suggested. "Follow the pencil with it, then when you finish a word you can keep track of the spacing by putting the pencil up to it before you start the next word. Take your time—the furrows will guide your pencil."

"What shall I tell them?" Larry asked the question desperately. He didn't want the lieutenant to leave him.

"The truth," said Atkins. "Say what you have to say." He went out and closed the door.

The pencil moved, but it might have been the pointer on a Ouija board, for it wrote on its own, without Larry's conscious control . . .

DEAR DAD:

The last letter I got from you said you had a promotion. I'm glad to hear this, Dad. It will mean a lot to Mother and you.

Dad, I'm here in Valley Forge Hospital. I'm sending this to the plant to you. When I tell you the truth, I'm sure you'll know how to tell Mother. Don't shock her, Dad. You'll know what to do.

I was hit in France by a sniper. He got me through the temple. I'm not hurt bad, but my eyes are gone. I don't mean gone entirely. I mean I'm blind. Completely blind. But I'm already learning to get around. I wrote this myself. Give Chris my love and tell her too. You're smart, Dad. You know what to do.

The lieutenant came back and sat down at the desk. Larry pushed the letter across.

"Is that okay, sir?"

Atkins chuckled. "You'll have to ask Corporal Flagg, Larry. I just work here. They gave me mine at Anzio—the .88 blues. I'm just as blind as you."

## 5. ANOTHER WALL

TIME was slipping by slowly. Out of the blackness a pattern was emerging. At first it was a jumble—a great mass of unrelated sounds and objects which Larry could hear, smell, taste and feel. The sum total made no sense, for all of it was dominated by darkness.

A blind man might recognize a jar of dried beans by feeling its shape, by plunging his fingers inside, and by listening to the swishing rattle of the contents when he shook the jar. That didn't prove he could ever learn to identify a single bean, once it was hidden with others in the jar.

Yet the beans began to grow and change as days went by. With their growth, they took on different shapes, losing their puzzling similarity. Then the pattern began to emerge. There were far more things beneath the sun than met the eye.

Corporal Jim Flagg became a set of footsteps that walked with unusual sureness, a laugh that was throaty, a voice that was smooth and could express great sarcasm without apparently changing tone. By the length of his stride when walking beside him, Larry learned that Flagg was tall.

The officers were taking form: Colonel Green, who never hurried you, who showed such interest in your eyes and your family; Colonel Waters, who could make a fellow without a

face go home looking like Gable. Colonel Waters was easy to
spot by the tone of his voice when he called you "son."

Captain Phelan, in charge of the ward, was another easy
one. At times his voice was tired, at other times it was quick
and decisive. He had an unexpected laugh that went off like a
gun.

Lieutenant Conklin and Lieutenant Harkness shared the
same office in Ward Fourteen. They were in charge of training and travel—which wasn't exactly travel, but meant getting
around on your own. Both had worked with the blind before
and come up from the ranks. Conklin was fast on the uptake
and expected the same. Harkness was full of patience. Together they made an ideal team. Like Atkins, they had lots
of understanding and could make you believe that blindness
was really fun.

Larry discovered that the pictures forming in his mind had
actual substance, but apparently the substance differed greatly
from anything he had ever seen, for the ingredients were different.

Miss Bailey, the night nurse, became identified with time,
appearing at seven in the evening and vanishing at seven in
the morning. Miss Ryan and Miss Douglas were equally em-
blems of day. He decided that Miss Bailey was prettier than
either of the day nurses, but he couldn't say why. Her beauty
had nothing to do with coloring or form. It was merely an
impression gained from the surety of her touch, the lightness
of her footsteps, and the poise reflected in her tone.

Yet Miss Douglas was his favorite of the three. She was
older, perhaps, and exceedingly kind. Her footsteps were solid,
her discipline firm. Miss Ryan was a little too pert. Larry filed
her away as the youngest, admitting that she knew her business thoroughly.

Later, when he got up courage to question Flagg, he was
glad to have the corporal confirm his impressions of the three.

Standing in front of the mirror one morning while shaving,
he tried to reconstruct a picture of himself. He had been a

stringy, introspective boy, overtall for his age when inducted. His dark brown hair had been smooth and thick, his brown eyes large. Chris had called them dreamy.

He had been good at track, although he was never terribly fond of athletics, running more for the honor of school and college than because he loved the contest. He was fond of reading, a taste that Chris, in spite of her profession as a teacher, found difficult to understand. Books meant work to Chris. She preferred a good hot band. Not that Larry disliked a band, but dancing was a pastime. There had been many evenings when he wanted to talk, to park someplace and just sit quietly discussing things, and holding Chris's hand.

The memory of himself was misty. Perhaps, while he was able to do so, he should have studied his features more. Army life had toughened him and filled him out. It would have been nice to know better how he looked now, even with a disfigured eye. Then as he grew older he might have pictured the changes better. Now he'd never really know.

He scowled at the unseen mirror. Chris had a trick of irritating him when he was angry by saying, "I don't care if you're mad at me, honey. You look so handsome when you frown."

Now he was building portraits of people and places without his eyes. Larry Nevin would join the gallery. He ran his hands up and down his firm slender body, then touched his nose, his ears, and his hair. Suddenly he laughed. He was "brailling" himself. The word had become an integral part of his language. He had taken his place in the world of touch and sound.

Flagg came to get him for Lesson 5: Muscular Memory and Obstacle Sensation.

It occurred to Larry that in four short lessons he had mastered an amazing number of strange new feats.

The ward with its walls and its forty-nine beds had become as familiar as the palm and fingers of his own right hand. He had brailled it half a dozen times, learning his locker, the drinking fountains, the position of pipes in relation to doorway and wall. The route between the bed and latrine, which

had seemed so long his first morning there, he now traversed
without thinking.

But the world had expanded.

His next step had been a large flat board laid out to scale
in a wire-strung model of buildings and paths. On it, with his
fingers, he followed the whole vast layout of the hospital's
hundred and forty-two buildings, and the intricate system of
corridors and slanting ramps connecting most of the buildings.

At first it meant nothing. Larry felt that some horrible joke
had been played on him by the patient Corporal Flagg. It
was just as intelligible as attempting to follow by touch alone
every inch of a ball of yarn as you wound it off of a skein.
Then all at once, flowing from fingertips to brain, a set-up
emerged. He couldn't explain that either. Touch, plus Flagg's
explanations, began to combine in impressions.

Ward One was on the second floor of a building. It was the
end building in a row of twelve, all alike except for the one
at the other end. That was the Receiving Building, where all
new patients came in.

His first trip, hand tucked in Flagg's right arm, was from
ward to mess hall. Flagg had already taught him how to travel
with a guide, holding the guide's elbow, relaxed and confi-
dent, following half a step or so behind. That enabled Larry
to anticipate when Flagg reached steps, either up or down,
when turns were made, or a stop to open a door. Flagg kept
driving home the fact that Larry must never let anyone push
or propel him. If anyone insisted, Larry must suggest politely,
"If you don't mind, I'd like to take your arm."

To get to the mess hall you took a corridor in the middle
of Ward One. You couldn't miss that, for Ward One was in
the end building and the corridor only ran to Ward Two—
and on. You passed through Two and Three, easily identified
by sound and smell. Then you passed a right-hand corridor a
little farther on.

There you made a mental note. That corridor led down to
Surgery and X-ray. You passed it and went right on until

Wards Four, Five, and Six came along. Now you'd walked almost two city blocks and you were close to a corridor crossing at right angles.

Then you turned left. Now you remembered the model—well, after a few more tries you did. If you took the right it went to the Administration Building. You passed through Seven, Eight, and Nine if, instead of turning left or right, you kept straight on. Between Nine and Ten a right-hand corridor led down to the clinic and Colonel Green. That was a good one to know. You'd use it a lot. Two more wards and the receiving ward, if you kept straight on.

It wasn't so hard as it seemed at first, once the set-up began to form—six similar two-floor buildings built parallel to each other and hooked together by corridors through their middle on the first and second floors, so that half of each ward lay on each side of a corridor, upstairs and down.

Between the first three buildings and the second three, a right-hand corridor to Surgery and X-ray. Between the second three buildings and the third three, a corridor that was very long—Administration if you turned to the right, mess hall if you turned to the left and kept on going between the Post Exchange on the left where cigarettes were sold, and the Recreation Hall on the right where they had the soda fountain.

No, Larry decided, after he had brailled the model a thousand times and walked five thousand miles of corridor, it wouldn't be a bit of trouble to find the mess hall.

Of course, there were other things to remember—emphasis on holding the arm correctly in dangerous places (no groping); emphasis on exploration and sound interpretation and its use; width of corridors, and how hooked-open doors stick out from the walls.

He remembered those after he'd nearly broken his nose coming out from the mess hall. He also remembered what Flagg had said about mastering walking in a straight line, and when traveling alone of keeping twelve to eighteen inches away from the right-hand wall.

Then there were the sounds. God, how Flagg loved sounds!

"If you'd paid attention to those footsteps and voices, Larry, you'd have realized you were bearing too far to the left and you wouldn't have smashed into Lieutenant Atkins." Or, "Couldn't you hear that ventilating fan? It's overhead in the corridor you're trying to find. What do you think your ears are for?"

Echoes, fans, kitchen noises, terrain underfoot, smell to establish location and direction. Great God above! He was only through Lesson Four, without a cane. There were twenty-two and a test to pass before they'd let him go home.

And now he was starting on Lesson Five. Flagg was talking:

"This muscular memory varies, Larry. I've seen some fellows get it instantly. Some never do. You'll get more of it when you get up to Old Farms Convalescent at Avon."

"I'm not out of this dump yet. You mean I'm to go up there for more of this training?"

"Eighteen weeks of it, Larry. You're lucky. They'll teach you anything you want to do."

"I want to get out of the Army and get home," said Larry. "Then I want to sit on my tail and do nothing. That's all I'll ever want to do."

"That'll be your privilege, once you're out. Right now, you're still in, and we're talking about muscular memory and obstacle sensation. Muscular memory is a way of fixing movements by linking those movements together. If you're good, you can automatically get to judging distance. Lots of fellows can light a cigarette by just striking a match and putting the flame to the right place. They've done it so many times before."

"I get it," said Larry. "What's the other?"

"Obstacle sensation?"

"Yes."

"It's sometimes called 'facial vision'—the unexplained ability of some blind people to sense obstacles in front of them."

"Oh! Like I busted my nose on that door?"

Flagg laughed. "Well, not exactly. With any facial vision training, you wouldn't have struck the door. You'd have stopped."

"Why?"

"Nobody exactly knows. They're working on it at Avon now. One scientist called it the interpretation of sensations in the skin—"

"On the nose," put in Larry.

"Only these are from external cues," Flagg finished. "This is the gym, Larry. We're going into the handball court. Lieutenant Conklin and Lieutenant Harkness are there. They'll explain what you're to try. Come on in."

"I want you to stand here, Larry," said Conklin when the door to the court was closed. "Now walk very slowly forward until you reach the wall. Keep up your arm. That's it."

Larry tried it without speaking, stopping when his arm touched the wall. Flagg guided him back again.

"Now you're in the same spot," said Conklin. "Try it with your arm down. See if you can remember when you're near the wall."

Larry walked forward, then gaining assurance, increased his pace. He should have counted his steps at first. It would have fooled them all. He stopped, then reached out a hand to check his distance. He was very close to the wall.

"Splendid," said Conklin. "Now walk back here toward my voice. Good. Now I'm going to turn you around. Try it again."

He felt himself given a couple of turns, then he stepped out full of confidence. Anyone after walking it twice could remember the distance to a wall.

Suddenly he stopped. Strong as the touch of an invisible hand, a shadow had dropped across his face.

"What's the matter?" asked Lieutenant Harkness. "You only traveled half the distance."

"Do you want me to butt my brains out?" asked Larry.

"You're smart, Sergeant." Conklin chuckled. "You knew we

headed you in another direction, didn't you? You were taking no chances. Let's try again."

Flagg brought him back, leading him over a zigzag route around the court. Conklin started him off again.

Larry took three swift steps and stopped.

"Now what's the matter?" asked Conklin. "You can do better than that, Larry."

"I'm afraid I can't, sir. The wall's just in front of me, less than three feet away."

"What makes you think that, Larry?" Flagg's voice was tense.

"Hell," said Larry. "Why shouldn't I stop? When I get close to it, I feel the wall! Something tells me there's something in my way."

## 6. A GUY NAMED JOE

LARRY had a gift. Of course, he'd had it all his life, as most people have, but had never had occasion to use it. It was one of those latent senses which the blind sometimes develop through sheer necessity—assuming they have the required sensitivity, persistence, and keenness of ear. Captain Phelan and Colonel Green called it facial vision. Larry didn't know what it was, except that when he drew very near certain objects, he *knew*.

There had been a discreet amount of well-suppressed excitement among the staff after his tests in the handball court. Colonel Green had gone over his eyes again and rendered a verdict of no light perception. Lieutenant Conklin, accompanied by Harkness, Flagg and Captain Phelan, had taken him back to Ward One and started him walking.

He had bumped into a bed and been roundly bawled out by a man who was sleeping. They had tried him again, changing his direction, this time with Lieutenant Harkness rhythmically tapping a cane on the floor in a corner.

Larry stopped a foot from another bed.

They moved out into the corridor and turned him loose between Ward One and Ward Two. That was a route he had covered many times before. Lieutenant Harkness tapped the cane. Larry walked off full of confidence and stopped a yard from a barrier of chairs that Flagg had placed in the way.

Harkness let out pent-up breath. "How did you know those chairs were there?"

"I could feel them."

"Where?" Lieutenant Conklin put in.

Larry thought awhile. "I'm not exactly sure, sir. There was a change, somehow."

"What kind of a change?"

"A feeling of pressure against my cheeks."

"Pressure?"

"Almost like a change in the currents of air."

"Did you feel that when you stopped at the bed in the ward?"

"Yes, sir, I think so. The cane was tapping behind me. I felt the pressure there when I neared the bed, but not so much as now. It seemed that the cane taps changed too."

They knocked off then, but took it up the following day. Afterwards he talked with Lieutenant Atkins, who possessed a strong sense of the same facial vision. The blind officer pointed out that the Army was making the first real efforts to train the blinded veterans in something that everyone possessed in a greater or lesser degree, following up experiments made at Cornell. The difference between sighted people and blind was merely that sighted people had the sense but never used it.

Larry was a little let down to find that in 1872 a blind man, W. Hanks Levy, had written extensively about his keen ability to distinguish many objects.

Larry asked the officer, "When you get close to something, how does it feel to you?"

"Like I'd wet a finger and held it up in the wind," Atkins

told him promptly. "Only the feeling comes against my cheeks."

"Why doesn't everyone have it?"

"I'm sure it has to do with sound waves and hearing," the lieutenant explained. "It's some kind of auditory phenomenon. They're making experiments at Avon now, using a scientific machine to test hearing acuteness. Maybe we're lucky, Larry, to have ears that are keener than average. You'll know for sure when you get up there. Meanwhile, keep practicing. I've found my sense develops with practice. It will be a lot of help to you."

It seemed incredible to Larry, thinking it over afterwards, that Lieutenant Atkins could be blind. The officer moved around the hospital at a faster pace than many of the patients with full vision. Several times he had taken Larry to the PX for cigarettes and bought him cokes in the recreation hall.

Atkins had told him a lot about Phoenixville, the nearest town to Valley Forge. Larry's initial two weeks of tests would soon be finished. Then he would be entitled to three evening passes a week to go into town, returning by midnight on the eleven-thirty bus. It was about twenty minutes' ride. In addition he could get a monthly week-end pass allowing him to make a trip to New York or near-by Philadelphia from Saturday noon to Monday morning.

What seemed still more incredible to Larry was the subtle change within himself. He was suddenly quite anxious to get a pass. A week before, he hadn't cared. What the hell good was a pass to a blind man who had to grope his way around?

Now the pass had become important. He was Larry Nevin, possessor of facial vision. Besides that, he had heard from other fellows about the Columbia and the Victory Bar over in Phoenixville, the dances at the U.S.O., and the girls to be met.

The fellows in Ward One and in his classes had become important too. At first, they had been less than shadows, moving things to be bumped into if you weren't careful. Gradually some had come out of eclipse and taken on the form of individuals. He discovered them to be different from the members of the hospital staff. They were more like Atkins, holding his interest and attention by a common bond.

Larry found himself creating them bodies, but he never asked Flagg about them as he had about the nurses. These men were becoming his companions and friends. They were growing to life from little attentions they showed him, directions given when he was lost in the halls, aid while he was in the workshop busy with modeling clay.

Some he thought dumb, some smart, some vulgar, some full of fun, some overserious. Their identification had nothing to do with any persons he had seen before his blindness. Rather, the stress was laid on character, interpreted and classified by actions and words.

Possibly he was most unfair, but he didn't think so. New standards were forming. Dumbness meant lack of interest and had nothing to do with a fellow's appearance. Smartness meant a desire to learn and master new things, no matter how long a time it took. Larry didn't realize it then, but non-essentials such as surface beauty, colors, and form, important to a man with eyes, were rapidly being cut away.

Normally he would have felt like a fool in the hospital zoot suit, a combination of red corduroy trousers and short red corduroy jacket. Now he walked about everywhere wearing one and without any trace of self-consciousness. He'd have gone into town just as readily in the hospital gray pajamas, providing he found them warm enough. Clothes had become a means of protecting the body from heat or cold. They all looked the same to Larry, night or day.

He regarded his fellow patients with much the same outlook.

John Masterson was a technical sergeant blinded in Italy. Johnny was a couple of years older than Larry. He had been through Dartmouth and attracted Larry because he was smart. Johnny's talk was mostly of subjects which Larry had studied without much interest in college—politics and economics. They assumed more meaning when brought up backed by Masterson's pungent language. Larry felt that Johnny Masterson had a right to be as pungent as he wished. He had driven a truck in Italy and stepped out on a land mine which had blown his face away.

Masterson fitted in a group of three. The other members were Private Oscar Hamilton and Corporal Ivan Stern. Hamilton was the oldest. He had been blinded in Italy by a German booby-trap, a neat device that had killed eight men and blinded four.

While occupying an Italian town, the Germans had unearthed a case of old Cognac which an Italian innkeeper had buried under the floor. Instead of drinking it, they had carefully removed a portion of each bottle and added methyl alcohol. The innocent innkeeper, delighted with the American occupation, had dug up the loaded case and served it to some jubilant soldiers.

Hamilton termed it "a contribution of Nazi chemists to the cause of modern war."

Ivan Stern, blinded in France by a rocket, was a Jew, and just as blind as Larry or Oscar Hamilton or Johnny Masterson, who had been through Dartmouth.

In fact Larry, who couldn't see Ivan's markedly Semitic features and curly hair, might never have known that Ivan was Jewish if it hadn't been for a guy named Joe.

Larry, for all his keenness in facial vision, had a habit he was finding very hard to correct. His tendency was to bear to the left, and not walk a straight line as he thought he was doing. This badly violated Flagg's warning about keeping twelve to eighteen inches away from the right-hand wall when traveling alone, a precept set forth in Lesson Four.

He was leaving the PX one morning, walking a mite too fast for safety and yawing badly, when he banged into another fellow. Larry's arm, half out in front, received a jolt. The other boy dropped a cane and started groping for it on the floor.

The cane had rolled against Larry's foot. He picked it up and said contritely, "I'm sorry. Here's your cane. It rolled against my foot. Did I hurt you?"

"You nearly knocked my teeth out," the other told him with a laugh. "You're way over to the left." Larry thrilled to the softness of the laugh. There was home in the Southern drawl.

"I'm Larry Nevin. You're from the South, aren't you?"

"New Orleans." The other laughed again. "I'm Joe Morgan."

Larry learned a lot of things from Joe.

Joe more or less took him in hand, picked up several things that even the conscientious and well-trained Corporal Flagg had missed. After all, Flagg wasn't blind. Joe, blinded during training on the California desert by a faulty land mine, had been in Valley Forge for a long time. Plastic work, he explained to Larry. Colonel Waters had built him a brand-new nose and quite a workable jaw.

Joe had a cane and knew his way around. The cane came with Lessons Seven or Eight. Joe had passed them months before. He had also held down a job in a war plant in Phoenixville for six weeks while his last operation was healing. He not only knew the hospital, he knew his way around in town.

He got Larry straightened out in his walking by describing his own feelings accurately when he had first started to yaw. Larry got the idea. In a couple of days he was walking the halls with nice judgment, following a course a foot and a half from the wall.

Larry made his first evening trip into Phoenixville with Joe. They were at the end of the Administration Building ten minutes before the bus was due to arrive. Joe kept chattering on, full of excitement at planning their evening, kidding back and forth with civilian employees on their way into town from work, wise-cracking with the civilian military policeman on duty to check passes.

It was very cold. The waiting passengers gradually huddled

inside of the vestibule at the end entrance to the building. Someone lit a cigarette. The policeman made him put it out.

Three more boys arrived, laughing at some joke of their own. One of them had a cane. Larry found that out as they squeezed by him. He wasn't sure that they were blind, for many of the patients with leg wounds used canes, and he didn't want to ask Joe.

Finally the bus turned in from the main road some distance away, announcing itself by a crunch of gravel. The waiting crowd moved back, Larry with them.

The M.P. said, "You boys first," and a hand touched Larry's arm.

"That means us," said Joe.

Larry found a handrail, climbed steps and located in his pocket what he thought was a dime. He blushed when the driver told him kindly that his dime was a penny. He'd never make that mistake again. He sat silent on the ride into town, conscious of people watching him for the very first time.

Joe must have sensed his embarrassment at his mistake, for he chattered all the way into town, getting a laugh from other passengers by pointing out landmarks which Larry knew Joe couldn't see.

Larry felt nervous as the bus neared Phoenixville—the nervousness of any passenger nearing a destination. Now it seemed doubly enhanced.

"Are we nearly there, Joe?"

"Not far. We just turned left at the Fountain Inn. This is Gay Street."

"How do you know?"

"You will next time, won't you?"

"Yes. I guess I will."

"I used to count my pulse when we turned," Joe told him. "The stop for the Columbia Bar was about seven hundred beats from the Fountain Inn. Now I just know." He got up suddenly. "This is Bridge Street. I'll show you the Victory, then the U.S.O. Then we'll meet Charlie."

"Who's Charlie?"

"He's bartender at the Columbia."

They got off. Larry was surprised to find that ordinary things comprising the night life of a little town were giving him a brand-new thrill. Maybe it was because the tawdriness was missing. Maybe it was the keen enthusiasm of Joe.

Whatever the cause, the beer was cold and biting, better than he'd ever drunk before, the laughter in the bars was infectious, the bowling alleys smelled clean and woody. He liked the deep-toned radio in the U.S.O.

They caught the 11:30 bus back. The evening had been a revelation. In France there had been no safety, no comforts, no drinks, and little laughter. Now Army discipline had begun to relax. Blind he might be, but Larry felt he was beginning to live.

He said to Joe, "We can get another pass day after tomorrow. Let's come in again."

"I'm leaving for Avon day after tomorrow," said Joe.

Larry suddenly thought of Jimsey. It reminded him that he was still in the Army, where friends must come and go. The laughter of the men on the bus sounded out of place. The Army had no right to tear another friend away. He didn't want to lose Joe.

"Damn it," said Larry. "Do you have to go? We've had such fun."

"You'll be up there yourself before long," said Joe. "We'll go in town again."

"And how," said Larry. "Write me about it, Joe."

"You bet," said Joe.

The following night they were sitting together when a bunch of new arrivals was brought in. Joe was to leave at six in the morning. Larry was feeling low.

"I hear that three of those new guys are niggers," said Larry. "I didn't know we had niggers in this ward."

"I've been here seven and a half months now," said Joe.

Larry lay awake for half the night, his mind whirling diz-

zily with a bright new pain. Over and over he dropped back
to childhood and followed through his life, to war and the
end in Valley Forge.

The answers didn't add up straight. Blindness didn't end
with blindness. Life that had been so simple, had turned
complex. Now there was humiliation to bear, perhaps even
ridicule.

He'd gone downtown with a nigger! Worse than that, he
liked the guy. The South was burdened with Negroes. He
knew all about it, and how to keep them in their place. What
the hell was the Army doing allowing them to associate with
white men who had lost their sight? Negroes should be earmarked somehow, maybe made to wear a bell.

What hurt him more was his own stupidity. He should have
known. Any kid could tell a nigger, if only by the smell. That
was a simple fact of life pounded into his head since his very
first day in school. Niggers didn't talk like whites, or act like
whites, or think like whites, or smell like whites.

Then, by all the glory of unsullied Southern womanhood,
how did they think and smell? It was too much to bear. Maybe
Joe Morgan thought Larry was a Negro too!

He felt himself enmeshed in a foul dark net of ignorance.
Part of his life, entrenched in his mind more strongly than
sight, had been ripped away in an instant. His eyes were gone
and his remaining senses had tricked him. Should he believe
the senses that, until death, he must rely on? If he did, then
every iota of schooling and childhood training must be wrong.
Yet, if he doubted the senses left him, he felt he couldn't go
on. Training or senses, which should he cling to? He had to
choose and, God in heaven, he hadn't the ability to do so.
Everything he had learned in life was smashed to pieces. It
was the world that must be wrong.

Tempestuously, he lashed back at his mother, blaming her
most because she was closest, damning her and his blindness
together, as though they might be one, cursing her for the
training that had made her son a fool.

"Damn my mother, the ignorant bitch!" He'd have killed anyone for saying that, and still he couldn't wipe it from his mind. This wasn't blindness. This was the sharp hot light of a mental hell. He'd found and lost his first firm friend in the land of darkness. Joe wasn't dead like Jimsey. He was worse than dead; he was black. Larry would never be able to go out with him again.

## 7. JUDY

"HELLO, soldier. Why so glum?"

The voice filtered through the music of the detachment band playing for the regular Thursday night dance in the Phoenixville U.S.O. It was a nice voice, not too girlish, not too young. Even in the single sentence Larry detected overtones, a warmth and a shading. It wasn't exactly sympathy. Rather, he felt the question was sincere, as though the speaker really wanted to know.

He didn't answer. The band crashed in, hitting an arrangement that entirely eliminated the melody of a current tune. The drummer took over. The shuffling feet thinned out on the dance floor, replaced by two or three couples whose dancing needed room.

Larry could picture their gyrations, the snap at the end of outstretched arms, the twirling girls with billowing skirts showing white lengths of bobby-soxed legs, the boys in khaki quick to recover after a twisting turn.

The deep couch sagged a little as someone sat down beside him. "Don't you feel like dancing?" It was the nice voice again.

He got up quickly and went outside. The air was stingingly cold, far below freezing. Larry stood on the corner and breathed it deep, enjoying the sharpness in lungs and nostrils. Lingering with him was a clinging odor of delicate perfume.

He walked down Bridge Street toward the station. Phoenixville had become familiar, now that he had a cane.

Three long weeks since Joe had gone.

Damn the nigger! He'd made Larry curse his own mother, made him write his parents he didn't want to see them until he got home. He had to think, and thinking was hell. Thinking was loneliness.

The lingering perfume was still in his nostrils. He'd been a stinker to a friendly girl he couldn't see. What was the difference? He'd been a stinker to everyone since Joe had left for Avon.

Masterson and Hamilton had followed Joe ten days later without bothering to say good-by. Only Ivan Stern was left, and Ivan had practically abandoned all attempts to be friendly. Stern was a Jew, so what the hell!

There had been a little nigger boy he'd played with in Palatka. They had fished for catfish in the river. Larry's mother had stopped them from playing together. There was something awful about niggers. They smelled. You couldn't eat with them in restaurants. You might patronize them and work them cheap, but you never rode in the same car on a railroad train.

How did you know a nigger was black, when you couldn't see? How did you know that Stern was a Jew, unless by his name? God almighty, he'd never be able to tell a Jap if the Jap spoke English. What did kids do who were blind from birth? Everyone in the world was a single color—black. That must be one for the blind kids' mummies to explain.

Larry went up the steps to the Columbia Bar, testing the way with his cane. On the porch of the old hotel he stopped. He'd run into fellows in the bar, or have to talk to Charlie. Tonight he wanted to be alone.

He went into the restaurant side. Harry Gleason, the owner, spoke. "Hello, Larry. You all alone?"

"Yes," said Larry. "I want to be if you have a table." Gleason must know he'd been alone for three weeks now.

"Some of the boys are in the bar."

"So I came in here," said Larry.

"Sure," said Gleason. "I understand. Sit right down here and I'll bring a beer."

"Rye," said Larry, "and water." He couldn't tell Gleason he had to think. Gleason was kind, but he'd never be able to understand that a mind could whirl in blackness. Nobody living could understand. Larry had to get himself in hand. He'd end up in the N.P. ward, crazy as a parakeet, if he didn't stop the whirling in his brain.

The rye came. He drank it and ordered more. The juke box was busy swallowing nickels. In the adjoining bar he could hear the sliding noise of weights in a shuffleboard game.

The rye sent fire through him and with the touch of the fire his brain began to work clearly, perhaps for the first time since his blindness.

The weeks of darkness became a camera box, a light-proof container of part of his twenty-three years. Now and again the shutter snapped and he had a picture of something to come, or something gone. Those pictures were all in color: gold, white, blue, yellow, red, and vivid green, but mainly flesh.

They were pictures with form, but the form was hazy. Or was it hazy? There was every chance that he was seeing it all far too clearly and with too much exactness. The pictures were dirty. At least his father and mother would call them dirty. Dr. Bannerman would call them dirty.

Everything in life was dirty. Dirt was black. Now everything in life was black. He couldn't tell black from white. If he had to go through life in blackness, he couldn't keep thinking that everything black was dirty.

He finished the second whisky.

Maybe his father and mother were wrong. Maybe Dr. Bannerman was wrong. He hated Dr. Bannerman anyhow. He could admit it now, for no one would ever know. The hate was shut tight in the camera box that would be his life forever.

Dr. Bannerman swayed Larry's father and mother. Dr. Bannerman, strong in the might of God, was certain that niggers were dirty because niggers were black. Now God was black.

The only thing white in the whole wide world was a woman's flesh. Chris would think that was dirty, but somehow Larry didn't care. Somehow he knew he was finding truth. God was black and a woman's breasts were white and soft.

He wanted their whiteness, wanted their fullness between his hands to mold and fashion, the breasts of a hundred pin-up girls that he'd never see. He wanted to bare them gently, to depress their perfect roundness with his finger, knowing their shape would always return to be depressed again.

Across the room a girl was laughing.

Her bottom was probably round and full, its contour depressed against the seat of her chair. Her legs were crossed. Her ankles were slim. Her calves were smooth, with a tempting slope that called for the touch of exploring hands, hands not afraid to creep higher, hands that would fight her resistance, hands that were full of the fire in Larry, burning hands that could never stop until they'd probed and loved and caressed her everywhere.

Larry groped for his cane and his fingers shut tight on the smoothness of the crook. His left hand gently stroked its length. Somehow he had to get home to Chris. His lessons must be learned. He'd concentrate on what Flagg had told him:

LESSON 7. *How to use a cane:*
    The cane is held with the hand well up in the crook and with the crook turned outward to protect knuckles from sharp edges and hot pipes. Tip of the cane is held close to the floor (one or two inches) and about eight to fifteen inches in front of the foot opposite the hand which is holding the cane, and extending one or two inches past the body.

If he was near the girl, he could raise her dress by raising the tip of the cane. The crook could be used to stop her if she screamed and started to run. The flesh would be white above her stockings. He could bury his face there, feel the warmth against his cheeks, hide there forever, and she'd never see his sightless eyes, never know he was blind.

The hand holding the cane is from twelve to eighteen inches in front of the hip. The cane is used as a bumper and never as a probe. It must not be depended on as a feeler.

Damn the cane! It was white and red-tipped, as though the end had been dipped in blood. Flagg had told him. What woman would ever want him now, with his puckered eye and his dead blind stare?

"Hello, soldier." It was the voice he'd heard in the U.S.O. A chair moved out beside him and a girl sat down.

The delicate perfume was strong again. His mind was full of overtones and shadings. Larry translated them into curves of her body and gleams of light making shadows on the soft wave of her hair. With such a voice, she must have lovely hair.

Gleason was beside him, removing empty glasses. "Larry, this is Judy Greene. She wanted to meet you. She's been awfully nice to a lot of the boys."

"I'll bet," said Larry. He held tight to his cane. "She followed me here from the U.S.O. I've got to go." He started to rise. Fingers touched the back of his hand. The fire inside him burst into a sense-consuming flame. He relaxed in the chair.

"I'll bring some beer," said Gleason.

"Whisky," said Larry, "and water."

Judy said, "I'm buying these, since I'm horning in, Mr. Gleason. Make mine the same."

"Most of the blind boys are pleasant, Larry," she went on in her level tone when Gleason had gone. "You're just insulting. What's the matter? Are you frightened of something, or playing some sort of a game?"

"I think it's you who's playing the game."

"Why? Because I asked you to dance?" She laughed, and the fire in Larry burned brighter. Her voice was warm, but the laugh held promise and passion.

"Because you followed me here. Hostesses always ask us to dance in the U.S.O. They give us a workout on the floor, then go home and tuck in bed alone. God's in his heaven, all's right with the world."

"What do you expect them to do?" asked Judy.

"Nothing," said Larry bitterly. "My parents taught me that babies came in flowers. Two years of college taught me to be a gentleman and never to think. The Army has taught me there's nothing in life but one small thing—let's call it the old Army game."

Gleason came with the drinks. Larry reached for his wallet, but Judy stopped him, a hand on his arm. He wished to God she wouldn't touch him. He'd broken bounds on two small drinks. If she touched him after the third one, he wouldn't be to blame.

"You're thinking tonight," she told him. He heard her lift her glass and swallow, heard the slither of silk on skin. "Two years of college may have taught you to be a gentleman, but you seem to have forgotten the teaching. I'm not a hostess."

"What were you doing in the U.S.O.?"

"I have a friend who works in there. I happened to drop in." Judy paused. "You looked lonely."

"Maybe I am," said Larry. He swallowed his whisky in a single gulp and the fiery drink felt cool. He could reach out his hand and touch this girl, find the bulge of a rounded breast beneath her dress, press his fingers against her thigh, concealed by the covering table. Somehow he felt that she wouldn't move, and somehow he knew that he couldn't touch her.

You had to see a woman's face to read the permission in her eyes, to feel her lips against your own and sense their yielding. God in heaven, you couldn't reach out in blackness and grab her! That was rape. He was dying for her slowly, but how did a blind man begin?

He decided to hurt her. "You'd be lonely if you knew that every dame who spoke to you was on the make."

"You're bitter, Larry. They're really not."

"You learn the truth when you lose your eyes. They're all after dough. If they have to tow a blind guy around, they expect to be paid. Ask any of the fellows."

"I've talked to many, Larry. Some of them are married."

"Why not?" he asked abruptly. "Some dames would marry a gorilla with two hundred bucks a month for life coming in."

"Do you think I'm like that, Larry?" Her voice was almost tearful. He was pleased with himself for getting under her skin.

"They're all like that."

She pushed back her chair and stood up quickly. "It's getting late. I have to get home."

"No. Wait!" He reached out in the dark and closed his fingers on the coolness of her arm. Desperately he pulled her back again. Once she was gone, he could never see to find her. "I didn't mean it, Judy. I'm crazy, I guess. I've had too much to drink." He got up and stood quite near her.

She was silent except for her quickened breathing. Then she loosed his crushing fingers from her arm. "You can walk home with me, Larry. I have a small apartment a few squares from here on Gay Street. I'm secretary to the manager of a plant in Phoenixville."

They went out into the biting air, Larry clinging lightly to her arm. The streets unrolled beneath his feet until finally she stopped and said, "We're here," and he knew she'd let him kiss her.

He drew her close. All the pain of the evening was in his embrace. All the desire was in his kiss. The passion caught her, starting her lips to tremble. Her arms tightened fiercely.

The shutter clicked open within his brain and pictured a face with a puckered eye hanging above a woman. The cold crept in and the passion was gone.

"I'll see you again," she whispered, and ran up the steps.

He walked to the corner to wait for the bus, shivering in terrible ague. He could have had her for the asking, but knew that he couldn't take her. Blinded eyes stood in between. His country had not only taken his sight, it had taken his manhood. His reward was a phallic symbol, a white-painted bloodtipped cane.

## 8. IVAN STERN

IT WAS raining. Miss Bailey had announced the weather when Larry got up in the morning, a custom which at first he failed to understand. Gradually he began to realize that sunshine made him feel buoyant, particularly when a snap was in the air. Conversely, rain, fog, and dampness were lowering to the spirits. It was obvious where the expression "dampening his spirits" came from. It was conceived in the weather.

Strange that even though you couldn't see it, it was important to know the type of day. Of course, it affected the way you dressed. Once out of uniform, it would do so still more. It also might affect one's plans. Who wanted to go swimming or picnicking on a miserable day?

Now it was Saturday, nine days since he first met Judy, and the rain had messed up his week end for fair. They had been out four more evenings together, danced some, had drinks and a dinner, and attended a picture show.

Since the first night they met, Larry hadn't attempted to kiss her again. It wasn't because he didn't want to. It was incredible to him that a voice and a body he couldn't picture could be so exciting. Too exciting, maybe. Perhaps that was the trouble. Perhaps his mind was picturing her body far too well.

He liked to think it was the rain that had made him refuse a week-end pass to Philadelphia. Judy had asked him to stay with friends she had there. It wasn't the rain. It was fear. He just couldn't face a night in a house with Judy.

She'd offer herself to him. He wanted her so badly that the very thought was killing, but the chill that had seized him the night they met was still more deadly. If he tried to caress her, he'd start to think she was yielding out of pity. He was afraid of that, afraid of the lens in the camera of blackness. Most of all he was scared he might try and fail.

He was sitting in a corner of the sun porch off Ward One listening to the rain patter above the muted radio when another fellow came in, touched Larry's leg with a cane, and asked, "Who's that?"

"Larry Nevin."

"I thought you had a pass." Larry recognized the voice of Ivan Stern.

"I didn't go."

"Why not?" Stern sat down beside him.

"I don't know. The rain got me down, or something. I've been feeling low."

"And taking it out on all of us," said Ivan.

"I didn't know it."

"That's what I told Masterson and Hamilton before they left for Old Farms. You started off by being a pretty decent sort of a guy. You were tickled about your facial vision and seemed like fun. What happened?"

Larry switched off the radio. The rain pattered louder. "I don't know."

"Something happened." Ivan's voice was sympathetic. Larry found himself thinking that Ivan might have more than average understanding. He needed some such person to talk to, someone who couldn't see the puzzlement which he felt was marking his face more every day, someone who couldn't see his puckered disfigured eye.

Larry said, "I met a guy named Joe."

"Joe Morgan?"

"Yes. How did you know?"

"We're quite good friends. I heard about it. Those things get around. What upset you?"

"I didn't even know he was a—" Larry broke off in the middle, for the first time in his life conscious that a word might brand the user as stupid and ignorant. Weren't all

black people "niggers"? Now what the hell had happened?
He found himself incapable of applying the word to Joe.

"So what?" asked Ivan. "You didn't know he was colored,
and went downtown with him. What part of the South were
you brought up in?"

"Florida."

"Miami?"

"No. Palatka. It's a lumber town in the northern part of
the state."

"I've heard of it. It made the New York papers some years
ago. I was a kid, but I heard my father talking about it.
Twenty-seven floggings and a couple of killings by the Ku
Klux Klan."

"You have a good memory."

"I have to have," said Ivan. "My race in some respects is
worse off than the Negroes. I'm a Jew."

Larry felt deeply embarrassed. There were only a few Jews
in Palatka, although he understood they had completely
ruined Miami Beach. He had gone to high school with a
Jewish boy, and one day even hunted with him. The hunting
trip had never been repeated. He'd been uncomfortable all
afternoon, afraid he was going to say something quite innocent
that might offend the boy. Now the same embarrassment had
carried over, and he realized that it was an ingrained hesitancy
in mentioning Ivan's race in Ivan's presence. He felt as if
Ivan had lowered his pants in public when he'd come out
flatly and stated, "I'm a Jew."

"I'm afraid I don't understand what you mean," he said
to Ivan slowly. "How could you be worse off than the Negroes?"

"As a race we're better-educated." Ivan gave a laugh that
sounded bitter. "It's a paradoxical fact, Larry, that the higher
your education, the more you're ridden with painful emotions.
The Negroes want, and badly need, better education, but
once they get it they'll pay by being racially hurt still more.
They hurt us by discriminating against us too."

"I don't get it," said Larry frankly.

Ivan told him, "Look at what's already happened to you."

"What?"

"You're getting better-educated because of your blindness. You're getting hurt worse too. You've been a perfect bastard to everybody since you found that a Negro boy could be just the same as a white one. I'll guarantee it's something you never thought of in your life before. It's upset all your precious Southern teachings, all your background of foot-burnings and lynchings. It's tough to take. Then one thing leads to another."

Ivan stopped to light a cigarette and give one to Larry. "You get interested in race prejudice. The next thing you know you're discussing it with a Jew."

"I have thought of it," Larry protested. "I wondered as a kid why I couldn't go fishing with a little black boy I liked so much. Then I wondered later why my father could go fishing with a black boy to row the boat and everything was okay so long as he paid the black boy a buck a day. Then there was a Jewish boy in high school—"

Ivan waited, quietly smoking his cigarette.

"I guess I have changed," Larry admitted at last. "I couldn't have possibly talked to him as I'm talking to you. Maybe it's because I can't see you, Ivan. It's like holding a conversation over a telephone with someone that you're scared to meet face to face. Your voice is impersonal, but it carries more weight. It's like listening to a commentator speaking on the radio."

"Damn it," said Ivan. "You're a lousy, inhibited, ignorant Southern Christian—which in my life is three steps lower than any Negro who ever lived, or any Jew. My blindness has done something to me too, Larry. I actually like you!"

Larry accepted Stern's statement thoughtfully, feeling that behind the banter was more than a seasoning of actual truth. A common bond had ironed out a possible enmity, no fault of either, which might have stood forever as a barrier between them. Instinctively he realized that back of Ivan's glib expounding was a search for truth, sincere and real. With it was a search for a friend in a life that had been very lonely.

Larry asked abruptly, "Ivan, what are we going to do?"

"About what?"

"About life, I guess, and blindness. I've seen more in a single month than I ever saw before, learned more than I ever did in two years of college and all the other years of school. I see what you mean when you said it would make me unhappy. I'm miserable."

His cigarette was smoked too low and burned his fingers. He dropped it in the big metal ashtray beside him, where it fell with others to smolder into a pungent little fire.

"About Joe?" asked Ivan.

"Not exactly. It's more about my father and mother, and Chris, the girl I'm going to marry. They wouldn't like you, Ivan, any more than you'd like them. They're just what you called me a minute ago. They'd die if they knew I'd been seen in town with Joe. I lay in bed and cursed my own mother, Ivan, damned her for having made me so unhappy by the things she taught me, cursed her for having reared me into a fool."

"You might have included your father, your girl, and your teachers," said Ivan, "and added a few hot ones for everyone else you ever knew. Did you ever read Hale's 'The Man Without a Country'?"

"I had to memorize part of it in school."

"You would," said Ivan. "A young officer got mad about something and said, 'Damn the United States; I hope I may never hear its name again,' or something equally asinine. So what did they do? They cut off all his buttons and sent him on a battleship and kept him there for life, clipping the name of U. S. A. out of all the papers, and never mentioning it in his presence. He died on the ship after many years—a fact that might make a fine memorial for Nazi Germany.

"That's a piece of crap that the country's been cramming down every kid for years to teach him what will happen if he dares to think or criticize. Most of the country, North and South, hates the Negroes and the Jews. Some sections pick on the Japs, even though we had one in here just before you came who had lost his eyes fighting for the U.S.A. like me and you. Some sections throw in the dumb Irish and all the Catholics, just for good measure.

"You're learning to examine yourself, Larry. God knows you got it the hard way, but I'll admit right here that I did too. I used to hate the United States because the people were so damn dumb. I don't any more. Since I lost my eyes, I've learned that people can't help themselves. They're a mob, Larry, and all mobs are dumb. You have to think like a Southerner, or they'll put you on a ship and keep you there for life. I have to think like a Jew. That's your fault and mine, and yet it isn't. We can save ourselves."

"How?" asked Larry.

"By determining in our own conscience whether or not our thinking is right or wrong. I'm smart, Larry, but there's one smarter Jew I can never fool, and his name isn't Jesus. His name is Ivan Stern."

Larry was silent. The rain increased its patter. Shadows that he'd never see began to grow long.

Ivan asked, "Do you get it?"

"Yes," said Larry. "You mean that we can't do anything until we decide within ourselves the difference between right and wrong." He was silent again.

Finally Ivan asked him, "Now what's bothering you?"

"A girl," said Larry. "A girl and the question of what is right and wrong. Have you slept with a girl since you lost your eyes, Ivan?"

"Yes," said Ivan. "Two. One's in Philadelphia, the other's in New York. I've been trying to work up something here in town."

"Then you don't think it's wrong?"

"Great God!" said Ivan. "Sex doesn't exist in the United States. It's not recognized officially by Army, Navy, Church,

Red Cross, or Marine Corps. How can anything that doesn't exist be wrong? Surely your family taught you that all the teen-age girls spreading venereal disease around the country caught it off of toilet seats. I'm thinking of a bill right now to abolish the modern toilet and have the country use nothing but logs. I'm going to run for Congress on it when I get home to Chicago."

"I'm not fooling, Ivan," Larry said desperately. "A girl asked me to spend this week end in Philadelphia. I turned it down."

"You're crazy," said Ivan.

"That's what's worrying me." Larry paused. "I was afraid of what she'd think about my blindness. It stopped me the other night. I thought maybe she was—hell, I don't know—pitying me, I guess. I grew cold all over. Did you feel like that at all?"

Ivan reached out and put a hand on Larry's arm. "The only thing I lost in France was eyeballs, Larry. Let's go eat. It's nearly suppertime."


## 9. DARKER THAN BLACKNESS

LARRY was learning that the world of movement stopped with blindness, and that life itself stood still except for sound. Outside of the hospital windows no one went by. Rain might patter, but it didn't fall. Snow was a miracle, appearing by magic on the ground.

A bus was full of rattles, groans and bounces, twisting him sideways and straightening him up again, but the scenery was missing. Traveling, except on foot, had a beginning and an end, but nothing in between. You got on a bus at the hospital and after a proper interlude of sheer discomfort, you got out again and found yourself in town.

Such a static quality of living produced a terrible boredom. Action and amusement during every waking minute became a vital necessity for keeping up his spirits. There was no rest, for once he relaxed, his brain kept galloping onward. With nothing to distract him, he kept on thinking. The effort was unusual and consequently tiring. His failure to reach conclusions invariably depressed him.

Shortly before his furlough he unloaded the problem onto Judy.

They were sitting out a dance together in the Victory Bar, crowded close behind a tiny table. Whisky gave him courage to talk, but not to touch her. Her nearness was burning through him. Dancing was different. Moving about on the crowded floor he could lose himself in the music and hold her close without the sharp desire for her driving him on too far.

"I wish we could stay here forever, Judy."

"It would bore you, soldier. There's nothing more deadly than morning in a night club—cleaning women and no one to tend bar."

"You're wrong," said Larry. "There's nothing worse than—" He stopped, full of sudden self-pity.

"Than what?" she demanded.

"Sitting and thinking."

"I wonder," said Judy.

"You've never sat in blackness waiting for the hours to drag along."

"There are different kinds of blackness, Larry."

"None as black as when your eyes are gone."

"I know one worse," said Judy softly. She lifted her glass and brushed him with her arm. "I watched it grow in a small New England town— Suppose we dance."

"Suppose we don't," said Larry. "What blackness is worse than blindness?"

"Are you in love with someone, Larry?" she asked abruptly.

The question upset him. He didn't want to think about Chris. He was here right now with Judy. God, she was just like all the rest, looking for marriage. Couldn't she tell he liked her? Wasn't that enough for the moment?

He liked her voice and her friendly laugh. He liked her dancing. He liked the way she offered her arm and led him around without being awkward. He liked everything about her. Now she was going to spoil it all by deliberately pinning him down.

"There's a kid, Chris Paterson, home in Palatka." He tried to laugh, but choked it off with a swallow of whisky. "We've kicked around together a lot. It's one of those things. What about the blackness in your small New England town?"

"Maybe it will help if I tell you, soldier. That's why I asked about the girl. If you've happened to love someone yourself, you'll understand better."

As though he didn't understand about blackness. She was being very difficult tonight, almost patronizing. He wished he could see her, study her expression, read the look in her eyes, watch the fullness of her breasts in their rise and fall.

He wanted to say, "I suppose there's another fellow," but she saved him the effort.

"I was born near Winchendon, Massachusetts, Larry—Toy Town, they call it. I loved a boy. His name was Paul."

It was running true to pattern and Larry had an instant of smugness at his own sagacity. There was always a boy. All that was needed now was to kill him off in the war.

"That's blueness, not blackness, Judy—worrying about a boy."

"The blackness wasn't mine, Larry. That is, not at first. I just watched it develop and spread about Paul and his family. I can't remember when I didn't know him. We went to school together. When he was fourteen years old he stole a car."

"Kid stuff," said Larry. "That gets knocked out of them in the Army."

"I thought it was kid stuff too. My mother's been dead for many years. My father ordered me not to speak to Paul, but I kept right on. I couldn't very well help myself. He kept getting into one scrape after another. After each one he'd always come running to me. The blackness grew, Larry, and ;pread like a plague. There was nothing I could do about it— nothing his wealthy family could do. After a while the blackness enveloped the whole of the town. Since I loved Paul very dearly it was doubly black for me."

"You mean that things got worse?"

"When he was seventeen he killed a girl. He died two years later in an institution for the criminally insane."

"Christ!" said Larry. He heard her swallow, heard the clink of her glass as she set it down. The band went into a number.

"So maybe you're lucky, soldier," she said through the music. "The privilege of thinking can't be bought. The faculty of reasoning comes from heaven. You've lost your eyes, but you're very much alive. All your life you'll have money enough to live on simply, and time enough to study and learn. Paul was dead before he died. Utter and hopeless blackness, Larry, is blackness of the brain."

Larry finished his drink and asked her to order another. She did without question, but he felt that her tone to the waiter held a hint of disapproval. The fact that he noticed it worried him, warned him that he was becoming conscious of her every inflection.

Why the devil should he care what she thought about his drinking? He scarcely knew her. He'd drink himself stupefied if he felt like it. It was none of Judy's business. He hadn't known before tonight what town or state she came from.

She was cutting the ground from under his feet and he didn't like it. He didn't want entanglements; he wanted fun— plenty of dancing and drinking. He didn't want to be told he was lucky. That was a hell of a thing to tell a blind man who'd given his sight for his country.

Chris, at least, would be secure. He could count on Chris. She'd never trot out a yarn about some crazy murdering boy to upset Larry and remind him that he had a working brain.

He was a little drunk right now, but it was helping him to
get things straightened out. Okay, if she wanted him to think,
okay. She was just another pick-up in Phoenixville. He didn't
intend to sit there and let her make him compare her with
Chris. It was like something or other—being unfaithful to a
faithful wife, maybe—or lusting after a dame.

She was getting protective, that was the trouble. She was
going to protect him against himself, and he'd be damned if
she was. She was going to make him have fine thoughts, noble
thoughts, thoughts above the body, thoughts far superior to
rolling in the hay. Useful thoughts were what she demanded,
brilliant thoughts, elevating and beautifully constructive,
worthy to flow from a blind man's brain.

He'd get the hell out, leave her sitting there alone, never
see her again.

That was a crack if he'd ever heard one. If he'd never seen
her, how could he never see her again? It was Chris he'd never
see again. Then how could he compare the two—Judy and
Chris? He needed to know more about Judy. Knowledge was
the blind man's friend. Once he knew more about her it
would be as though he'd seen her. Then he'd be in a position
to never see her again.

"You're very quiet, soldier."

"I was thinking about that boy. What happened afterward?"

"I told you—he died."

"To you, I mean."

"I left home instead of going to college. I took a business
course in Philadelphia—living with the friends who invited
you in for the week end. They advanced me the money. When
the war broke out I got this job in Phoenixville."

"What about your father?"

She was silent while she lit a cigarette. "He's still in
Winchendon."

"Don't you miss him? Being home, I mean."

"No. My father and I disagreed on many things. He owns

a manufacturing plant. There was a strike several years ago."
Smoke drifted toward Larry. "He thought I was far too young
to know that he was in the wrong. He never quite forgave me."

"He must be cleaning up now," said Larry.

"What's the difference?" Judy laughed shortly. "He'll be
just as unhappy paying extra taxes. He loves money, not
living, Larry. A man such as that can't win."

"Maybe not." He was thinking of Chris's father and the
barrel plant, and the wages that were kept so profitably low.
"Some of them make an awful lot of dough."

"Yes," said Judy. "My father built himself a brand-new
house. It was finished a month before Pearl Harbor. He had
planned for years to have his daughter make her début from
the mansion. She wasn't even there to help him move in."

"But don't you miss him, Judy?"

"I miss what he might have been to me. Don't worry about
him, Larry. He isn't lonely. Now that I've left him he's quite
convinced that I drove young Paul insane. For that matter,
so are most of the people in Winchendon. It's a tragic fact
that whenever anyone commits suicide, or loses his mind, society insists that some individual—probably someone who
loved the victim—shoulder the blame. Society's always perfect, Larry. In war, in hunger, in destitution, society's never
to blame."

She had spoken with such sincerity that the words were
sinking in. "What about my blindness?" he asked her. "Isn't
that son of a bitch Hitler to blame?"

"And so are you, and so am I," said Judy. "We're little tiny
units of the civilization that put Hitler into power. You just
can't duck your own part, soldier, any more than I can duck
mine. You should have started thinking earlier in life about
the causes of lots of things, Larry. Or someone should have
made you, if you were too immature to start thinking on your
own."

"You mean that kids should be taught about politics and

economics and international affairs and that sort of stuff? Hell, I don't understand them now."

"Yet you've had more education than most boys in the armed forces. Learning comes harder, Larry, after we're grown."

He fell to picturing Chris again, thinking of her teaching the kids in school. Suddenly he wanted to ask Judy about her and found he couldn't. Other things flooded into his mind— Joe and Ivan Stern.

In the space of a second he'd grown tongue-tied, ill at ease, with the girl beside him. She knew too much and thought too clearly. There'd been a professor in college like that, a man whom Larry admired above them all. For two whole years he had vainly wanted to discuss many matters with the instructor, but never could bring himself to it. He was scared that he'd feel like a fool. Just about the time his awkwardness was vanishing he was sucked into the war.

He touched his Braille watch, then got to his feet, feeling a little dizzy. "It's getting late, Judy. I better catch the next bus back." He gave her some bills. "Pay the check, will you?"

She was back in a minute to lead him out, his hand tucked under her arm. He was conscious of her heartbeats as they waited for the bus in silence.

He heard the whine of the tires two squares away, but made no move to kiss her.

"Good night, soldier." She pressed his hand briefly against the warmth of her coat. A single teardrop fell against his fingers.

"Good night, Judy."

The bus doors closed behind him. Maybe life in darkness was much like traveling—a beginning, an end, and no in-between. He didn't know what he wanted. He didn't know anything. What had Judy told him?

"Utter and hopeless blackness, Larry, is blackness of the brain."

# 10. THE TEST

THE plastic operation, which Larry had secretly dreaded, had proved to be comparatively minor. Ten days after it, the bandage was off and Flagg told him the eye looked fine, scarcely a trace of any scar.

Larry had learned to believe in Flagg, who recognized that confidence in an instructor was half of a blind man's training. Larry had found that Flagg would tell him the truth even though it was unpleasant.

He wanted the truth. Already he had met visitors at the hospital and people in town who thought they were being helpful by telling some of the patients how well they looked when it wasn't true. It would have been far more helpful had the subject been dodged entirely. A fellow might be blind, but that didn't make him an idiot. A blind man was quite well able to realize that he might look like hell if half his face was gone.

There were other well-meaning visitors who persisted in thinking that blind men were deaf men too. One of the boys had tubes to breathe through where his nose had been shot away. Lying helpless in bed, his overkeen ears caught all kinds of thoughtless remarks. "Oh, my God! Isn't that horrible!" a passing visitor remarked one day.

Larry knew that the remark was involuntary, nothing more than a startled reaction of sympathy. Nevertheless it hurt him. He was certain it hurt the boy in the bed much more.

Sensitivity to his own appearance was reduced a lot when Larry got his plastic eye. The eye was light in weight, and according to Flagg, an excellent match to the remaining real one. What was still more important, it was almost unbreakable.

Old-fashioned glass eyes broke when dropped. The new ones of plastic just bounced if they fell on the floor. They fitted better too. In fact, any place that might prove in time to be uncomfortable or irritating could be handily smoothed with an ordinary nail file.

He was still more pleased when he found he could move it, although sometimes lying wakeful at night he wondered why. You couldn't see anything with it. Still there was a certain satisfaction in being able to turn it from side to side. It made it more human and eliminated the feeling that he was staring out glassily at nothing. He disliked dark glasses. Now he felt no need for them with his movable plastic eye.

The eye was another milepost. Larry had been in Valley Forge for six weeks. He was beginning to discover that his blindness was a road lined with mileposts. Events which might have been of minor importance in an ordinary life assumed great proportions in a world of darkness—the importance of events in childhood, Larry decided. After all, he was still a child in the world of sound.

Lying in bed the night before the final test which would earn him his furlough if he passed with credit, he reviewed the high points starting with Captain Phelan's gentle breaking of the news that Larry Nevin would never see again. There weren't so many, but each was vivid in a different way— Corporal Bruce's whistle, Larry's own first trip from bed to latrine, his first meal in the mess hall, his discovery that he could stop when close to a wall.

Still more important had been his meeting with Joe Morgan. Judy, maybe, was even more important than Joe, again in a different way. It was hard to explain. How could a child tell if his first day in school was more important than his first circus, or maybe his first pair of glasses?

Six weeks was a very short time when one faced a lifetime in a brand-new world. His talk with Ivan Stern had ripened into a sincere friendship. That had made an impression. So had his plastic eye. Lots of things were making impressions; that was all that he could honestly say.

Now he was close to going home. That had seemed of paramount importance at first. Chris; his mother and father; the warmth of the South and his own home town; the smell of the cypress; Dr. Horton, the dentist, who knew more about hunting turkeys than any man in Palatka.

Then the impressions had flooded in and decreased the great importance. He was getting used to Valley Forge, used to Flagg, to Phoenixville, and Ivan Stern and Judy; used to his bed, the ward, the nurses, the doctors.

Outwardly he must show excitement. It wasn't natural not to show excitement at going home. In fact, it wasn't decent. As well admit that the food in the hospital mess hall might be better than his mother's, or that Judy had thrilled him as Chris never had—of course, again, in a different way.

Inwardly, fear had tempered excitement. At Valley Forge and Phoenixville the people were well conditioned to maimed and blinded veterans and the set-up was all for their treatment and comfort. What was it going to be at home? There, people were concerned with their own affairs—ration coupons, lack of gas, shortages of meat and butter. There, people had to make a living by working every day.

Deep in his heart Larry knew quite well he was frightened to death of furlough, filled with panic at seeing his family. Tip, his dog, was getting old and his nose was bad. Maybe even Tip wouldn't know him.

There were trains, and strangers, and dining cars, and pitying people. There were stations, conductors, M.P.'s and girls, more soldiers, and friendly sailors. There were Travelers Aid workers, and Red Cross workers, and social workers, all eager to meet and help him on his journey.

God in heaven, how could he face it?

Valley Forge was his home, where darkness was born. He wanted badly to stay.

Then the test came and he wanted just as badly to pass it. Maybe he was anxious to show that he was as quick as the others—Johnny Masterson, Oscar Hamilton, Ivan Stern, and

Joe. Maybe inside he was really burning with desire to get home.

The test had sounded simple when Flagg read it:

*Hospital Travel Test*

Patient will leave bed and proceed to mess hall, then travel to the PX and buy a Coca-Cola. Return to the bed, then travel to the workshop via outside route.

Easy? He had made the trip a hundred times, alone and with other blind boys, with and without his cane. Now all he had to do was cover the same familiar route, this time using his cane.

But this time, Flagg was following behind, watching and making notations.

Notations burned into Larry's mind:

Patient makes turns into corridors well.
Checks wall with cane not oftener than necessary.
Handles strange situations well.
Looks for familiar landmarks.
Knows routes well.

He had followed the mat, turned right where a breeze from the corridor had brushed his face, turned left and found the staircase.

The stairs were simple. The cane was held straight out in front to clear each step by inches.

Descend without counting. The cane would strike its tip and warn you when you reached the bottom.

There's a wall. A right-hand turn on a landing. More stairs down. The cane has struck again and you're on the ground floor. Now you turn left and check the wall, then cross and touch the right-hand side. Now straight through five more buildings, with your cane held right and following a course (without touching) eighteen inches from the right-hand wall.

Simple as hell! Simple as walking blindfold through the halls of some inferno!

*Handles strange situations well.* There are voices ahead on the right-hand side, talking but not moving. A group of people? Three men on litters? Or nurses and doctors talking, maybe off the corridor? No, that can't be. You're not close enough to a ward right now. They're standing in the hall.

Closer and stop. Feet move, and someone says, "Okay." Eighteen inches. Check with the cane.

*Looks for familiar landmarks.* Spots them with his plastic eye. Take it slow, for somewhere near is a bunch of pipes and a fire valve. You've bashed into it a dozen times. Now the cane has touched and you've cleared it.

*Patient moves steadily.*

*Uses ears.* Listen to the wards go by! Listen to the dishes, the moaning over a dressing. Listen to footsteps ahead of you. You're overtaking another guy. Listen to water running. Someone's using a drinking fountain, bent over so he can't see you. Circle it, and in again. Eighteen inches from the right-hand wall. Listen to Flagg in back of you, busy making notations.

*Patient recognizes terrain through shoe soles.*

*Uses echoes, wind and air currents to locate places and objects.*

*Is composed.*

*Is courageous.*

*Is co-operative.*

Here's the turn where the mats are crossed, recognized through the shoe soles. Make a note to take a shoe to Colonel Green and have him fit it with a plastic eye.

Keep your mind on your work, Nevin. There are doors ahead and the main crossroads of Valley Forge where the traffic's so thick they have traffic cops. There'll be litters there, rolling by swiftly on silent wheels, and blind men training, and guys with one leg learning to walk, and nurses with trays, and doctors, and fathers and mothers and sisters and brothers and sweethearts, every one of them hiding a tear.

Your cane's found the doors. The traffic M.P. says, "Come

on, Sergeant." He's talking to you. That's one on Flagg. Thank God, that crossing's by!

You pass the PX and into the mess hall and find your table, and out again. Remember the door where you cracked your nose? That baby's still there, but you class it under familiar landmarks now, and don't knock out your plastic eye.

In the PX, Flagg's not beside you. He's hanging behind you making notes. You grin as you order, "One coke, please, miss." If Flagg wants one, let him buy it. So you spilled some water. The hell with that. The return trip's easy. Like a horse going home to its stable.

And now there's only the downtown test:

Patient will leave bed and proceed to the bus stop in front of the Administration Building and travel to a designated spot in Phoenixville, and return via bus to ward. While downtown and waiting for return bus, the patient will be given a test of traveling with a sighted attendant who has followed at a close distance throughout the above test. The latter test will consist of maneuvering curbs, turns, steps and doorways without verbal help from the attendant.

Thank God the snow's nearly melted. The snow is hell in Phoenixville, hiding the curbs, concealing the gutters, doing everything possible just to confuse a guy. All snow feels alike when you feel with a cane, and approaching tires sound different. Then sometimes there's ice and wind, all most confusing.

But today is nice, and Florida's warm, and you want to get home. So you listen for traffic and cross the streets and lead Flagg into the U.S.O. and the Victory, and the Recreation Hall. You show him the turns, and you go up steps, and you end with a drink in the Columbia Bar—a drink for yourself, since Flagg's on duty.

And all the way back on the bus again you wonder.

Patient knows route.
Moves cane smoothly in front of body.

Finds landmarks easily.
Checks traffic movements.
Walks straight line.
Gets into bus without difficulty.
Fixes cane properly before stepping up on curb.
Locates curb easily.
Follows straight line.
Enters business buildings without undue difficulty.

"Pretty good, Larry," says Corporal Flagg as you get off the bus without his help.

You're going home.

The bricks are warm on Lemon Street. Tip will know you. Chris will love you. Your mother will kiss you, and Dad will shake you by the hand.

You've learned to see a lot of things looking out of your plastic eye.

## 11. "GOIN' HOME"

THE station platform at Paoli was crowded. Larry was conscious of people all around him, shuffling their feet, lifting bags and setting them down, striking matches to light cigarettes.

He moved back from the platform's edge, gauging himself with his cane, and held a little tighter to Flagg's arm. The crowd might close in on him carelessly, push him onto the tracks which ran so close to the platform. That would be too much irony, to be run over by his furlough train.

Funny what excitement there was in waiting for a train. Double now since he couldn't see it. The people around him breathed more quickly, talked in unnatural voices. Some of them laughed at nothing. Others spoke in a monotone, probably saying good-bys to someone.

Through the cold, an early spring sun shone warm against his face.

"What time is it, Flagg?"

"Fifteen past twelve."

Larry checked his Braille watch to verify the corporal's statement. Down the track a whistle blew. Rails began to hum and loudened into a tangible vibration. Air rushed at him. Cars clanked and rattled and thundered by in a frightening rhythmic procession. Larry tasted smoke against his tongue.

"Was that it?" His stomach had tightened. He hoped he wasn't going to get the G.I.'s and have to keep trotting to the men's room all the way home.

"Take it easy," Flagg cautioned. "Paoli's on the main line, Larry. A freight just went through."

"When's mine due?" His mind didn't seem to be working clearly. He had asked that question a dozen times during the forty-minute taxi drive from Valley Forge.

"Twelve-nineteen." Flagg was very patient and went into more elaborations. "We get into Thirtieth Street, Philadelphia, at one. Your train for Palatka leaves there at one forty-two."

"I get home tomorrow morning?"

"Ten-thirteen. Your family's been notified to meet you. You don't have to change at all."

Two G.I.'s were making remarks about a WAC who had just passed by. In back of Larry, a woman was giving writing instructions to her husband above the plaintive cry of a very young baby.

"This is late, isn't it?" Larry touched his watch again.

"A few minutes. It's a local. An electric."

"Couldn't we have gotten a train from Phoenixville?"

"Only at ten-eleven. You'd have had a three-hour wait in Philadelphia."

"Three bucks for that cab is plenty."

"It's quite a drive, Larry."

"I sort of wish you were going with me, Jim."

"Thanks, Larry. You'll be okay. Your seat's reserved and

your baggage all taken care of. If you need anything, there'll be M.P.'s on the train. I'll see you to your seat okay."

The crowd fell back and the rails began to hum. Noise and air rushed past him and slowed. The shadow dropped across his eyes, warning him of a wall in front.

The train was there. Electric trains were different from steam—not so much bluster. Steam felt as though it might run you down wherever you stood. It panted and hissed and coughed like something human. It was everywhere. An electric train was smoother, more like an automobile. It slid into place with businesslike swiftness, and without such an awe-inspiring roar. It started smoothly and got you there.

People pushed up into a knot around Larry and Flagg, then silenced and fell away. A man shoved rudely, and a woman near him muttered, "Shame!"

Larry could have struck her. He was pleased at being shoved around. It meant that the shover had not observed his blindness. Why did every moment of triumph have to be killed by some sympathetic dame? She'd probably like to provide Flagg with a town crier's hat and a bell.

Flagg led him up steps, through a door, and into an alley of sitting people. They found a seat together. A whistle tooted twice shrilly. The train moved off.

Larry lit a cigarette and was careful to keep the ashes from his clothing.

"How do I look?" he asked Jim Flagg.

Flagg waited a moment and said, "Just swell."

Again he was grateful that Flagg was honest. He had spent a long time on dressing and shaving, on shining his shoes and knotting his tie. His hair had been cut the day before. He had brushed it hard with a touch of tonic, testing the part with his finger. It waved in front, but he couldn't help that, for the wave was natural. He wanted to look his very best. He knew if he didn't that Flagg wouldn't hesitate to say so. The thought made him feel just swell.

Flagg kept pointing out sights to him on the ride into

Philadelphia, sketching pictures of main-line towns and countryside in short concise sentences.

"This is Villanova. Pretty country in spring and summer. Lovely trees, bare right now. There's a college here, and a prep school too, I believe. Lots of stone fences."

"This is Bryn Mawr. The famous women's university here. More stone fences. Beautiful homes, the kind with big glass hothouses. There's still some snow on the ground."

The train seemed to poke along. To Larry, the stations were endless, packed close together to taunt him. Every time the train picked up speed he'd feel the brakes clamp down. A moment later, they'd stop, and more annoying people would climb off and on.

He smoked without cessation. He had bought a lighter in the Valley Forge PX. There was a fascination in twirling the little wheel and holding his finger above the flame to make sure the wick had caught.

Cigarettes helped to pass the time. Each one was an adventure, a tiny item marking his progress toward muscular coordination. Privately he was practicing lighting them just to be knowing when the flame was held in the proper relation to the cigarette's tip. Sometimes he puffed vainly; occasionally he lit one too close to his lips. But his average was improving. He knew he was getting on.

The Thirtieth Street station proved boundless when they finally arrived. Larry was anxious to try navigating it on his own with the aid of his cane. Its size was apparent from the sound of his voice when he spoke to Flagg. The challenge was strong to braille this great terminal, to see how well his training in watching others by sounds and footsteps had taken hold, to test more fully his power of facial vision.

The time was short, though, and he wanted some food. He went to the lunchroom guided by Flagg's familiar arm.

He ordered a chicken sandwich and coffee, a snack that could be eaten in a hurry. Flagg sugared and creamed the coffee for him, and stirred. The sandwich was good, but after the first mouthful Larry discovered his appetite was gone. He forced himself to eat the remainder and drink his coffee. Diners on the trains were crowded.

"We'd better go, hadn't we?" he said to Flagg. "My watch says nearly one-thirty. We haven't much time."

They went out into the station together. Larry suddenly found himself resentful of the people about him, resentful of his dependence on Flagg and on time.

The people moved with easy strides, hurrying trainward, stopping to buy tickets, glancing casually at the station clock which he knew must be on the wall. They could hurry if they saw they were late, or read from a blackboard where trains were posted that the train they wanted had been delayed. They could find a gate, walk to the proper platform, and take the proper train.

A blind man must always have extra time, time to ask questions, time to make errors and time to correct them, time to eat slowly, time to walk slowly.

They went up a ramp to the platform. He was a fool to leave Flagg, a fool to start on such a journey. Why hadn't he told his father to come and get him? The family wasn't as broke as that. His dad was making good money, had sent him fifty bucks just for expenses. Now what good was the fifty bucks? He couldn't even get to a diner to eat without Corporal Flagg. He couldn't get anywhere, if the truth was known. He'd sit in a corner the rest of his life without Flagg, his Seeing Eye.

Warm arms went around his neck. Warm lips pressed against his own.

"Larry!"

"Where did you come from, Judy?" He felt that his face was terribly red. "This is Corporal Flagg. Miss Greene."

"I nearly missed you, Larry. I thought you'd come in by Phoenixville."

"We took a cab to Paoli. How did you get here?"

"The Philadelphia and Western from Norristown."

They were discussing railroads—the Philadelphia and Western, the Reading, the Pennsylvania.

"Your train's a little late," said Flagg, speaking as though it were something momentous. "I'll go and talk to the train man."

"What's the difference?" Larry protested.

"I'll be back, don't worry," said Flagg. He was gone and Larry was alone with Judy again. You were caught up in tricks such as that when you roamed around in an invisible world. Events were beyond your own control. A moment of safety could become in an instant a moment of chaos.

A puppet on strings, that's what he was: a robot. "Here's Larry Nevin, Miss Greene. Keep him for me for a few minutes, will you? Mold him. Upset him. Bend him to your will."

"What time do you reach Palatka?" Judy asked.

He'd forgotten entirely that she knew where he lived. "Tomorrow sometime. I'm supposed to get in at ten-thirteen."

That was a matter of vital importance. A girl kept turning up in your life, popping into your scheme of things out of unexpected places, reminding you what a dope you were, diagnosing your dread disease—blackness of the brain.

Didn't she know you were pledged to Chris? Didn't she know you were bursting inside to get back home and take up the pattern of life once more where the war had forced you to drop it?

He was Larry Nevin—gentleman and hero, returning to the girl he loved. He was future General Manager (and possible owner) of the Paterson Barrel Factory—Roll Out the Barrel. Give the Greene dame the brush-off, toots. There's a nice deal waiting in the sunny South. Tell her how you feel about her—and her story about that crazy lug who was criminally insane. Why the hell couldn't you shake that guy, banish him out of your mind forever? Why couldn't you be honest instead of helpless? Why did you have to tell her about the arrival of your train?

"I brought you a little present, Larry. It isn't much. A box of candy and some cigarettes."

"You shouldn't have, Judy. You need the smokes worse than I do. I know how tough they are to get."

"I want you to have them."

"I'll take them then. That's swell of you."

He took the package and held her hand. It was firm and smooth, with tapering sensitive fingers. The palm was soft and warm.

The physical contact filled him with a sudden great contentment. Without being actually conscious of dawning affection, he realized dimly that every time he touched Judy clouds of doubt and confusion were swept away. Yet, inwardly, he fought the pleasant contentment. Somehow it seemed disloyal to Chris, and Chris was a symbol of home and marriage and children—everything that a soldier dreamed of in battle. Such an idol wasn't to be toppled in a day.

"Write me, won't you, Larry? Just a line on a postcard to let me know how you are." She tightened her fingers around his hand. "I'm not going to write to you. Somehow it makes you seem too far away."

"Sure, I'll write you, Judy." His quick relief made him eager. He'd been worried about getting letters from her while he was home, and hadn't known how to tell her. They'd have to be read to him by someone, and even his mother would have asked too many questions.

A loud-speaker blared, announcing the train. He released her hand as Flagg bustled up. "I have your traveling kit, Larry. I'll put it in the rack above you. The rest of your stuff is checked right through to Palatka. You have your ticket?"

"Sure, Jim, and the baggage check. Everything's okay."

Judy kissed him. "Good-by, Larry."

He pulled her close against him. "I'll be back in a month, Judy."

The train rolled in.

"I'll miss you, soldier." She kissed him again. Her footsteps moved away. Somehow he felt the kiss would always stay.


## 12. THE TUNNEL

THE tunnel stretched from Philadelphia to Palatka, from Pennsylvania to Florida. It was the longest tunnel in the world. All the stops were in the tunnel—Baltimore, Washington and points south, which was probably a very good thing. Stations, on an average, weren't places you wanted to see.

Riding a train in the tunnel, a white man might be subjected to a great indignity by finding himself a passenger in a Jim Crow car. Of course, a blinded Negro, such as Joe, ran the same chances. Well, not exactly the same. Joe would be elevated by riding in a car with white people, elevated and highly honored. Joe's education would be improved by listening to the conversations born of white education. . . .

From across the aisle: "This closing up the joints at midnight's a lot of malarky, if you're astin' me. Whassa idear? I'll tell you whassa idear. Ast John L. Lewis, thassa idear. Shorta coal. Make the people think we're shorta coal. Then out go the goddam miners. Thassa idear."

From down the aisle: "And I sez to him, so my husband's overseas, wolfhound. See if you can figure that one."

From farther back and across the aisle: "The last time we went to the races I started with five bucks and ran it up to ninety-four. Even then I didn't dare mention it to Steven. I told him I'd been saving out of the household money. Then when I dropped it on that parlay—did I have to think fast then! It's gotten so now you can't get a bet down on anything. It's a bad mistake to kill all the fun in a nation. We're getting just like Germany—all the time work, and no fun."

Larry began idly to picture them to himself.

The man so concerned about the welfare of the miners had a valve-shaped voice with hexagonal edges. His words fitted in with the rattle of the train. "Whassa idear?" Clackety-clack. "Thassa idear." Clickety-click. His face was square and closely shaved, and his nose was marred with blackheads, probably from mining coal. There was every chance that his nose was shaped like a piece of coal. His hair was close-cropped. His neck was dirty from coal dust. He wore a dusty diamond in his tie. His soup-stained belly shook like jelly.

The woman so concerned about her husband's welfare was scarcely more than a girl. Her hair was frizzy and over-waved. She wore a single-piece sleazy dress with nothing at all underneath it. As the train sped on, her dress slipped up, revealing yellowish skin. Her breasts were flat and boyish. Her voice was made of filings—tiny steel filings that burst from her mouth like splinters from an .88. The constant eruptions of filings had worn away her chin.

The lady who loved the races was packed tight into a girdle that stretched one way and hurt her middle. Her teeth were large and even. Her nose was straight and even. Her hair was straight and even. The seams of her stockings were straight and even. Her legs were long and bony, and vanished into the girdle. She had bright red hair and horns on her forehead and wore a goatee. She cheated at bridge and gin. She had no breasts. She couldn't have babies on account of her girdle. If she had one she'd have to nurse it from the goatee on her chin. She was talking to a deaf mute who couldn't reply.

"You asleep, bud?"

The voice beside Larry was round as a dollar. The man was solid and sweaty. He wore a watch chain of solid gold across his vest and a five-hundred-dollar gold timepiece on each end of the chain. A tablecloth of solid silk was tucked around his collar. He drank lots of beer and belched with dinner. The war was a personal annoyance, and he liked to ask soldiers about it. Soldiers always knew about a war—when it would end and the next one would begin. What they didn't know, the fat man would tell them.

"Nope," said Larry. "I'm not asleep."

"I thought not. It's hard to tell with you chaps. They do a job on you today. You *are* blind, aren't you? I saw a fellow bring you in."

Larry nodded. "Yes. I'm blind."

"I'm Ernest Somerset." He announced his name as though ready to be friendly, since Larry had confirmed his judgment. "I'm pretty tough to fool. You have to be to get along in my line with things as they are today."

Larry didn't ask what Mr. Somerset's line was, or how things were today. It was much more fun to have pictures in the tunnel. They were all your own, shared with no one. It was obvious that Mr. Somerset made one-winged bombers. He was in partnership with Dr. Bannerman and was going to Florida to see the unctuous minister. Together they manufactured bombers that came home on a wing and a prayer. Mr. Somerset made the wing, Dr. Bannerman the prayer.

"I rode back from California on the train with some of you fellows a couple of weeks ago. I'm supposed to have a priority, but too many armchair officers ride the planes. Those fellows were going to some place near Hartford."

"Avon?" asked Larry with a touch of interest.

"Uh, yeah. Something like that. You been there?"

"Not yet. I'm just going on furlough."

"Anyhow, I started to tell you I saw they were blind right away. I told them all they could have jobs in my plant after the war—assuming these fellows in Washington don't take it away."

"I don't understand," said Larry. "Is the government trying to take it away?"

"Hell!" said Mr. Somerset. "They're taking everything away. You fellows in the Army are lucky—er, that is, you don't have to worry about a business. I manufacture medical equipment. The boys need it overseas. You fellows will need jobs after the war. I'll give you my address. Of course, there'll be a change in the rate of pay."

Larry closed his eyes and leaned his head back. It didn't

make any difference. Mr. Somerset was unquestionably very
sound—sound as a dollar. It would be a pity if the government
took his medical business away. The fellows in Valley Forge
needed a lot of medical equipment. The blind needed jobs.
War must be a wonderful thing. It made lots of business for
men like Mr. Somerset, supplied lots of blind to work in his
plant.

"You sleepy, bud?"

"No," said Larry. "I just rest better this way."

"I was saying that on the top of taxes, we have headaches
like this Wagner-Murray-Dingell Bill. I'm making a trip to
Washington now to have my say. I'm speaking for the N.A.M.
Put crackpots like Wagner in the Senate and that's what you
get. Interference with business. So much interference I'll have
to run down to Florida for a couple of weeks to get a rest. If
I was let alone I could carry on. Now I can't even get a Pullman. Have to just ride anyway."

A baby somewhere began to cry, at first just a whimper.
In a second or two it really started wailing and yelling. It was
probably sick. Maybe right this minute it needed some of Mr.
Somerset's precious medical supply. Maybe its mother was ill
and couldn't feed it. Maybe it was a little pig like the baby
in *Alice in Wonderland,* or *Alice Through the Looking-Glass,*
or *Alice Blue Gown.* The beautiful mother, all dressed in blue,
holding tight to a little pig that was very ill and spanking it
when it sneezed. The baby gurgled and quieted down. Maybe
it was a little duck with a Wagner-Murray-Dingell bill. What
the hell was a Wagner-Murray-Dingell bill?

"—too many free handouts," Mr. Somerset was saying. "Did
boondoggling and the W.P.A. stop this war? It did not. We
have a Social Security now, and what good is it? Now this
Wagner wants to take care of people from the cradle to the
grave. Well, people don't want to be taken care of. It stops
them saving. If men won't work for a fair price and save their
money for a rainy day, let them starve. If they get ill, there's
a county hospital they can go to. Socialized medicine, that's

what it is. Well, I'm telling you, young man, doctors aren't
going to throw their lives away working for no-accounts. The
people who are worth saving with decent medical treatment
have saved up money to pay."

In Italy, there had been a kid with a swollen belly. It had
cried like the one a few minutes before. Only the dago kid
had kept on crying. It wouldn't eat. It had cried all night and
cried all day until after a while its cries grew faint, and quit
altogether.

In Italy, a man had taken out thousands of lira notes that
he'd buried under his little house and burned them. They
made a fire to keep him warm on a bitter night. He'd saved
himself from freezing with a lifetime of savings. The lira might
have been dollar bills, for the lira couldn't buy anything, and
neither could the dollars. Nothing was left for money to buy—
no food, no clothes, no milk for the crying baby, none of Mr.
Somerset's medical equipment.

Now at home the dollars couldn't buy butter or meat, or
typewriters, or aluminum, or refrigerators, or radios, or auto-
mobiles, or Mr. Somerset's medical equipment, or Mr. Somerset's peace of mind.

There was a day way past when Larry's mother was very ill.
She was very ill for a long, long time. Larry's father hadn't
any money to pay, yet he'd worked very hard since he came
out of the Army in the First World War. Larry must be wrong,
but he felt that his father was quite a decent man. His father
had even worked quite hard building roads on the W.P.A.

Now Mr. Somerset's precious medical equipment was available in France. As a matter of fact it was free to the users,
along with a lot of doctors who were working for peanuts night
and day. Larry had made use of it, and Masterson, and Hamilton, and Ivan Stern, and even black Joe Morgan. He wondered
if Joe had saved up money to pay.

Three thousand men in Valley Forge had used Mr. Somerset's medical equipment, forty-five hundred in Halloran, thousands in Dibble and Rhodes, and England, and France, and

Russia, and China, and more on ten thousand islands ,and
ships in the Pacific (whose name means not belligerent). None
of the men that Larry knew of had saved up money to pay.

"—this country was built on the fact that every man has
a chance to make a fortune," Mr. Somerset was saying. "Rob
a man of initiative and he's no damn good. Half the men I
have working for me and drawing outlandish wages are no
damn good anyway. Now this Wagner wants to give them
handouts. Well, I'll tell you, young man, the country won't
stand for throwing more money away!"

You could blank your mind in the tunnel. You never needed
to pull down shades. The sun never struck you in the eyes
to wake you from dreams.

Half the fellows Larry knew weren't any damn good anyway. Jimsey wasn't any damn good, nor half the fellows at
Valley Forge, including Larry Nevin. It wasn't any wonder
that Mr. Somerset was irked about the handouts they were
getting. They'd be robbed of initiative for the rest of their
lives. Two hundred a month to Larry Nevin, who didn't even
have eyes to work on a W.P.A.

And doctors too. All the medical care you needed to fix your
eye when your eye had been shot away. Hell, the trouble was
with his mother. She should have been hit by a gun.

It was very puzzling. If your teeth got shot out, they fixed
them. If they just fell out in normal course, you must save
up money to pay.

If you killed a thousand Germans at a cost of a million dollars, you were pensioned for life. If you saved a thousand
Americans at a cost of a million dollars, you were stepping
on Mr. Somerset's business and throwing money away.

And suppose we'd saved a thousand Germans before they
grew big enough, or hungry enough, to hate us and started out
gunning for Larry Nevin's eyes? Or a thousand Japs, or a
thousand Italians? Or suppose his mother had taught him that
the little Negro boy he'd played with was just as good as he
was, and the country had spent the cost of ten thousand planes

on food and education for the Negroes in Palatka, or a single billion for education about truth in general, telling the nation that Jews were really people?

Would Mr. Somerset be so bitter?

Would Joe Morgan be lost as a friend forever?

Would Valley Forge be filled once again with maimed and bleeding soldiers?

Would Larry Nevin be blinded for life?

You could sleep and dream when you went through the tunnel. There was no night and there was no day. None of your fellow travelers really existed. They were only voices with bodies you gave them. They had no minds, no thought, no conscience. They spoke without grimace or waving hand. You weighed their words for sincerity and tried your best to understand.

Some made sense and some didn't. Maybe most of them never would. So you faced a life of darkness because most of them lived, like Somerset, in desperate fear of money thrown away.

The tunnel was long, and your blinded eyes found it hard to tell night from day.


## 13. BEGGAR ON HORSEBACK

MR. SOMERSET departed at Washington, neglecting to give Larry the address of his plant where jobs for the blind would be forthcoming after the war (at slightly lower rates of pay). Mr. Somerset would have his say about the Wagner Bill and leave for Florida later on.

A woman took Mr. Somerset's seat. She sounded elderly and a trifle oversympathetic when she started to tell Larry about her son, an officer in Patton's division who was practically directing the entire push into Germany.

Why couldn't people be normal with him? He was still smarting from Somerset. Now the woman beside him was babbling on. Didn't she know that under her garrulous cheerfulness Larry could tell she was thinking, "I simply must be bright and cheerful with this poor blind boy!"

He was unresponsive to a point of rudeness. Then that began to worry him. Damn it to hell, you couldn't win! A fellow without any arms could be tired or disagreeable, or get oiled in a bar without every old hen in the country clucking about the rudeness and immorality of men with no arms.

But the guy without eyes was out of luck. If he didn't feel like talking, all blind boys were boors and slightly queer. If he wanted a couple of shots too many to forget for a while that the world was dark, all blind men were dipsomaniacs. The Anti-Saloon League, or the Federation of Non-Alcoholic Sons of Dr. Bannerman, or some similar collection of emasculated old poots bent on having another bloody try at Prohibition would point with disgust and try to prove that the kid was blind because he drank whisky in his beer.

He had joined a club when the sniper hit him. What Larry Nevin did, all the blind did, as long as it was something the public disapproved of. But just let him work a little better on a job than any man with eyes, or learn a little faster, or think a little harder, and instantly he became outstanding. The public flatly refused to accept the fact that a boy who was bright when he had his eyes continued bright without them. The same thing went for the boy who was dumb.

Yet the sympathy of the elderly woman next to him was real. That's what made it tough both for him and the woman. If he tried to explain that he didn't want sympathy, she'd never understand.

She was thinking of her own son, somewhere in France, dreading in her heart that he might come back blinded someday. How could Larry tell her that if such a tragedy happened, her misplaced sympathy would ruin her own son's confidence in himself, break his morale, make him want to seek a secluded corner and stay there for life?

How could he tell her that blind Larry Nevin was already

beginning to feel himself better than Larry Nevin with eyes? That his brain, for the first time in his life, was beginning to accept and reject things, to carefully sort and analyze? How could he make her understand that her very speech stamped her as being ill at ease, as Mr. Somerset's words had stamped him as a thoughtless selfish man?

The woman beside him considered herself a perfect lady, well schooled in dissimulation. She thought herself tactful, believed herself a hostess who would never knowingly give offense to anyone. She would cut off her hand rather than bring pain to a wounded boy.

Mr. Somerset fancied himself as a high-powered business executive. He was a positive man, fighting for Mr. Somerset's rights, which he was certain were good for his country. He dominated friends and employees, and browbeat opposition and enemies into submission.

Larry Nevin with eyes would have taken both as he saw them, been charmed with the lady's perfect manners and gentle deportment, and overawed by Mr. Somerset's wealth and belligerent air.

Blind, he found himself overawed by his newly developed powers of classification. He had listened to Mr. Somerset and found him wanting. He had listened to the woman beside him and found her stupid. She had refused to take the trouble to treat Larry Nevin as Larry Nevin. Instead, because it was easy, she was treating him as she thought all the blind should be treated, chattering on as one might to the village idiot, without giving him any chance to reply.

By the time an M.P. rescued Larry to take him into the dining car for dinner, the woman had made her son in France so obnoxious that Larry hoped a land mine would get him. Deep inside he felt that the boy in France wouldn't care. Her entire concern was getting her precious boy home again. There wasn't a thought in her motherly head about the causes that might have sent him there.

All during dinner Larry wondered about causes. The effects,

so far as the soldiers in Valley Forge were concerned, appeared
to be quite obvious. The effect on himself was apt to last a
long time. How could he blame the talkative woman for not
thinking about causes? His own mother hadn't thought about
them. He hadn't ever given them a second of time himself
until he suddenly discovered that both his eyes were gone,
and Judy had started thoughts about causes pounding in his
brain.

Now some kindly stranger next to him in a dining car was
cutting up fish for him and removing the bones. He had been
brought in to dinner by a military policeman, led through
cluttered aisles of staring people who fell silent as he passed
with his escort. The M.P. would take him back to his seat
again after making a stop at the men's room.

Were the staring people or the fish-cutting stranger thinking about causes? The effect was right in front of them. What
about the M.P.? Was he thinking about causes, wondering
what the hell had taken him from a home somewhere and put
him into uniform so that blind Larry Nevin could hook himself onto his arm?

With dinner inside, Larry determined to be more sociable
with his traveling companion, but she'd fallen asleep when he
got back to his seat. Maybe it was just as well. The tunnel was
getting on his nerves. He hadn't had to stay in one place so
long since he was hit in France. If the woman started gabbing,
he'd get irritated all over again.

The car began to quiet down. The mass of breathing around
him changed, settled into a pattern of long regularity, then
seemed to merge as though he were listening to a single giant
sleeper. Conversations held in whispers became unnaturally
distinct, yet none of the words were quite distinguishable.
The rustle of turning paper grew less. The baby whimpered
sleepily. Everything was dominated by the rattling of the
train.

Years before, he'd seen a moving picture called "Beggar on
Horseback." He'd never exactly understood it, and perhaps

because he hadn't, it had made on his memory an unforgettable impression.

It had to do with the saying, "If wishes were horses, beggars would ride." In the picture, the hero had a dream. In beggar's rags, on a beautiful horse he rode into a world of distortion where everything assumed the shape the hero had given it in his mind.

The thought came to Larry that he was living in such a world himself. He had given a girl in back of him horns and a red goatee. He had drawn a picture of the woman beside him busy through life with having sons and ignoring causes. He had pictured Mr. Somerset as something like Thor, snuffing out lives with a deadly hammer.

He leaned his head back and tried to sleep, but sleep crept on at odd times since his blindness, without any light to guide it. It was far away now, for his brain was busy with causes.

Why was he suddenly so obsessed with causes? They had grown up into things alive, each assuming an entity. It was very late now to think of causes. He should have thought about them in college. His mother should have studied them closely, given them deep consideration while Larry Nevin could see.

Mr. Somerset was going to Washington to have his say for the N.A.M. Larry had heard of the N.A.M. in college. It stood for the National Association of Manufacturers, if he remembered rightly.

Was the N.A.M. a cause of his blindness, or was it a cause of Mr. Somerset? He didn't know. What the devil did a National Association of Manufacturers do?

Right at the moment, it brought up pictures of other letters that had been in his life. Tonight in the tunnel they marched like men, and with just as little meaning. A legion of letters marching to war to be blinded. N.A.M., W.P.A., O.P.A., N.R.A., A.A.A., F.S.A., C.L.U., T.V.A., T.N.E.C., H.O.L.C., C.I.O., A.F.L., C.E.D., N.L.R.B.

Were all those letters causes? Had they banded together hand in hand for the blinding of Larry Nevin? Christ, his

mother wouldn't know the meaning of one of them, unless it
was the O.P.A. He wondered how many his father knew. Or
the woman sitting beside him with the son in France. Or the
people sleeping noisily in the blackness of the car.

Yet all of those people voted. They voted for more letters,
more taxes to pay for blinded boys, more restrictions for boys
like Joe. They voted for less money for hospitals, less money
for teachers, less money for feeding the big-bellied kids in
Italy. They voted for millions and billions and trillions to
blow more people away. Mr. Somerset voted. I'm a member
of the N.A.M. I'm on my way to Washington to have my say!
Millions. Billions. Trillions. Blow it up to hell and gone with
blood and guts and the eyes of Larry Nevin, but in Christ's
sweet name don't spend it on making paupers well. That's
throwing money away!

And what had they taught Larry Nevin of causes?

The farm bloc was some kind of a fort where the farmers
stored up grain against the Indians or a rainy day. It was
square and had big spikes on top to keep unfriendly voters
from climbing inside and eating.

Shakespeare wrote plays, and said, "Yond Cassius has a lean
and hungry look; . . . such men are dangerous."

The National Chamber of Commerce published a maga-
zine and was larger in size than the ones under beds in the
country.

Russians wore beards, danced with their boots on, drank
vodka, and would fight America after the war to make it a
Communist nation.

Einstein and Steinmetz were Jews.

Lobbying meant hanging around lobbies with money in a
small black bag.

If you played with frogs you got warts, and with yourself
you got pimples.

Unions were groups of racketeers banded together to get
niggers into Southern plants on a par with white men so the

niggers could intermarry. All union men had been run out of Chicago by the F.B.I.

No gentleman ever let his wife know when he went to a whorehouse.

Senators kissed babies and handed out cigars, voted for higher taxes to put in useless waterways, and supported the farm bloc.

The government killed hogs that were needed to feed the poor, dumped oranges into the river that were needed to save children from rickets, supported all people who wanted to idle, and kept electing Roosevelt, a mental defective, despite the fact that nobody in the country wanted him for President.

The "free press" was the mainstay of the nation, because the only truth to be found was in the paper you subscribed to. All other papers published lies.

The only gentleman was a Southern gentleman, and sometimes when they slipped their granddaughters had coal-black babies.

The North gave niggers a free hand because the people didn't know how to treat them and were never kind to them. Southern gentlemen on northern trips knocked down niggers in subways and washrooms, thereby averting a second Civil War.

New York, the movies, all clothing stores, and most of the government agencies were entirely controlled by Jews.

If you fed a man who was hungry, he'd never work again.

The machine never put anyone out of work, because it made more jobs for industrious people.

A gentleman always gave a lady his seat in a streetcar, except now the streetcars were gone.

Wanamaker sold shoestrings.

Rockefeller saved his dimes to give to little boys.

Carnegie worked hard day and night to buy libraries.

Larry Nevin didn't know a goddam thing about anything. He'd been misinformed by ignorant teachers, ignorant friends, and ignorant parents. He'd been pumped full of unadulterated crap in primary school, in grammar school, in high school, and in college.

He'd been told that he had lost his eyes to save his country. Now that he was totally blind, he could see quite well that the statement was just another goddam lie.

He could only save his country by learning and thinking. He could only save that whimpering baby behind him from losing its eyes by learning and thinking.

If he'd lost his sight for anything, it was that he might see more clearly. That might save others. He didn't know. He fell asleep determined at least to try.

BOOK THREE

# Furlough

## 14. SUNLIGHT

THE air was getting warmer. Someone fastened back the door to the car. A breeze blew in and the chill was gone. Warmth was everywhere, peaceful and lulling. The train slowed down as though ripping through such balmy stillness was sacrilege. It shuffled along like a lazy boy plodding barefoot on a country road to kick up tiny dust clouds. The smell of resin from stacked-up boards seeped into the car. A saw whined shrilly. Hot sun struck against Larry's cheek, and suddenly he could see.

He was blinded, not blind. The only things that had changed in life were the unfamiliar. The things he had known for twenty-three years would remain the same, unchanging forever, like the lichen-covered wall in France. Those were the things that, encountered again, he would always see.

The pine mill with the whining saw which the train had passed was very clear. He could see the piled-up sawdust burning slowly with an endless invisible fire that sent an acrid smoke plume out to fog the air. The mill was built high up on logs, an open-sided building covered with a corrugated iron roof. A grinning Negro rode the shuttling carriage, flashing back and forth with dazzling speed, moving levers that fed the log to the whirling saw. Boards fell off, moving slowly away in a tired procession, carried along by an endless chain to be piled where their resinous odor might mingle with smoke from the sawdust fire.

The crawling train stopped. The talkative lady pushed by

his knees with a long farewell and scraping him gently with
bundles.

He said, "Good-by," and sat silent.

Baggage trucks were running swiftly along platforms outside. The Negro porters, riding standing in back of the speeding trucks, dodged people and each other with frightening
skill.

The voices outside, loud with excited greetings, were familiar. He could see the faces, watch the embraces, follow the
people out through the station into their cars and travel home
with them through Jacksonville.

Bay Street was bright in the sun.

"Larry!"

"Who is it?"

The kiss said Mother.

"Who's with you, Mother?" He clung to her tightly.

"Your father and Chris."

The handclasp was Dad's. The second kiss belonged to
Chris. The sunlight was playing in her hair.

"Larry, dearest!"                   .

"Hello, Chris. You're looking prettier than I ever saw you.
Umm . . . Maybe a little stouter."

"Why, Larry Nevin, how you do go on!"

Now how in hell did he know she'd say that? Didn't she
know he could see them, every one?

"We just couldn't wait until ten-thirteen, Larry. Chris got
gas from the ration board and we came up in her car. Dr. Bannerman was simply dying to come along with us. Insisted it
was his duty. Sometimes I just simply can't understand your
father. He just wouldn't let him come. I said, 'Lawrence
Nevin, I don't know what you're thinking of. The minister
himself!' It made no more difference than it ever does when
your father gets one of his spells on. I said, 'What do you
think our boy will . . .'"

The sunlight glittered on his mother's glasses as her head
bobbed up and down. It touched the lines on his father's face,

heightening the crow's-feet at the corners of the patient understanding eyes.

"Let me take your arm, Dad. Walk a little ahead of me. You
can go ahead at your regular pace. I've been trained to get
around. You needn't worry about the steps. As long as I have
my cane with me, I'm a whiz at going up or down."

His father's suit was the gray one that he'd had five years.
Larry knew it by the patched place under the arm. They went
down the steps together. His dad was as good as Corporal
Flagg. His mother was talking behind them, telling Chris
something about getting his luggage. Funny how well he could
see them all.

Larry said softly, "Thank you, Dad," as they stepped from
off the bottom step.

"Okay, old man."

Both of them knew that the word of thanks concerned Dr.
Bannerman and had nothing to do with Larry safely reaching the ground. A brand-new bond had formed between them.
It was the first time in his entire life his father had called him
"old man."

He saw the station as they all walked through—the ticket windows to the left, the Western Union straight ahead, the maga-
zine-covered newsstand. Outside the doors, the parking places
were to their right, alive with sun that was streaming on
asphalt and glittering cars.

Confusion came when he tried to get into Chris's car with
all of them helping. He dropped his cane and tangled with
Chris attempting to retrieve it. In the front seat beside her,
at last, he found that his hand was shaky. He offered Chris a
cigarette, took one himself, and pushed the lighter on the
dash.

Behind him, his mother quit talking, but the silence was
worse than her chatter. He was glad when the cigarettes were
lit and Chris had started the car.

"How did you know where that lighter was?" Chris turned

the car deftly onto the viaduct. She had always been smooth
at driving.

Larry turned his head as though to look closer. The wind
would be whipping her golden hair. The freckle on her nose
would shine with that tiny spot of golden brown.

"Maybe you don't remember me. I'm Larry Nevin. I've
ridden more than a hundred times in this car."

"Don't be foolish, dear. Of course I remember." They had
reached the crest of the viaduct and started down.

"—and the biggest batch of biscuits that the stove will hold.
Of course, there's the problem of butter, Larry boy. There's
been practically not a piece in Palatka even with ration points.
I drove over to East Palatka yesterday just to see if I couldn't
get some from Mrs. Stewart Brown. She's having a lot of
trouble herself getting decent feed for her cows. Had to sell
three of them just last month. You and your father know
what that means. Butter and milk are both cut down. Not
that I ever like to pay the black market prices asked by her
and Stewart Brown. I'd churn myself, if I had the milk and
cream to spare. Heaven knows I've—"

"I'm taking up golf," said Chris, and checked herself
abruptly.

The car was running out Riverside toward Ortega. He
could see the trees, and down to the left between stucco houses
the flashes of the St. Johns River. The river ran north, rising
way down the state in a lake called Helen Blazes. The whole
thing was crazy. When you went up the river, you really were
going down.

Shortly they would strike the road that used to be brick,
the road that led through Orange Park, where the loose bricks
rattled in front of the peaceful Moose's Home. It might have
been nice to sit forever smoking a pipe and feeling the sunshine on his face in front of the Moose's Home.

The trees were thick along the road and shadows dappled
the roadway. He could see the picture clearly. Only now the
road was wider for the traffic to Camp Blanding.

"I'll take up golf myself, Chris. They'll teach me to play if the course is open when I get back up to Valley Forge. I can keep it up when I get to Old Farms. We can have a lot of fun."

"Of course," Chris told him brightly. "It will be a lot of fun."

His mother had stopped talking.

"I bowl," said Larry, and remembered that there had been no alleys in Palatka when he left there. "I hear there's good fishing at Avon Old Farms. Trout in the Farmington River that runs through the grounds—it was a boys' school. There's bass in a pond. How about some fishing while I'm down here, Chris?"

"I'd love it, Larry. That would be fun."

He knew how she looked without being told. She was very beautiful. A flush of red was in her cheeks. Her eyes were blue and sparkling. Her lips were red and kissable. Her slender legs stretched out before her were the shapeliest he'd ever seen. Her sweater was tight over swelling breasts.

The road swept down to the bridge over Doctor's Inlet. Beneath the bridge, the water was choked with hyacinths. The hyacinths were decked with tiny flowers. Later on the flowers vanished, leaving nothing but a solid mass of vivid green. Beneath the hyacinths which choked the river were fish that you couldn't get to.

Beneath the darkness, choking the light, were things that you couldn't get to.

They'd been told not to ask him questions. They'd been told to be bright and gay. They were watching their steps. Only his father was human, and he was the one who had never had anything to say.

Maybe that's why he'd never known his father. It was strange how quickly he'd learned to know him today. His father came from New Jersey. After being discharged from the First World War, he'd moved down South to stay. Gas, or something. Larry had never been curious, yet he had followed his father's pattern in many ways. He had the same moody

reticence, the same desire to read a lot. He had his father's
Northern speech, and had never adopted his mother's Southern accent. When mad at them both, she called them Yankees.

"—so I've arranged a little party tonight and it's just for
you, Larry boy. Now if you don't like anyone coming, all you
need to do is say so and I'll simply send them away. I really
mean that, Larry dear. I'll simply send them away. Of course,
they're simply dying to meet you, and every single one of
them wants to give you thanks for what you've done. Your
father and I are so proud of you, Larry, we really don't know
what to say. And Chris is proud of you, aren't you, Chris? And
if Larry doesn't want to come to the party, if he wants to be
alone with you, you simply take him away. I know you feel—"

They were pulling out of Green Cove Springs, where the
live oak trees made tunnels over the roadway. In places, the
Spanish moss hung so low the tips would brush the car. The
sun never quite got through the trees, and parts of the town
to Larry had always been gray.

There was a bathhouse where he used to swim. The water
from the spring was sulphur, and it bubbled up from deep in
the earth to form a pool of translucent emerald green that
still was crystal-clear.

Chris would dive, and the naked lines of her girlish body
would show like something fluid beneath the water as she
swam. She always seemed to belong there, to have a home in
the pool so cool and clear. Larry always dived in to join her.
For an instant they'd swim together, and sometimes he'd touch
her, and she'd seem very near.

She slowed the car, and her hand brushed his knee as she
shifted gear.

"We just passed the pool where we used to swim, didn't we,
Chris?"

"The things you remember, Larry!"

They'd told her to be natural, not to mention his blindness
and not to avoid it. Why the hell couldn't she be herself? She
was stiff as a poker—"The things you remember, Larry!" She

was going to be sweet or bust a gut. She wasn't going to stare at his plastic eye for fear he might see her.

They'd told his mother to be casual, probably Dr. Bannerman. "Be casual, as if nothing has happened, dear lady. Just trust in God, and let your mother instinct guide you!" Well, her instinct was certainly guiding her wrong. She was talking his goddam head off, boring a hole in his ear.

He sat silent without listening.

The car passed fields where he'd hunted for quail, endless stretches of cut-over land where Tip had run, putting up covey after covey and ruthlessly tracking the singles down.

They were near Tocoi. He had driven that road with his father when the road was nothing but hub-deep ruts that bounced you up off the seat of the ancient car. They had stuck one night in a mudhole and waited for dawn, and Larry had cried at the hooting of an owl.

A short bridge stuttered. They'd crossed Rice Creek. Palatka was very near.

"We can try the fishing in Rice Creek soon. How'd you like that, Chris?"

"That *would* be fun, Larry."

The car sped on. He'd never go fishing with Chris again. Something was wrong. The car rolled in on familiar roads and stopped at home on Bronson Street. Neighbors yelled from the Nevin front porch that was shining in the sun.

"—now they're all just dying to see you, Larry boy."

His father spoke up in a voice that Larry had never heard. "Sit right where you are, old man. Mother, you and Chris get out."

"Why, Lawrence Nevin, you've lost your mind! Your boy's just home, and people are waiting."

"Mother, you and Chris get out, and goddam quick. Larry and I are driving downtown to have some whisky and chase it with some beer!"

"DAD."

"Yes?"

"Here's looking at you."

"Good health, Larry."

"I'm really looking at you, Dad. You look just the same as when I went away."

"I'm a little grayer, Larry. Time marches on."

"Dad, are we alone?"

"There's just Tod Wimer back of the bar."

"Can he hear us?"

"I don't believe so. Why?"

"I don't know. I'm glad you brought me here for a drink. Tod knew me right away, didn't he?"

"Why shouldn't he? You look just the same too."

"Bartenders aren't the same as other people, are they? There's a guy named Charlie in the Columbia Bar at Phoenixville. The fellows like him. He seems to understand."

"Bartenders see a lot of fellows with their hair down, Larry. They hear a lot of stories."

"Dad, order us another one. I feel sort of funny inside after that train ride. A couple of drinks may settle me down."

"Sure thing, Larry."

His father left and returned again. A radio started playing. Larry decided it must be in back of the bar. He located the glass on the table. It had made a noise when his father set it down.

"Here's looking at you." It was a very nice toast—a toast with a comforting sound.

"And you, old man. Drink it down."

"Dad, what's the matter with Mother?"

"Nothing, Larry. What makes you ask me that?"

"She's different, Dad. Something's cockeyed. She never talked like that before."

"Talked like what?"

"Gabbling on about nothing—butter and milk from Stewart Brown. She talked without stopping on the whole drive down from Jacksonville."

"Your mother was always talkative, Larry."

"Not like that. You know it as well as I do. She'd say her piece when she got mad about something, but then she'd quit. She seemed—"

"What, Larry?"

"Not glad to see me." Larry finished his beer. It was warm and the dregs were bitter. "She's changed, Dad. Chris has changed. The whole damn town's changed. Everyone except you, Dad."

"Are you sure about me?"

"Certain."

"Think now. Have we ever talked this way before? Ever had drinks together in a bar?"

"No. I guess we haven't."

"Then I've changed."

"Hell, I guess you have, Dad. That makes it a hundred per cent. Changes in everyone. Changes in the whole damn town. I suppose it's the war. I've dreamed of coming home, Dad. Pictured how everything would be. I never believed that Mother could change, or Chris. Mother was cold this morning, Dad. She was— God, I don't know, hard inside as if she'd never had any love for me."

"And what about my changes, Larry?"

"At least you didn't let me down."

"Your mother hasn't changed, old man. She loves you more than anything in the world. She hasn't let you down."

"She didn't seem very glad to see me."

"Neither was I. Did you expect us to be?"

"I thought—"

"—that we'd be overjoyed to see you coming home blinded,

Larry? The only child we have? You don't give much credit
to your mother and me. It's tough for you, son. Tough as hell.
You can't laugh that off, but it affects your father and mother
too, and all the folks who know you. Your mother's been
under a terrible strain. She had to be brave with all the neighbors watching. She's had to be brave for a long, long time.
She did her crying in private when you went off to war. Now
she's talking awfully fast to cover up tears that choke her. You
should thank her for the beautiful act she's putting on, instead of getting sore."

"I'm not sore, Dad. I'm just sorry that it seemed that way
to me."

"Nothing's changed at all, Larry. The town's the same old
sleepy place. Maybe a little sleepier since the cypress mill
shut down. Your mother's the same, loving you as she always
did, maybe a little more. I'm the same, except that we're a
little closer. You're older now, and you've been through battle,
and the same thing happened to me. Chris is the same."

Larry lifted his empty glass and put it down. "She's not
the same to me. It's something inside her that's changed, Dad;
nothing I can see."

His father left and brought more beer. "I was engaged to
a girl in Princeton, Larry. All the time that I was in France,
she wrote to me. Her letters were full of Princeton—places
where we'd ridden horseback together, places where we'd eaten
together, news about the students, the baseball games, and the
ivy-covered walls in spring. I knew from the letters that the
girl was in love with me."

"I didn't know that you went to Princeton, Dad."

"I didn't. I went to war."

"You've never talked about it much."

"Maybe I tried to forget it, Larry. Maybe no one was interested enough to ever ask me. Maybe that's why I'm telling
you now. In a very short time you'll be a civilian and your
ribbons and chevrons will all be gone. You'll only have your
blindness to show. I didn't even have that. I had only bad

health from gas in my lungs. It made me find a living in a climate that was warm, but it wasn't very interest-arousing. Think me tough if you want to, but in three years' time your eyes won't be interest-arousing either. That's one thing I'll guarantee."

"So you married Mother instead of the girl."

"That's right, old man, or you probably wouldn't be sitting here with me. In the Army I had a lot of dreams. I suppose you've had them too."

"Lots of dreams, Dad."

"You're damned unlucky, Larry. You're a lot like me. I dreamed of going to Princeton, with all its background and ancient halls, and of all the things I'd do when the girl and I were married. We'd travel together abroad—I was going to be highly successful—we'd visit the East together and see Japan and the cherry trees. As a matter of fact, there was little we wouldn't see."

"But you had to move South." Larry heard his father drink deeply of the beer.

"That, of course. Then I met a girl in London. She was very exciting and very sweet to me. The letters from Princeton began to change. I went back to France and both of the girls kept writing. Fellows I knew kept dying. I still longed for Princeton, but some of its vital importance had faded.

"When I left the Army I hurried home. My mother had died in an auto crash, and my father had been dead since before the war. The girl was still there, but the girl had changed. Her kisses weren't the kisses I'd dreamed of, not nearly so warm as the girl's in London. Princeton had changed. The great stone buildings were smaller. The ivy was dusty from cars on the highway. The trees were stunted and not actually green."

The radio back of the bar flared up, and was quickly lowered again.

Larry said softly, "I think I know what you mean."

"No," said his father. "I'm telling you this because you don't know what I mean. Nothing had changed at Princeton except the contents of a dream. The great stone buildings were just as large measured inch for inch. The ivy was thicker, if anything. The trees were fuller, spreading wider, and just as green. The girl was just as much in love with the Lawrence Nevin who'd kissed her good-by and gone to war, but the Lawrence Nevin who went to war never returned. She couldn't love the bitter stranger who came back. That Lawrence Nevin was a man she'd never seen."

"It was you who had changed, Dad?"

"That's your danger, Larry. I was smarting under injustice. I hated everyone for the goddam dumbness that had wrecked my life, killed my comrades, ruined my marriage and sent me down to another state to make a living at any work I could find there. I hated people who let wars come. Now you hate people who let wars come."

"That's had me frantic already."

"And others beside you, Larry. Others without so much cause to be bitter. I've talked to boys who've been overseas and felt their animosity, their hate, in fact. They don't know why they hate me, but I do, Larry. They hate me because I hated people who brought on wars, and myself did nothing about it. I lost my chance with the other soldiers who came back in 1918. Now you're blind and hating too. You're blaming me and your mother and Chris, and the people here in town. Everything's changed, yet nothing has changed except Larry Nevin."

"What in God's name can I do, Dad? I met a blind Negro in Valley Forge and didn't even know he was black. I liked him. We kicked around together in Phoenixville. I got to thinking about Mother forbidding me to play with a Negro boy when I was a kid. She told me all sorts of things. Now I know that they're none of them true. I've been stewing about it on the whole trip down."

"You've helped already."

"I don't see how."

"By merely realizing that you're facing a problem far too big for just me and you."

"You mean there's nothing I can do?"

"There's a lot you can do, if other blinded boys will help you. You have power now, Larry—much more power than I ever had."

"But I'm blind, Dad."

"That's what I'm referring to. You can make friends with this Negro boy. You say you like him?"

"Yes. I certainly do."

"Then go around with him. Get other white blind boys to do it too. There's nobody in the country will ever dare to raise a voice against you."

"But why did Mother teach me it was wrong?"

"Because she was taught it was wrong, Larry. I was too. Your mother had to live down here where most people think it's wrong to be social equals with a Negro."

"Why do they think it's wrong?"

"You did, didn't you? It took a frightful thing, Larry, to make a change in you. You're still young."

"That's strange, Dad. I heard almost the same thing from a Jewish boy named Ivan Stern."

"He probably knows, Larry, since he's a Jew. As I said, you're young. Now, you'll have enough money coming in to at least eat on for the rest of your life. I had to make a living, son, to buy clothes and food for your mother and you. I was in the South and I had to have jobs. Let a man get branded as a nigger lover and he's bucking a system. A system can starve you and put you and your wife and your children out on the street. A system can wreck a woman socially, take all her friends away. It can do much more than that, Larry. It can start wars too—wars between classes, wars between races, wars between countries, wars that kill millions, and blind boys like you."

"You think I can help because I have a pension and because I'm blind?"

"I know it, old man. You can if you want to. Public opinion changes. Just a few years ago, drinking in a decent bar was wrong."

"But you couldn't fight race prejudice, even if you wanted to?"

"It would have ruined me, son—ruined your mother and you."

"I think I'm beginning to see things clearer, thanks to you."

"I owe you some sight, Larry. There might have been a lot of other things I could have thought about and worked at to save you."

"Dad, what makes people so dumb?"

His father was silent until the rest of the beer was gone. "How much French do you know, Larry, outside of 'Voulez-vous promenader avec moi ce soir?' and 'Hinky dinky, parlez-vous!'?"

"Not enough to read a menu."

"Well, think this over. It's a little French verse that may interest you:

> "Ce monde est plein de fous,
> Et qui n'en veut pas voir
> Doit se renfermer seul
> Et casser son miroir."

"I understand enough to get that, Dad. Let's go. I'd like you to drive me around the town before we go home."

It hadn't changed at all. River Street was just the same, and Lemon Street, and all the streets he knew. When they stopped at the house he got out alone and found the steps without his father. He knew by the silence that Chris and the neighbors had gone.

It was easy to walk down the long straight hall to where dishes clanked in the kitchen.

"I smell biscuits, Mother. I haven't had a bite to eat for nearly three years, and Dad gave me a little verse to recite for you—

"The world is full of fools,
And not to see one pass
You must lock up yourself alone
And break your looking-glass."

She took him quietly in her arms and said, "Baby!"


## 16. "LARRY-BOY"

THE prospective gathering his mother had arranged for the evening worried him all afternoon. Finally he summoned nerve enough to plead he was tired. He couldn't face a group of townsfolk gathered to thank him for what he had done.

He slept in his own bed, yet it wasn't his own. He'd dreamed about it for far too long, shivering and twisting on the floor of a truck, never quite free from danger. No bed in the world could ever meet such a build-up.

It was shorter than he had thought, and the mattress had lumps and buttons which he couldn't remember ever having noticed before.

Tossing restlessly, he heard his mother and father come up-stairs and pause for a moment's conference in the hall. After a little his mother came in and crossed the room, bumping into the chair where he'd hung his clothes. He fought an in-sane desire to ask her why she didn't turn the light on. When she kissed him and tucked the covers closer around him he muttered in feigned sleepiness.

After she left, he was irritated into further wakefulness at his own unreasonable conduct. "It took a frightful thing, Larry, to make a change in you," his father had told him that morning. There was something still more frightful which his father had overlooked: he didn't want to change.

He wanted his mother to be the same, someone he could turn to in every trouble, someone he could follow unthink-ingly without the creeping doubts that were plaguing him now. He wanted to hold forever to that single restful moment when she'd taken him in her arms at lunchtime and called him "Baby."

Yet that was gone, as his home was gone. He knew it, bitterly, now that he was there. The confines of the house had shrunk, as his bed had shrunk. They were part of the town, and all of Palatka was smaller. What had his father said about Princeton? "The great stone buildings were just as large, measured inch for inch. Nothing had changed—except the contents of a dream."

But everything in Larry's past life was the contents of a dream. He could never measure bed or buildings inch for inch. That was a property of vision. He could only remember that once he could climb to his mother's lap and she'd kiss his tears away; that once he found wisdom in every word she had to say.

He could never measure Chris by inches. He could only dream that once she was shining beauty, and once he had thought her wise and witty. Now, in a day, he found himself comparing her with another girl, and Chris had shrunk in stature.

Or maybe Larry had grown since he'd been away. Maybe he'd built a yardstick in his maturing brain. If so, it was something he hated. How could there be a yardstick in the love of a son for his mother or the love of a boy for his childhood sweetheart? What arrogant egotism had come alive inside him that would force him to question the thinking of older people or the wisdom of his own home town? If it was manhood, he wanted none of such unhappiness. He wanted to be a boy again. Blind, the status of manhood was far too heavy to bear.

Tomorrow he'd renounce it. He'd take up with Chris where he last left off. Mr. Paterson was giving him a party—maybe to announce his engagement to Chris. He'd go and have fun, be normal, show them what a blind man could do. Everybody in Palatka would be there.

After dinner he could slip away with Chris in the car. . . .

"Are you in love with someone, Larry?" That was Judy and

she had no right to be there, speaking out of the darkness. His bedroom was sacred, the bedroom of a little boy. Maybe he should call his mother. His mother would banish her quickly, send her packing back to the Victory Bar.

"Yes, I'm in love with someone," he mimicked half aloud. "I'm in love with the girl I'm going to marry."

Judy was nothing but a shade, anyhow. Chris was real and beautiful, with sunlight in her hair and a father who owned a barrel plant. He'd close the deal tomorrow and never think of Judy again. Judy was too much responsibility for a little boy.

His sleep was fitful, peopled with some of the old excitement that had kept him awake during long past nights when a fishing trip was planned for early morning.

He woke before eight, touched his watch, and lay still awhile hunched under the covers, wondering about the state of the weather. Outside Tip barked desultorily at some imaginary quarry, then quieted at a word from Larry's mother.

Her solicitude for his comfort annoyed him, and again his own unreasonableness was brought to mind as it had been when he lay in bed the night before. His mother's motive in quieting the dog was certainly natural and kindly. What the hell was he griping about?

Everything seemed cockeyed since he got home. God knows he'd never read motives into other people's simplest actions before. Now he was projecting himself into everything, developing a sensitivity that could drive him crazy.

Suppose his mother had let Tip bark.

Larry thought that over and decided he'd still have been sore. He was forced to admit that it wasn't his mother's actions that upset him, it was his own unsettled state of mind. He wanted mothering, yet he didn't. He needed consideration, help, and guidance. Let anyone offer those necessities and immediately he rejected them with anger.

The answer was clear, yet he hated to admit it. Every innocent courtesy, every gesture of love and protection was reminding him of his blindness. He simply had to quit weighing each attention, analyzing it with cynicism to judge if it was offered only because his eyes were gone.

Yet when he got out of bed he moved on tiptoe, frightened that his mother would hear him and come upstairs to guide him to the bathroom door.

In the bathroom he found his electric razor, plugged in the cord, then closed and bolted the door. An unaccustomed modesty had grown during the past few weeks, another trait he had never been conscious of before.

Again his blindness must be to blame. If Army training discouraged anything, it was the practice of false modesty. Countless times Larry had stood stripped before a hundred equally naked men, nonchalantly talking, with no more thought of his nudity than one of a group of urchins cavorting around a swimming hole.

At Valley Forge the feeling of watching eyes had come to life and grown, a sensation of marked discomfort which made him awkward, the sensation of a typist trying to work with an onlooker standing behind the chair. It persisted while he was eating too, robbing him of normal ease and causing him to spill an occasional mouthful that was handled with an overdose of care.

The hum of his razor brought his mother halfway up the stairs.

"Are you all right, Larry-boy?"

He could feel her unseen eyes, full of worry, peering through her twinkling glasses, peering through the railings, boring through the sanctity of the bathroom door.

"Sure, Mother. Everything's okay." He unplugged the razor, stopping its sound-killing whir.

"I have waffles for breakfast."

"That's fine, Mother. I'll be right down."

"Are you dressed yet?"

"Five minutes, Mother." He reconnected the razor in token of dismissal.

"Larry!"

"Yes." The razor was silent again.

"You can eat in your bathrobe, honey."

"I'll dress first, Mother." He waited to hear her footsteps, but she lingered on the stairs—both of them waiting, he to hear it and she to say it. It was hellish—that knowledge of what she was going to say.

"Can I help you, Larry?"

"No, Mother. Everything's okay."

"Well, if I can help you, Larry-boy, just call." Her footsteps descended slowly, doubtfully, unwillingly—down the stairs, dragging out to the kitchen along the downstairs hall.

His fingers trembled as he plugged the cord on the razor again. Christ, he was a stinker! He'd led her on deliberately, planned everything that she'd said to him from her very first call. Why, in the name of heaven, why? Only a monster could hurt a mother who loved him, bait her with cruelty, mock her affection.

Was he trying to show his own cleverness, or to tickle his lousy vanity because he could outthink her? No, by God, it wasn't that. It was something far deeper—some horrible change that had made him unnatural, made him want to hurt himself. When he hurt his mother, he was the one who suffered worst of all.

"Well, if I can help you, Larry-boy, just call."

Shaving in darkness, he flailed himself with the words still ringing in his ears. What did she think? That he'd wet the seat or mess his pants in the bathroom? Or shave his behind instead of his face?

Couldn't she give him credit for being a man, even though he must grope through life in blackness? That was what hurt him—the fact that he knew she didn't believe he was grown up and would always offer to help him, the fact that he could anticipate her offer.

Shushing the dog—calling off the party the night before because he said he was tired—"—if I can help you, Larry-boy, just call!"

Suppose he took her at her word—"Okay, Mother darling! You gave me a pair of eyes at birth. What about another pair?" That should keep her quiet and stop her futile offers of assistance. Yet he'd never say it. Instead he'd skillfully hurt her with silence, kill her with cleverness, torture her with the lifting of a disapproving eyebrow.

His hands were still trembling when he finished shaving and washing. He clung to the railing as he made his way to his bedroom at the end of the upstairs hall. His dressing was noiselessly furtive and done with meticulous care.

Somehow he had to show her, prove his worth, convince her that he wasn't a helpless changeling. His appearance had become a challenge. If he appeared at breakfast without a flaw the fact might finally convince her that her son was a man quite able to do anything at all.

In the dining room the smell of coffee calmed him, coupled with the ease of locating his chair. There were flowers on the table. He drank in their fragrance, found his napkin, fresh and clean, and smelled it too.

"Mother, I'm down."

"Coming, Larry. Drink your orange juice. I'll be right there."

He reached for the glass with caution and closed his fingers around its icy smoothness. The first sweet sip was full of overpowering flavor and brought the peace that he'd missed for years.

This was his home in Florida, his mother's house, built for him and his father by loving care. Maybe he couldn't see it, but with overwhelming suddenness he woke up to the fact that he was there. Nowhere else was the orange juice acrid and sweet as honey, lingering long on the tongue. Nowhere else was the linen cool and creamy and caressingly smooth to his fingers.

This was breakfast at home, his mother's breakfast. Instead

of smoke and death and blood, the air was filled with flowers and coffee. This, at last, was a dream come true.

His mother came in and set the waffles before him. "I cut them up, Larry, and covered them well wtih butter and syrup. Is that all right?"

"All right, old lady? It's swell!!"

"I'll 'old lady' you, young man."

He reached out an arm and circled her waist as she stood beside him, then drew her close and laid his cheek against her arm. "You didn't kiss me good morning!"

"I didn't know that you wanted me to, Mist' Nevin, suh!"

"I allus kiss the servin' maids, Missus Nevin, ma'am!"

She held him close and kissed his lips in a game they hadn't played for years.

"Larry, your coffee!" She freed herself and used both hands to thoroughly rumple his hair.

When his coffee was poured and sugared and creamed, she sat across the table, taking his father's chair. He knew she was watching, but now he didn't seem to mind. It was part of something he'd longed for, just to have her there.

"What are your plans this morning, Larry?"

"I'm going shopping with my mother." His mouth was over-full of waffle. He swallowed some coffee and searched with his fork for another morsel of waffle. She didn't offer to help him. "Want me to go shopping with you?"

"You know I do, Larry Nevin. I'll be the envy of every woman in town."

"Humph!" he grunted. "Maybe I'll make you let me drive the car."

She was silent an instant, then he heard her push back her chair. "No," she said, "but I'll let you dry the dishes for me, smarty. And one thing else—"

"What?"

"If you're going downtown with your mother, you'll have to brush your hair. I've rumpled it into a terrible mess, Larry-boy." She went out into the kitchen.

He sat searching idly for a last piece of waffle that wasn't there, knowing full well why she'd mussed his hair. It was already mussed. In spite of all his careful dressing, he'd forgotten to use a comb and brush before he came down to breakfast. She'd always call him "Larry-boy." He didn't care.

## 17. HAIL THE CONQUERING HERO!

THE porch swing had a creak in the chains when you moved it backward, but when it swung forward the creak was a groan. A vine grew on one end of the porch, almost closing it in. There were pungent flowers on the vine which attracted bees. Now and again one of the bees would knock off the job of collecting honey and go exploring, zooming around your head. A bee could sound monstrously large when it was cloaked in darkness, and it carried a sense of danger with it. You didn't dare fan it away. Waving a hand, you might inadvertently hit it and get yourself stung.

Chris was due to pick him up at half-past four.

The proper thing was to keep a lover waiting. A lover's heart expanded, thumping wildly at his loved one's expected arrival. The dragging minutes provided him with time to dream, painting exquisite pictures on the canvas of his mind. Eagerly he checked the shadows, lengthened by the dropping of the sun.

Ah, sweet misery! Mayhaps she languished in the arms of another! Mayhaps—

A car turned in to Bronson Street two blocks away, slowed at the corner and went on by. That was the eleventh one.

It was nearly five.

His mother was moving about upstairs, humming a little tune.

He wished he had a good stiff drink. He was turning into an awful lush. Booze for breakfast, booze for lunch, and booze for suppertime! "My precious boy ended in the gutter at twenty-three!" So he liked his liquor. So this, so that, so what? It never kept him waiting. It loosened up his tongue and innards. It made him feel swell.

Booze was like cursing, an easy outlet that never failed you. You couldn't talk and couldn't think, so you drank and swore. Boy, did that get their attention! They weren't sorry about your eyes; they were sorry about your morals. "That sweet boy gone to perdition—and blind with it all!" He hoped it worried their asses off. He liked to annoy them. What the hell!

He felt his watch. Five past five. Maybe the stinking thing had stopped. He held it close to his ear and heard it ticking. People thought that clock-hands moved slow when they watched them!

Judy had never kept him waiting, but Judy was only a voice, an echo at a table in a bar.

His mother came down and sat in the swing beside him. "Chris is a little late, Larry. I guess she's dressing."

"Probably, Mother." What did he care if Chris was dressing? He couldn't see her if she arrived stark-naked in her car.

"You look very nice in your uniform, Larry."

"And I suppose the black glasses make me look like a movie star."

"They are rather attractive. Certainly they're not conspicuous at all."

A car pulled up to the curb and he heard the slam of a door. Chris's light footsteps clicked up the walk and onto the porch. Larry kept time with them, tapping with the tip of his cane.

"You look lovely, darling," his mother said.

"Thank you, Mrs. Nevin. I'm afraid I'm a little late. I picked up two of the girls who are coming to the party—Eleanor Ruckeiser and Maud Sloan. They teach with me at school. I hope I haven't kept Larry waiting."

Well, by God, she had kept Larry waiting—stolen time from his precious furlough. And where the hell did she think *he*

was? Inside the house? Half a mile down the street? Or maybe
she thought his mother had stuffed him and fitted him with
nice glass eyes and mounted him on the swing! "I hope I
haven't kept Larry waiting," indeed. He had an inclination
to tell her he wouldn't go. He hated nitwits who discussed
him as though he wasn't present.

"Did you get that dress in Palatka, Chris?" She might realize
he was still alive if he said something.

"Jacksonville, darling." Her laugh was nervous. "I bought
it just for the party."

So neither his mother nor Chris was going to describe it.
Well, mindreader Nevin would create his own description and
see how they liked it. "It's sharp," he said, bending forward a
trifle. "The neckline's good and the skirt flares out just right
at the waist. And I've always liked that particular shade of
green."

A bee buzzed loudly through the silence.

His mother said, "But, Larry-boy—"

"As a matter of fact," Chris told him slowly after a wait,
"it's sort of a red."

"Come here." Larry stretched out his hand.

Chris stepped closer, but he sensed her hesitation. Deliberately he appraised the fabric with his fingers, found her waist-
line and smoothed the filmy dress down firmly over her un-
girdled hip and thigh. She stiffened under his pressing palm.
Her marked embarrassment pleased him. She was uncomfortable under his mother's eyes and afraid to move for fear of
hurting his feelings.

Sadistically he prolonged the situation, moving his hand
significantly downward until his little finger slipped over the
hem of the dress and came in contact with her knee. It was
the first time he'd touched her in years, and then never with
such familiarity.

What puzzled him was that he experienced no thrill. She
was firm and vibrant and warm, but he might have been
stroking a marionette for all the kick there was in it. All he

wanted was to see how long she'd stand there, rigid and suffering. Somehow he just felt mean.

He moved his hand below the dress to the smoothness of her stocking, knowing that the gesture would start her soft cheeks flaming. She had always blushed very easily.

"Whatever you tell me," Larry announced with a grin, "that dress will always be green to me." He suddenly wanted Judy. Judy would grab him and kiss him with quick possession if he stroked her thigh and pressed his hand against her knee; Judy would— Hell, she'd understand that a blind man had to braille the things he couldn't see!

Chris had pulled away hastily. "I'm glad you like it anyhow, Larry." Her laugh was forced and full of ripples. She was mad as blazes. "You and Mr. Nevin are coming to the party, aren't you?"

"Of course, Chris, darling. But it may be late. Lawrence's hours are long at the plant, you know. Don't you children worry about us."

He'd upset his mother too with his foolishness. She never referred to his father as "Lawrence" unless something had gone wrong.

"We have to run," Chris said quickly, and put a hand on Larry's arm. "Come along, dear. The girls are waving at me."

"Have a good time, Larry-boy." Her voice showed concern.

"Yes, Mother."

As Chris took him out to the car he determined to have a good time or bust. He was the newcomer to Palatka, when all was said and done. Why did he expect others to act normally when he wasn't normal himself? Two years ago, a year ago, he'd have been petrified at the thought of entertaining a blind veteran newly come home.

Eleanor Ruckeiser put him all off again when Chris introduced him as they got in the car. He didn't know Eleanor Ruckeiser from Adam, nor Maud Sloan either and couldn't figure why Chris had brought them along—unless it was to exhibit her hero so word could get around the school.

Miss Ruckeiser gushed and addressed him as "Mr. Nevin" over a limp frightened hand. Larry felt sorry for the kids in her class who wouldn't recognize a sergeant when they got out of school.

For a wonder, in his state of irritability, he liked Maud Sloan. Her voice was assured, with even a hint of mockery in her greeting.

"Hi, sergeant."

He maneuvered a seat beside her by insisting he'd prefer to ride in the back of the car. She sat just close enough to be friendly and to let him know that he wasn't riding alone. He offered cigarettes. She let him light hers and his own and wordlessly guided his hand to a pull-out ashtray.

"How do you like being home?"

"I haven't been here long enough to know. It's like waking up in your own bed after some horrible nightmare."

"That's what Tom said when he was home on leave. Do you remember him? Tom Davis? We're engaged. He knows you."

Larry said, "Sure," stirred by a faint recollection of a long-legged incorrigible boy who had been in a scrape for breaking windows in the Mellon High School. "Is he in town now?"

"He left a month ago. He's in the Third Marines."

Larry said, "Oh." News was filtering in from Iwo Jima and there wasn't much more he could say. He wondered if Chris had talked about him to other fellows home on leave, and if they'd said "Oh."

"I'm keeping my fingers crossed, and praying," Maud remarked softly. Larry felt that she was looking at his own black glasses and that the glasses didn't matter. "All I want is for Tom to come home."

The car jounced and her knee touched Larry's. He thought of Judy. Everyone was reminding him of Judy. Or was it because Maud and Judy talked much the same?

He tossed his cigarette out of the window. "Sometimes I get hunches, Maud. Did you know the blind got hunches?"

"What kind of hunches, Larry?"

"Good and bad. This one's good. I have a hunch that Tom will be okay." He didn't add that Tom Davis must know he'd be a blithering fool to stop a bullet with such a girl at home. That was the knowledge that helped a soldier play the stinking game.

There were voices and hellos from the porch as the car pulled up to the Patersons' house on the edge of town. Some of the voices were hazily familiar. A couple of them, Dr. Bannerman and Chris's mother, Larry placed right away.

Accompanied by the minister, Mrs. Paterson came down to greet Larry at the car. He had a picture of her thin patrician face, the black velvet ribbon circling her throat, and her expensively waved white hair.

"Why, Larry Nevin, I do declare but it's good to have you home. I was just this minute telling deah Dr. Bannerman—"

He wasn't interested in what she was telling dear Dr. Bannerman. Her effusiveness wasn't like Mrs. Paterson, who was usually formal to a point of being cold. He'd never met her when she wasn't quite aware of Mr. Paterson's position in the town. She'd overshot her mark, tipped her hand in the very first words of greeting. She was having a social fit at the thought of her precious daughter, Chris, tied for life to a helpless blind man.

Dr. Bannerman was helping Larry from the car, turning on a thousand-watt charge of ministerial charm.

Inside of himself, Larry froze. He shouldn't have come anyhow. This party wasn't given for him—it was a wake for his blindness, a token by the Patersons that, come what may, they always did their duty. He knew it, knew that the thought had been eating him all afternoon. There'd have been no party for Larry Nevin, filling station attendant, home with eyes and no money. He'd bet a buck there had been no party for Maud's marine, Tom Davis, when he was home.

He didn't like Dr. Bannerman, and walked up the path to the porch in silence, resenting the minister's fatherly hand on his arm. If the minister wanted to sell religion, he might learn how to guide a blind man without pushing him along.

The porch was full of chattering women—elderly women waiting for their husbands, younger women waiting for their men to be killed or come home.

Larry found his face was set in a fixed mechanical smile. Chris had disappeared somewhere, leaving him trapped in the magpie cage alone.

Even the kindly voice of Dr. Horton, the dentist, failed to relax him. He felt that the dentist was under a strain when the talk turned to hunting. Larry Nevin's hunting days were done.

Someone passed cakes and icy drinks which proved to be a mixture of fruit juices blended with an innocuous sparkling cider. God was present, stern and all-seeing, so you couldn't even have a beer. Why the devil couldn't Bannerman go home?

Chris bustled up from somewhere. "Are you all right, Larry, darling?"

"Fine, except I wish you'd spike my next lemon phosphate with a shot from your father's private stock."

Her voice lowered. "Larry! Dr. Bannerman's here."

"Don't I know it? Chris—"

She started away, but he reached out quickly and closed his fingers around her arm.

"More people are coming, Larry."

"The hell with that. Take me inside, Chris, where we can talk."

"But, darling—"

"Chris, I mean it."

"Well, come on, then. It isn't very nice." A hint of impatience was in her tone. She led him inside to her father's tiny office.

"Shut the door, Chris."

"What will the guests say, Larry?"

"I don't give a damn."

"Larry!" She closed the door.

"Now listen, Chris. I'm not fit for human company. You've given this party, but everyone here is scared to death of this blind man you're lugging around. Everybody's miserable, and that includes you and me."

"I'm sorry, Larry. I thought—"

"Don't be sorry. Listen to me. I'll stick through supper under one condition—after we eat, you take me out for a drive. We'll have ourselves a couple of snorts, then sit in the car and talk awhile."

"Larry, I can't."

"Maybe you don't remember, Chris."

"Remember what?"

"You used to love to have a beer and take a drive with me."

"But, darling, the people—"

"This doesn't concern the people, Chris. Tell them I'm ill, or anything. This concerns our life—just you and me."


## 18.  AND  GREAT  WAS  THE  FALL

BACK on the broad veranda unseen hands kept plying Larry with food which he didn't want. A table had been set up somewhere near the end of the porch and a buffet supper was being served. The clatter of knives and forks seemed loud, cutting through voices, shuffling feet, and exclamations of praise.

"Scalloped oysters! My dear, I haven't seen anything so good since the war. From Apalachicola? I don't know *how* you—"

"Umm! Homemade cake!"

"How are you making out, young man? It's been a long time since I—er—saw you. I had a letter from Phil last week. He's on WAC recruiting now. You haven't any coffee. Wait, I'll get you some."

"Uuh—oh, thanks." Now who the hell was that? And Phil?

Who was Phil? Larry was certain he should know. It was probably Phil's father—sore because Larry hadn't given him the double take. Whoever it was, he wanted Larry to wait.

Okay, he'd wait. God knows he couldn't do anything else but wait. Wasn't he the guest of honor? "That's him with the dark glasses on. Over there, sitting in the wicker chair."

A car rolled up and stopped. Maybe it was his father and mother. No. He doubted if his mother would let his father take her to the party. Neither of them liked the Patersons, although they'd never said so openly. She'd figure Larry would have more fun without his parents there.

Some fun! A Buddha riveted to a wicker chair.

"H'lo, Ed."

"Hey, Carson. And Dr. Bannerman. It's a pleasure, reverend. Hello, dear. Well, well, Larry Nevin! How are you, son?"

"Ed" was undoubtedly Mr. Edward Paterson. Strong, sure footsteps had crossed the porch to Larry's chair. "I'm fine, Mr. Paterson."

"Well, well, that's fine, boy. Good to see you again. Make yourself at home."

Larry groped for a table beside him and disposed of a plate he'd been balancing on his knee. He stretched out his hand, but no one shook it. Mr. Paterson had vanished into thin air.

To cover his confusion Larry found a cigarette. There had been matches and an ashtray on the table beside him. He reached for them gingerly, struck a cup of coffee and sloshed it lavishly over the table. Phil's old man, whoever he was, would have made a good waiter. He'd promised coffee, and brought it, by God, on silent feet. He'd set it down so carefully that Larry hadn't even heard him put it there.

A harsh resentment at his own helpless condition and at the stupidity of his fellow creatures came to a focal point in Larry to etch his soul with a drop of searing poison. The resentment was doubled, trebled, because this was happening to him in his own home town and at the house of the girl he had dreamed of marrying.

What a hell of a dream! What a hell of a party! It wasn't a party. It was a nightmare.

Voices and laughter were swirling about him, but never touching him, never taking him in. He was a sightless trunk spewed up out of battle into a world of people with eyes. He was something set apart forever, something the others could neither touch nor contact, although painfully conscious of his presence.

He clenched his fists to a point of hurting, and suddenly inside of him a great understanding was born, a tolerance created out of unbearable grief and pain. He was no longer Larry Nevin. He was Larry Nevin, *blind man*, earmarked and catalogued neatly by a system of abysmal ignorance. He was one, inseparable forever, with Joe Morgan, Negro, and Jewish Ivan Stern. Joe was a black man. Ivan was a Jew. Larry was a blind man. He had joined the legion of untouchables. Pity surged through him with the realization that Joe and Ivan bore crosses twice as heavy as his own.

Out of his new-born tolerance grew pity for the friends about him too. They were kindly people, sympathizing with his blindness, anxious to make his furlough happy. The wall which kept them apart from him was a wall of great futility, the same futility which silenced strong men in the face of death or fatal illness. They had been taught through life that certain conditions were hopeless—the conditions of blindness and blackness, and being a Jew.

Larry Nevin had come home blind. He was utterly hopeless. What the hell could the home folks do?

He had a thought, bitter as wormwood, that perhaps all the blind should be kept together, segregated like lepers in a colony of their own. It took time, but the people with sight did get used to the blind when a lot of them were constantly around. That had been demonstrated to him already in Phoenixville.

In Phoenixville he had had no sense of being stared at with curiosity and pity. He was served with understanding and without comment in stores, restaurants, and bars. He could walk the streets without self-consciousness, play shuffleboard and bowl without feeling as though he were some armless wonder on exhibition.

Yet Phoenixville was little different from Palatka—larger perhaps, but still an average American town. The blinded soldiers had been assimilated into its daily routine simply because, due to the near-by hospital, some of them were always around. That would never happen in Palatka. There, Larry Nevin would always be a problem, an outcast throwing a pall on fun and parties, an object of misplaced pity which, if he married, would inevitably grow to include his wife and children.

Sitting in the wicker chair with the Paterson party swirling around him, he saw without wanting to that he had to leave home forever. Palatka was used to the bats swarming out of the lumber piles. It would never get used to Larry Nevin.

He had a life of his own to live, ambitions that were setting and maturing. He was an individual with some kind of unknown destiny which he must fulfill. He'd take Chris with him, if she wanted to come. Otherwise he'd go alone. He wasn't going to be the problem of Palatka—"poor blind Larry," the hero of a little town.

A chair slid up beside him. Breaking into his reverie came the executive voice of Mr. Paterson.

"I've just been talking to Chris, Larry. She said I should pass it along to you." Mr. Paterson coughed as though the passing might be difficult. "I want to tell you, boy, that we're all very proud of you."

"Thank you, sir." Larry knew he wasn't helping much by saying "Thank you, sir," and waiting. He must look like a bespectacled owl. The porch had quieted as though the curtain had risen on a show.

"What I mean is," Mr. Paterson continued, "when you get back here from the hospital we want you to feel at home."

"Thank you, sir." (Welcome, little stranger! Feel at home in this brand-new town!)

"We—and I speak for every businessman here—intend to see that every boy getting out of uniform has a job. What I'm trying to say, boy, is there's a good job waiting for you in the Paterson plant. Ah-hum! It may take a little experimentation—I know you get what I mean, but we'll find out, Larry, the best thing for you to do."

("Look me up sometime," said Mr. Somerset. "The medical supply business can use some of you fellows—at slightly lower rates of pay.")

"I appreciate that, Mr. Paterson, but it's a little soon for me to make any plans. Maybe I'll decide to settle up North."

"Up North?"

"I don't know for sure, sir. You see, I might not be much good in a factory. I may want to go on with college. There are lots of things to consider. I need to find out more things that the blind can do."

"Perhaps you're wise to think it over, boy." (Was that relief in Mr. Paterson's tone?) "Whatever your decision, there'll always be a job of some kind here for you."

The time seemed endless after that until Chris and he were together in her car. Then it was brought to him, even more strongly, that everything was the same—but different.

He, not Chris, was the one who should have been driving, directing the evening, promoting the stop for a long cool drink at the bar. Picking the road and a quiet place for parking was a man's responsibility—a ritual recognized but never mentioned. For Chris to have to do those things was embarrassing to them both. His blindness was reversing the roles of boy and girl.

They sped out toward Interlachen, the warm air pleasant against his cheeks. Finally he brought himself to help her.

"I'd like to talk awhile, Chris. What about turning off somewhere?"

"Can't you talk while I'm driving?"

"I can talk, but my mind's on the road all the time. It's nuts, but I keep listening for other cars and trying to figure out where we are. I can't think very well."

He'd furnished enough excuse to overcome her proper protest. She left the smoothness of the highway for a narrow road of sandy ruts which bounced them badly. A branch brushed by the window. Chris stopped and cut the motor. A quail called softly, searching its covey. A mosquito droned.

Larry opened the door beside him.

"What are you doing, Larry?"

"I want to get out for a minute."

"Oh!"

"Don't get embarrassed." He laughed. "I merely want to feel a couple of trees and a piece of Spanish moss—maybe get a touch of turpentine on my fingers."

"Can I help?"

"No, thanks. Let me find them myself." He heard her light a cigarette.

After a little he got back in, trailing a piece of Spanish moss from his fingers.

"That's probably full of red bugs, Larry."

"I don't care. Someday I'm going to get a dog to lead me through the woods and another dog, like Tip, to find me quail. I'll come out here in the winter and hunt—shooting at sound. Maybe I won't kill anything, but I'll still be shooting at quail."

She was supposed to say something to that and didn't. Larry's own intuition began to worry him. A nasty new habit —this lately developed business of stripping a girl's mind instead of her body.

This was Chris with him, believe it or not. He'd known her for years, fished and danced with her, been proud of her, watched her progress in school, carried her picture and her letters with him into battle. How could she possibly be natural when he persisted in peopling her head with thoughts of his own? That was the prerogative of a girl—a *woman's* intuition was the proper term.

She'd said practically nothing, so he'd promptly decided she wanted nothing so much in the world as to drive him home.

Damn such strain! Damn his own unfairness! Damn this new business of being a seer in darkness!

"Larry—"

"What?"

"Why did you tell Father you might settle up North?"

"Don't you think it's a good idea?" He'd toss it into her lap right now. Maybe she was suffering as much as he was. This was the discussion he wanted, the long-awaited conversation. Maybe it would clear the air and get them back on a normal basis again.

"But you'd have a job here, darling. Father said so."

"It isn't the job, Chris. It's something else. I don't belong here—"

"That's foolish, Larry. Our families are here. That's a—well, a protection, if nothing else."

"I don't need protection, honey. Don't you get it? I have money coming in for life—"

"You don't want to loaf, do you, Larry?"

"God, no! But neither do I want protection—or jobs given me out of pity."

"Larry, how can you—"

"Wait, Chris. There are sheltered workshops for the blind. They offer protection—sitting on your tail and making brooms. They give you jobs because you're *blind*—not on account of what you can *do*. I have to be hired because I'm Larry Nevin, or I'll die."

"Why do you think that Father's making a place for you?"

"That's exactly what I'm driving at, honey. He's making a place for me. He said himself it would take a little experimentation, and I don't want to be an experiment. I want to be so damn good at something that employers will break their necks trying to hire me away from each other."

"Father's a businessman, Larry. You're unfair if you think he's offering a chance because he's sorry for you."

Mosquitoes were humming in the car. Larry brushed one from his neck and felt blood on his fingers. "I don't think he's sorry for me, Chris. He's sorry for you."

Suddenly the pity which had surged up in him for his friends in Palatka grew and enveloped Chris too. He reached out his arms and gathered her close, remembering the first time he'd kissed her. She'd been so slim and lissome and shy, a kid in white with a rose in her hair sitting out a dance at the high-school ball. The yielding touch of her lips had built castles, glorious places with battlements and shining windows. The castles had grown as days went by, breaking often into his studies, keeping him sitting silent in class, watching the towers and waving pennants throw shadows on the classroom wall. Sir Larry Nevin, the white-plumed knight riding to battle! A token, Lady Christine, before our castles fall!

Startlingly close to the automobile he heard the hoot of an owl.

"Let's get out of Palatka, honey. Anywhere. I have to be Larry Nevin."

She buried her face against his shoulder. "I don't know what to do, Larry."

She hadn't kissed him. He released her very gently. Everything of the castles was gone except a single lichen-covered wall.

## 19. TWO WORLDS

As HIS furlough sped along, he found himself developing a disquieting power of analysis brought about through contact with his own home town, with his father and mother and Chris, and with friends he had known before.

The patients and staff at Valley Forge had all been new, as had Judy, the people met in Phoenixville, and those talked to on the train. They had assumed proportions and characteristics all their own. Inevitably, some part of their make-up was drawn from Larry's background and experience while he still could see.

He knew that. An art teacher in high school had asked him one day to draw an imaginary animal possessing no part of any animal, fish, or fowl he had ever seen. He had tried and found it couldn't be done. His mind and the paper remained as blank as a darkened movie screen.

Now he faced a talking film cut off from light in the middle. To continue the story, he must follow the action of the introduced characters by their dialogue alone. Yet he could still picture those characters he had seen. New characters introduced by their dialogue into the talking picture presented a different problem. They must be furnished with bodies to fit their voices. Larry was faced with the problem of an author creating characters that embodied traits drawn from all the people the author had met and seen.

His world of sound was becoming divided, splitting between the visual old and the invisible new. There was a choice to be made, and he was finding the decision most upsetting. Sooner or later the old and the new would merge, and the stronger would predominate forever. He couldn't just keep hopping from one to the other, or hovering indecisively in between.

The decision was important. It not only affected his entire future, it affected the lives of others—Chris and Judy, his mother and father, Joe Morgan and Ivan Stern.

He didn't want to be a fool, locked up in a room with a broken mirror so that he couldn't look on his foolish face. Hell, he couldn't see it anyhow, even though the room was full of mirrors. Nevertheless, he'd know. His dad had admitted failure, and had put the problem squarely up to Larry Nevin._

His mother, for instance. He'd kept her in the old world of familiar things and found himself almost hating her. He'd never liked the complacent way she nodded her head and bobbed her glasses to give a silent "I told you so!"

Her amused and tolerant listening smile when his dad was telling a party story had always been a source of irritation. He'd never liked the endless doodads she spread around the sitting room, or the searching of his bureau drawers and the reading of his old letters.

Those were just a few of a thousand things that now he'd never see. What he had learned in his brand-new world was how long she spent in the kitchen cooking a hundred things he liked; how a hole in his sock was mended while he was asleep; how clean and cool the bed linen felt, and how fresh and sunny the towels smelled after her careful laundering.

When she held him close he felt how frail she was, and sensed the love and sacrifice that had occupied her entire life.

Again he had begun to wonder and find himself torn between loyalty and irritation, between the old world and the new. Was her mother love blind and selfish? Should she have pampered him a little less and thought a little more? Should she have trusted less in Dr. Bannerman and the minister's boss? Should she have been as much concerned, or even more, with his lessons in grammar school as she was with his lessons in Sunday school?

Were buttons and biscuits more important than sex and segregation of the Negroes and the Jews?

Was her husband's earning capacity more important than what had filled his lungs with gas in the First World War?

Could she look at her blind son's plastic eye and think she could kiss it well again, or deep inside did she have to admit, as his father had, that perhaps she owed him a little sight?

Was the blue star hung in her window a star from heaven for being a minor female deity, or was it a *summa cum laude* for being insufferably dumb?

Larry couldn't answer, for he didn't know.

He didn't know about Ivan Stern or Joe.

If he chose the old visual world to live in, he'd have to take

Ivan with him too. Then Ivan would be an old-world Jew. Now all the old-world Jews were short and fat and greasy. They had big bellies and curly oily hair and waved their hands while jewing you. They ate no pork, except on the sly, and ran secondhand clothing stores where they stood outside to drag you in. When they got excited they yelled, "Oi, Oi!" All their "W's" were "V's." All their "A's" were "E's"—"Dun't esk me vy!"

That was crazy, for Ivan Stern, his blind-world friend, didn't look or talk or act like that at all. Ivan spoke the most perfect English Larry had ever heard, strong perhaps, but perfect and without a trace of accent. His words made sense.

Ivan was tall, with a short straight nose, a nice tan face and brilliant dark blue eyes. His teeth were straight and even. There was a cleft in his strong, square chin. Strangest of all, he had a well-cut, carefully parted head of yellow Nordic hair.

Then there was Joe. Put Joe back into the visual world, and what had you? An ape man intent on nothing in life but marrying, or preferably raping, white women. Larry wasn't too old to remember lots of things he had heard before the war, or things pounded into him in school and college by other boys, or precepts taught him by his mother.

He wasn't too deaf to hear things being said all around him right now. As a matter of fact, his ears had grown abnormally keen. The Negroes were spoiled with high wages. They were getting too damn fresh, mixing equally with whites in the Army. They were already bringing pressure to bear for bills allowing intermarriage. Great God above, the next thing the bleeding South would find was a restoration of the Fourteenth Amendment to the Constitution! The only thing left after that would be restoration of the Ku Klux Klan.

Obviously he could never make friends with Joe Morgan of the visual world and go around with him, as his father had advised. *That* Joe Morgan was a great black shadow blotting out more sunshine than his blindness, threatening white supremacy too. Such things could never be.

But what of Joe in the brand-new world of blackness? What about the friend he couldn't see?

Larry would never forget the fellow he met in the corridors of Valley Forge, the boy from home with the chuckle and the welcome Southern drawl.

That Joe Morgan was tall and pale from illness, a lanky guy who needed more food. His own good humor and sympathy for others had tempered the shock of his blindness. His own strong spirit was helping him to bear up bravely. What was even stranger than Ivan's Nordic blondness was the fact that Joe Morgan had freckles topped by bright red hair.

Those were facts unchangeable. It would make no difference what anyone told him—Ivan was a blond; Joe had red hair. Both were boys he could associate with without any qualms whatsoever, boys his mother should be glad to receive as guests in her house, boys he could introduce anywhere.

Their bodies had been made by Larry Nevin.

Then there was Chris . . .

The furlough had settled down into an amiable routine. The mornings were full of the lazy droning he had dreamed of overseas: talks and shopping trips with his mother, the smell of grocery store and drug store, the zest of tasting his favorite food at breakfast, and the noonday meal.

At four o'clock, Chris would get away from school. Larry was always waiting, rocking quietly in the front porch swing. He'd be at the top of the front porch steps, tapping his cane, before she blew her horn. When she was still a block away, he could recognize the motor of her car.

There were cocktail parties and dinner, a couple of drives to Jacksonville and movies, one to a concert in Daytona, and an afternoon spent in brailling old Ford Marion in St. Augustine.

Chris was sweet, and had learned many things quickly. She paid him every attention, stayed by him at the parties and saw that his glass was filled. She accepted kidding about their approaching wedding, an event that was apparently set in the minds of everyone except the prospective bride and groom.

On a Saturday they went on a picnic to Cowpen Lake, a favorite spot they had often visited together.

Chris called for him early, half an hour before sunrise. The best bass fishing in the transparent waters of Cowpen Lake was late in the evening or early in the day.

During the drive, Larry sat in silence, picturing the sunrise, drinking in every landmark along the Gainesville road.

He wanted to get out quickly, to get tackle into the rowboat, to feel the scrape of grass along the gunwales and the first free surge as the boat was pushed from shore.

There was a pocket dotted with lily pads a hundred yards from the camping ground. He could drop a plug there blindfold, had done it on many a pitch-black night before the rising of the moon.

Chris was full of delay.

"What's the matter, honey?"

"I can't get this reel on, Larry."

"Give it to me."

"Wait a minute. I'll get some pliers from the tackle box."

There wasn't a breeze to make the slightest rustle in the leaves above them, but out on the lake there were splashes, tiny splashes as if some farmer had tossed away a handful of corn.

Minnows were jumping.

"Got it, Chris?"

"Don't be so impatient, Larry. We have all day."

"Give it to me, honey."

"Just a second, and I'll have it on. There!"

A splash much louder than the rest.

"Ready, honey?"

"Heavens, Larry, I hope I didn't forget those oarlocks! Now isn't that silly of me?"

"I'm afraid I haven't seen them, Chris."

"Larry, how can you say that, darling?"

The sun was warm against the back of his neck. An early morning breeze was whispering. A little higher and the sun would strike in the shallows. The big ones feeding would have their fill and head for the cool deep water. Fishing time would be gone.

"Larry, dear, are you sure you can row?"

"They had a blind crew at Valley Forge last summer. If I'd been there, I'd have been on it. Let's get the boat out, Chris."

"I'll push it out, Larry."

"Chris, I'm blind, not crippled. Show me where the damn thing is and let's get on."

Silence.

Silence while they pushed through the grass, and the plug got snarled pulling the rod in the water.

Silence while he tried to cast, to find that the boat was too close to shore.

Silence and darkness, while the sun crept up and the big ones were gone.

And suddenly he realized she was frightened, scared to death of this stranger with the plastic eye who was swinging a gang-hooked plug in the air, petrified with fear of this man she thought helpless, this blind Larry Nevin whom she'd never seen in her life before, and might someday be forced to marry.

"Chris, I think you're very brave. Let's go back to shore."

"There's nothing to be brave about, Larry."

"Oh, yes, there is." He laughed very softly. "You're very brave to let me try casting. It's dangerous, even if I had my eyes. I'm afraid I can't make it, Chris. See, I've backlashed again. Let's go in and just sit on shore."

He wanted to tell her about the two strange worlds and ask her advice about Ivan and Joe, but he never did. Somehow he felt she wouldn't care, and probably wouldn't know.

They lolled back under a tree together, and once just to assure himself he kissed her. She let him, even answered, and he felt again that she was very sweet and very brave. He'd never forget the ruins of the castle the night she hadn't kissed him in the car. He was glad when at noon it began to rain.

She came to the station to see him off on the day he had to go.

He shook hands with his dad, kissed his mother and held her close, and then kissed Chris.

His mother and father had moved in with him, been given new bodies and lovely new minds.

Chris was left. She'd always be part of the old world of vision, lovely and sweet. She'd never be part of the world of sound where Larry intended to make his home.

She'd never meet Ivan and Joe.

## 20. TRANSITION

NOT until he was back in Valley Forge did his furlough begin to integrate. Then it took several days for a concrete impression to form, and for a month of excited confusion to become entirely clear.

It was a shock to find that Valley Forge was more like home than Palatka. There was a feeling of surety in his quick navigation of the endless corridors, in his certainty of location around the hospital and Phoenixville.

Voices he had tabulated since his blindness proved easier to identify. That caused him a little worry, as though he were being unfaithful to old-time friends and family. He had found it difficult in Palatka to place certain voices that he felt sure he would know. Dr. Bannerman's voice had sounded nothing like the voice Larry remembered declaiming from the pulpit. Even his mother's voice had been different. He'd had to ask, "Who is it?" when she spoke to him on the train.

Yet Flagg, Ivan Stern, Miss Bailey, the officers and the doctors and many of his fellow patients with whom he was no more than slightly acquainted had only to speak to be instantly identified by name.

Thinking it out, he decided that the voices in the hospital had been catalogued in darkness, with a consequent greater attention to cadence and sound. They were also much closer in space of time. The voices in Palatka were memories from that long-ago era before the war when people spoke with care-free abandon. Now the abandon was forced, the voices unconsciously worried and shrill. Certainly they weren't the voices that Larry thought he remembered.

He discovered that he was thinking many things out since his return from furlough. Gradually he was accepting his blindness, adjusting himself to an ineluctable condition that was not of his own choosing.

On one of his trips to Jacksonville with Chris, they had been walking down Main Street. Larry had heard a woman say, "If that was my son, I'd rather see him dead!" While neither he nor Chris had mentioned it, he knew that Chris had heard it too. It had upset him badly, kept him lying awake at night, coloring his entire furlough.

Part of his adjustment came when he realized, after much painful consideration, that the woman who had spoken really meant it. She sincerely believed that she'd rather see her own son dead than blinded. She knew that she'd rather be dead herself than blinded.

There was the great impassable gulf between the sighted and the blind. Deep in his heart, Larry Nevin himself had believed it before he lost his eyes. The chances were that his mother, his father, and Chris all felt the same way. The sophism was that all sighted people considered sight essential to life. So long as their eyes were functioning, their brains would reason with a sighted point of view.

Larry was beginning to reason with a blind man's point of view.

Lieutenant Bob Atkins, blind himself, had told him about

the bats. The brain of man was geared to sight. It received the impressions of images through a neat mechanical device called the eye. But it was the brain that enabled man to see. The eye itself was merely a working camera lens which actually received impressions upside down. It was the brain that turned them right side up again. Destroy a tiny segment in the seeing part of any man's brain and that man would be just as blind as Larry. There were several boys in Valley Forge with perfect eyes that were perfectly useless as seeing devices. Those boys hadn't been hit in the eyes at all. Bullets or shells had injured the seeing part of the brain. Their perfect eyes were no more good than ones of plastic.

The brain of a bat was geared to sound. It received the impressions of images through a neat mechanical device called the ear. But it was the brain that enabled the bat to see. The bat uttered a continuous series of tiny squeaks when flying around. Those squeaks hit any obstacle and bounced right back again in high frequency waves of sound. Destroy a tiny segment in the hearing part of any bat's brain and that bat would be just as blind as Larry.

The seeing man had rays of light to show him objects in his path. The seeing bat had waves of sound. Experiments had been made with bats flying around a room strung with wires. Their eyes had been coated over with nontransparent collodion. They flew around with accurate and dazzling speed, never touching a wire. When their ears were stopped, they flew into wires and crashed into walls. Their sight was gone.

It was Atkins, in a follow-up, who interested Larry in the verb "to see."

According to Atkins, only one definition in Webster's Unabridged Dictionary had anything to do with the eyes. The next time a Gray Lady came to read to Larry he had her read them over. Later he pressed his Braille teacher into service, and had her write them down.

He still wasn't very good on Braille, but for a long time afterward he carried around the punched definitions, worry-

ing them with his unskilled finger until finally he had mem-
orized them completely:

> **See:**—1. To perceive by the eye; have knowledge of
> an object or of its existence or qualities through the
> action of light emitted or transmitted by it or reflected
> by it or reflected from it to the retina; hence to fix the
> attention upon, look at, view, observe.

That he couldn't do. He had lost his eyesight.

> 2. To perceive with the mind; have an idea of or per-
> ceive the meaning of; be cognizant of; understand; ap-
> prehend; comprehend; as to *see* the meaning of a remark;
> to *see* one's object or purpose; to *see* an advantage.

So he had lost his eyesight, and he was seeing a thousand
things today that he'd never seen before. He was perceiving
with his mind that the mind was the only thing to perceive
with. He was perceiving the pleasure of thinking, of thinking
not only at night, but in the daytime. There indeed was a
pastime he'd never indulged in before.

He was perceiving the meaning of blindness, a close brother
to dumbness. Blind as a bat held no terrors any more. Most
of the world was blind as bats, flying around with covered-up
eyes and stopped-up ears, flying around with brains that
weren't working, tangling up with wires of greed and smash-
ing themselves and their children against obvious walls of war.

He had cognizance of the woman's remark in Jacksonville.
What was more, he understood it.

He had apprehended his marriage with Chris, and compre-
hended her apprehension. He was beginning to see the meaning of words—at the age of twenty-three.

He had already discovered one marked advantage in losing
his sight—he wouldn't have to look again on the shambles of
a war.

> 3. To have knowledge of by effort or experience; ascer-
> tain or find out; also, to experience, undergo, or suffer;
> as, go and *see* whether someone is at the door; to *see* hard-
> ships.

God, he'd found out plenty! His trip down home had really been hell. If seeing was experience and suffering, he'd seen enough on that single furlough to last him a year.

Someday in some way he'd try to get across to ordinary people that a blind man wasn't necessarily afflicted with leprosy. Was every girl in the world like Chris, scared to death of a blind man? Of course, there was Judy—he'd have to look up Judy again. He'd called at her house the first night back and been told she'd gone away on a trip. It was a pity Judy couldn't have been in Palatka. At least, she would have shown them that Larry Nevin still had his feet and legs. Maybe he should have written her.

He'd danced three times while he was home, each time at a cocktail party to records on a victrola. One of the things that had burned him up was that Chris had always managed to duck it. The other girls were wives of friends. He certainly couldn't have forgotten. He was too well reminded by a constant fight to prevent them leading him, and the distance they kept while towing him around the floor.

Let people get a couple of drinks on board and they had no sense at all. They didn't have much sense anyhow. He'd been left high and dry, anchored to nothing a dozen times every day.

"Here I am, Larry, right over here!" That was certainly helpful as hell with two chairs and a table full of cocktail glasses in the way.

"If you're looking for your drink, Larry, I just gave you a refill. It's right over there." They might have added, "Excuse my pointing!"

It had been a swell month of blind man's buff—his hand stuck out with nobody there to shake it; nine of the people out of ten giving him hearty welcomes home on Lemon Street and vanishing without warning into the Florida air.

There seemed to be a conspiracy among every family he knew to feed him chicken, broiled or fried, and keep him away from bathrooms. Holy mackerel! The whole crowd ate around together. After they'd seen him tackle half a broiled chicken once, you'd have thought they'd catch on. Broiled chicken wasn't easy for a man with eyes to handle politely. Unless it was cut and the bones removed, the only nice thing for a blind man to do was to pick it up between his teeth and get down under the table.

And it was a little silly for Mrs. Daniels to get so upset because she forgot to lock the bathroom door. Why didn't she say something when he came in instead of holding her breath in panic? God knows he couldn't see her. How the hell could he know she was sitting there?

Maybe that came under definition 4—To call on or visit; interview or confer with.

Or maybe 5—To grant an interview to; have a meeting with; meet; receive; as to *see* callers.

He'd seen too many people. Until they took a course in seeing for themselves, he didn't want to see them again.

There were other definitions, several more:

To escort—to see a friend to the station. To accomplish some purpose, to *see* that the work was done.

*"Let governments see that labor is allowed to enjoy its full earnings, untaxed by war, waste, or protective tariffs."*

Lieutenant Atkins had given him that one to mull over, something right out of the dictionary, a quotation from *False Hopes,* written by some guy named Goldwin Smith, who seemed to have had his eyes opened in 1883.

*False Hopes.* That was a hot one! Thank God that civilization had progressed since 1883. Goldwin Smith should take a tour around Valley Forge and Old Farms Convalescent Hospital and see what science was doing for the fellows who had left their eyes kicking around in France, the Pacific, and Italy. Good old Smitty! He was nuts. Didn't he know that labor couldn't enjoy its full earnings without war and waste?

War and waste meant prosperity. Everybody had jobs, even in Palatka, where Larry's dad had worked on the W.P.A. Of course, the W.P.A. had robbed everyone of initiative. Mr.

Hines, who owned the local crate factory, had told Larry that while he was home. It wasn't patriotism that caused people to work. It was just big pay. Larry'd see for himself as soon as the war was over. (Definition #3.)

In the meantime everything was swell. The more ships you blew up, the more work there was building new ones. The more men you blinded, the more plastic eyes you sold.

Old Smitty was nuts. He lived way back in '83 when men were rugged and couldn't read. Now, five out of every hundred adult Americans had spent from one to three years in college. Larry was in the group and knew, and the colleges had actually graduated five per cent more. Why, damn it all, only sixty per cent of the entire country, of twenty-five years of age or over, had never gone beyond grade school!

It had Larry worried. Mr. Hines had talked to him as if he was the same Larry Nevin who had worked in a filling station a few years before.

He wasn't, and it wasn't because his eyes were gone. His father had realized the change better than anyone. His father had come back from battle too. But the country seemed full of men like Mr. Somerset and Mr. Hines, men who refused to face the fact that if you washed a teen-age kid for a long enough time in a porridge of blood and entrails you might turn out a cynical realistic man.

Those kids had been trained to recognize their enemies, to penetrate camouflage, and instantly to tell friend from foe even when the foe was speaking good English and masquerading in an American uniform. Those kids had been trained, not in the ways of polite diplomacy, but in ways of destroying a foe with a steady hand.

Larry was beginning to think that there were a hell of a lot worse headaches in store for Mr. Hines and Mr. Somerset than the Wagner-Murray-Dingell Bill.

He tried to reassure himself by taking it up with Ivan Stern one night in the Columbia Bar.

"Ivan, how old are you?"

"Thirty. Why?".

"Did you graduate from college?"

"Chicago."

"What did you do before the war?"

"I worked for a big accounting firm. I'm a C.P.A. Now what's worrying you? Ants in the breeches because your girl's away?"

"She's not my girl."

"Oh. Then you're worried because that luscious Florida tangerine's so far away?"

"I met a man named Somerset on the train."

"You meet the damnedest people, Larry. Who was this great brain?"

"He manufactures medical equipment." Larry refreshed himself with beer.

"God!" exclaimed Ivan. "Don't tell me this bastard started the war."

"He was worried about the Wagner-Murray-Dingell Bill."

"Turn around a minute," said Ivan. "I want to see if he stole your plastic eye. Hey, Charlie, fill 'em up again!"

Fresh beers came. Larry drank deep and traced his finger around a wet place on the bar.

"How can the country be so prosperous, Ivan, when we're wasting so much material—blowing up billions of dollars of stuff in this war?"

"Full employment," said Ivan shortly. "Overemployment, as a matter of fact. Two jobs waiting for every gal or guy. Everybody always wants everything to make their lives comfortable. Now everybody's hard at work, and they all have money to buy." He laughed. "When there's anything to buy."

"This Somerset said that the people won't stand for throwing money away after the war. How are we going to keep prosperous and still pay for the war?"

"Full employment," said Ivan.

"I don't get it," Larry admitted. "We'll be way in the hole.

Where's the money coming from to give full employment and still pay for the war?"

"Full employment," said Ivan. "Who the hell stopped to wonder where the money was coming from when we got into this war? We had to manufacture more stuff than we'd ever manufactured in our entire history, and damned fast too, no foolin'! Do you think Mr. Somerset was lying awake nights worrying about who was going to pay for his medical supplies, or about the size of the national debt? He was, like hell! He was wondering where he was going to get his raw materials and his manpower and galpower to work them up into lancets to cut out our eyes. You've got the cart before the horse like most people, Larry. Money doesn't produce full employment. Every bank in the country was busting with money during the depression until they finally busted entirely. It's full employment that produces the money, puts it into everybody's pockets, and then produces more when that is gone."

"That's true, all right," said Larry. He used his finger to draw a design in the wet spot on the bar. "But I'll bet my neck Mr. Somerset, and Mr. Paterson, who makes barrels in Palatka, and Mr. Hines, who makes crates, and a slew of other people will start worrying about money after the war."

"After what war?" asked Ivan coldly. "Mr. Somerset had better realize that a hell of a lot of tough bozos are moving in here who won't realize that the war is over until they have good jobs, a home and children, and money in their pockets. He'd better start worrying about putting them to work at damn good wages at anything public or private even if he has to lobby through a bill to build ten thousand hospitals from coast to coast and staff them with government-paid doctors to use his lancets."

Ivan slid down from his stool and finished his beer. "I heard ten years ago that Germany was helpless because she was broke as a nation. She hadn't any money, consequently she couldn't buy anything and could never start a war. Now I'm hearing that we're busted because we're billions in debt and can never put everybody to work to manufacture the things we need to win a peace. That was a hell of a lot of free metal that that son-of-a-bitch, Hitler, tossed at us, Larry. Neither of us can read a sign or find a door!"

When they got back to the hospital, Flagg told them that orders had been posted. Twenty new casualties were arriving unexpectedly. Beds were needed. Larry and Ivan and eight more blind were leaving in the morning for Avon.

# BOOK FOUR

# Old Farms Convalescent Hospital (Sp.)

## 21. THE GREAT UNKNOWN

THERE had been much talk about Avon.

Larry had been long enough in the Army to discount rumors. G.I.'s never knew anything, so they persistently—and with some justification—imagined the worst, and built it into news items. The distributing center was generally the latrine.

Picked up there and passed on with the usual elaborations, the most innocuous piece of misinformation could expand in a day to a three-column story of front-page proportions.

Old Farms Convalescent Hospital (Sp.)—the "Sp." stood for "special"—was an ordeal faced by all the blinded veterans in Valley Forge and Dibble. Eighteen weeks of rehabilitation training must be undergone before a man could be discharged to take up civil life again.

Letters had come back to Valley Forge from Masterson, Hamilton, and other boys. At first the letters were always bad. If later on the tenor changed to speak of good times and interesting valuable training, the good reports were quickly forgotten. The bad reports were retained, to grow and flourish.

The name of the place was unfortunate. "Old Farms" built pictures of an old men's home full of indigent ancients living on meager food and charity.

The fact that the Army had chosen with care one of the best-equipped and most picturesque boys' schools in the country meant little to the soldiers waiting to go there for training. The rolling acres bordering the Farmington River, the old world English buildings designed by Theodate Pope Riddle, an architect of genius and imagination, and the modern train-

ing equipment installed by the Army, were lost for a time
on boys who couldn't see.

According to reported letters:

Old Farms was stuck way out in the country, miles from
Hartford, with nothing exciting near.

The bus service was terrible. A taxi cost five dollars—if you
could find one. You faced a court-martial if you missed the
last bus and had to spend the night in town.

The snow was ten feet high. They took your canes from you
at Old Farms. Fellows stayed in their rooms all the time because they were constantly falling in snowdrifts when they
tried to get around.

Very few passes were given to go downtown.

You worked ten hours a day in classes.

There weren't any girls within twenty miles, and none were
allowed on the post.

You were subject to instant discipline if you came in smell-
ing of beer.

You were a guinea pig for Army experimentation.

Unless you passed a stiff examination in English, Math, and
a dozen other subjects you had to stay thirty-six weeks instead
of eighteen.

The food was awful, the officers and detachment men un-
sympathetic and brutal.

In short, any blind man was better off with eighteen weeks
in jail.

All the discouraging messages flooded back on Larry as he
sat in Broad Street station, waiting with the others to board
the train. Old Farms was part of the great unknown, part of
the unfamiliar future. That was the fact that tainted it with
fear.

This journey was different. The excitement of furlough was
missing, also the stimulation of going home. This was merely
a continuation of unwelcome routine, and at the end of the
journey lay strangers.

There had been excitement at the hospital early in the

morning: the roll call, the brief farewells and promises to write (and send the real lowdown), the collection of luggage, the assignment of escorts, one for every boy.

The morning, late in March, was very cold. Outside of the Administration Building, the party of twenty-one had split up. Sergeant Bill Kelley, the quiet N.C.O. in charge, finally got his group loaded into the heated ambulances for the drive into Philadelphia.

During the drive, the excitement hung on, but once in Broad Street station with the party reassembled, to Larry, at least, the excitement seemed to be gone.

He had noticed curiosity when he was traveling alone to Florida, a hush of voices as he passed, then conversations quickly resumed in a louder tone. Now it was multiplied tenfold, only the conversations were not resumed. Instead, the party of ten blinded veterans cast a tangible pall.

He knew there were lots of people around, but the silence just about where they were sitting was most depressing. He felt caught in the center of a spider web of speechlessness that moved out from him in concentric circles until normalcy was reached somewhere around the confines of the large waiting room. It was a pity people didn't know how much their actions affected other people who couldn't see them.

Sergeant Kelley had gone off to arrange the transportation and confer with the Station Master. Larry's sighted escort for the trip, seated beside him, was a P.F.C. named Adams. He had been wounded in Italy. Most of the sighted detachment men had seen service overseas and been assigned to duty at Valley Forge after a furlough home or a discharge from hospital. Perhaps their service made them sensitive too, for the reaction of the people in the station had subdued their normal joking with their blind charges.

Adams sat smoking, scarcely speaking to Larry, although he had been talkative enough on the ambulance ride in from Valley Forge. Larry was more than glad when Sergeant Kelley returned with the announcement that the Station Master was opening the gates half an hour before departure time so that the boys could board the train.

It was probably the lowest moment of his blindness when he touched his hand to Adams's arm and picked up his cane. No wonder the people watching that grim parade were silent. Deep in their hearts they were bound to feel some blame.

Larry's problems, and the knowledge of his helplessness to overcome them, suddenly appeared overwhelming. His shoulders stooped as though some insupportable weight had been rested on him to be borne forever. This wasn't a journey to Old Farms with nine other blind boys; it was a journey into life itself without any eyes to guide him. It was a journey into a universe of darkness where everything was unknown, where danger couldn't be recognized until you were close enough to touch it, where people drew back from you in a hush of terror.

This was the last parade.

A few years before, he had been full of great ambitions. Someday he'd be an architect, or an engineer, or a doctor, or a lawyer, maybe, or something great that would make the name of Larry Nevin known. He'd marry and raise children, have a house of his own and an automobile, and a boat on the St. Johns River. All of those things might not come true, but working in the filling station during his summer vacation it was his privilege to sit during his lunch hour and quietly dream.

They moved from the waiting room into the station and the gate clanged open. Sergeant Kelley said, "This way, fellows."

"This way." That was another joke. He clung tighter to Adams's arm. Now he couldn't even dream. He knew how a prisoner condemned for life felt when he was taken on board a train handcuffed to his guard.

Life was a joke—a corny one without much laughter. So he thought he was learning something at Valley Forge! That was a precious lot of hooey. He had learned to walk around corridors, mastered a dozen letters of Braille, and kissed a girl in Phoenixville whom he'd never kiss again.

And now he was well. His eye was healed. He had been home on furlough and was adjusted with his family. He had become socially conscious, built up sympathy with Negroes and Jews, delved into economic thoughts with the aid of Ivan Stern. He had served his country. Maybe he was a hero. At any rate they had given him a lot of pretty ribbons to wear.

He had facial vision, and an income for life. Well, the only things lacking to make him a perfect citizen were a pair of eyes and a brain.

Facial vision—he must develop that at Avon, turn himself into a batman. You could keep from running into a stone wall, but you couldn't get on a train.

Practice enough, and you could snap your fingers and locate a tree at twenty feet, or a fire hydrant, or a building. But you couldn't tell if a man was black, or kiss a girl again.

The car was cold, and the conductor very jovial. He had been properly trained by the railroad. He had carried lots of blinded boys between Philadelphia and Hartford. The railroad probably had a course called "Transportation of Blinded Veterans." It taught the conductors to be jovial and casual and save the blind boys pain.

Adams put him in a seat by a window and left. The conductor said, "There'll be heat in here shortly, and lunch at half-past eleven in the diner. Make yourselves comfortable."

Somebody sat down by Larry and asked, "Who is it?"

"Larry Nevin."

"I'm Carl Grebe."

Farther back in the car someone yelled, "Hey, Larry, are you on here?"

"I suppose so," said Larry. "It felt like it with my cane." He recognized Ivan's voice. Grebe, he didn't know very well.

Grebe asked, "Do you want to sit by Stern?"

"No," said Larry. "Stay where you are. We can change around later. I suppose we'll be hours on this train."

"Three o'clock, I think," said Grebe. "I was supposed to come up here months ago, but the plastic work on my face took longer than they expected. What ward were you in at Valley Forge?"

"Ward One," said Larry.

"I was in Fourteen. You haven't been there very long, have you?"

"Not very," said Larry. "Less than three months."

"You're lucky," said Grebe. "I've been in there nearly a year. I've been working in a war plant for the past three months; that's probably why I didn't see more of you. I don't know why in hell they're sending me up to Avon. I'm a machinist. My wife's working up in Wisconsin. I want to get home."

"I thought you got training at Avon," said Larry.

"What do I need with training?" Grebe lit a cigarette and gave Larry one. "It's just eighteen weeks more in the Army to me, and I'm losing money. I've been making over sixty-five a week in the plant at Norristown and a bonus. Now I have to waste eighteen weeks at Avon just to get it over with. After that, I'm coming back to Valley Forge again. More plastic."

"You must have gotten it bad," said Larry.

"Land mine," Grebe told him. "I'm glad to have a face again. I understand it looks pretty good. When my wife first came down to see me at Valley Forge, she and my face were both pretty blue. Now they're taking out the powder marks with a flesh-colored pigment of some kind. They tell me you can't see them on my forehead at all."

Pipes began banging, and Larry could feel the warmth of steam creeping into the car. He asked Grebe, "In that factory —what did you do?"

"I ran a punch press. Of course, I'd done it before and it was nothing new, only I'm better now."

"Was it hard to get on to?"

"Well, I was a little scared at first," Grebe told him. "Afraid I'd shove my hand into belts or things, but once I got over that I whizzed right along." The car jolted twice and began to roll. "I guess we're going."

Larry said, "I think I'll sleep awhile." His cigarette was finished. He dropped it on the floor between his knees and located it with the bottom of his shoe, then leaned his head back. The sun struck warm against his cheek and he pulled down the curtain beside him.

The waiting to start had given place now to the waiting for the midday meal. After that, it would be the waiting for the arrival in Hartford, and then the waiting to go to Avon, and after you were in Avon, the waiting to get through.

He didn't want to work in a factory. He hated machinery clanking around him. Fearsome moving belts, whirring in darkness—the frightful monotony of picking up something, putting it in a slot, pulling a lever, and pulling it out again.

What *did* he want to do?

Nuts to that job in the barrel factory! He didn't want to go home. It flooded back on him now that the entire stay in Palatka had been unadorned boredom: sitting on the porch waiting for Chris, hanging around the house waiting for biscuits for dinner, hanging around the bar waiting for another drink. Christ in heaven, he didn't want to do anything except possibly marry Corporal Flagg, who at least had a sense of humor and was skillful at leading him around!

Well, the hell with it! He didn't have to do anything. He had fifty bucks a week coming in for life, once he was out of the Army. He didn't even have to think if he didn't want to. By God, the country had blinded him, and now it owed him a living. Why should he worry about full employment, and Mr. Somerset, and Ivan Stern, and things he'd never thought of before? Why should he be upset at all by the thought of hauling himself out of bed at six o'clock in the morning and finding his way to some cheerless plant to nurse a clanking machine? Why should he think of anything? He'd tell them to go to hell at Avon, and sit on his tail. He was blind, and everything was very clear now. Even if he worked out all the problems in creation, there wasn't any way he could help. The easiest thing in life was sleep. There was nothing else in God's black world a blind man could so well do.

## 22. COLONELS DIE IN BED

LARRY awoke with a feeling of utter frustration. His neck hurt, his legs were cramped, and Carl Grebe had gone quietly to sleep with his head on Larry's shoulder.

Larry got up and straightened Grebe, who protested feebly in the middle of a snore, then pushed by Grebe's sprawled legs into the aisle.

Three or four of the fellows had started a song, and the sound annoyed him. What the hell were they singing about? It sounded like a bunch of high school kids on a picnic train.

He started for the men's room, steadying himself on the seat backs. At least, he thought it was the men's room. It didn't make any difference, for the entire car had been turned over to Sergeant Kelley's party.

One of the detachment men asked, "Can I help you?" but Larry refused him curtly. Since he had to grope through his life in darkness, he might as well learn. He could always reach one end of the car, and both ends were hooked onto the train.

Heaven knows, the place had a guiding smell that he couldn't miss. He was noticing washrooms and toilets more, and most of them were a bad reflection on his fellow citizens. The dirtiest dives he had ever used in the Army had never offended his nostrils like those in some public buildings and on the train.

Out of the place, he slammed the door behind him and passed the singers, seeking a vacant seat at the far end of the car. He heard Ivan Stern's voice, but he didn't pause. He had decided on a life of complete inertia. If he sat down with Ivan, he'd only get hooked into a conversation about something that he couldn't help anyway. Ivan's certified public accountant's mind thought too fast for Larry. Ivan made him lie awake at night wondering how, after the war was over, he could keep a lot of dopes from starving and getting into another one.

That wasn't good.

A sensible blind man like Grebe went to work in a factory and earned big money, or joined a Sheltered Workshop and made brooms, or comfortably rocked himself to sleep in his pension. Ivan was too hectic. He'd never be happy, and nobody around him would ever be happy. Larry didn't want to get himself upset all over again.

He located Grebe by the snoring, but kept on going, brailling for vacancies as he went along. Three seats ahead a pleasant voice said, "Sit down, Sergeant. I'm Arthur Diamond."

Larry slid in beside the speaker. "I'm Larry Nevin. Are you a detachment man?"

"No. A patient. Cigarette?" A case clicked open.

Larry found it and took one, then heard a lighter scratch beside him. He drew in and felt smoke fill his lungs. "You have pretty good vision, Arthur."

"Well, travel vision." The other laughed. "I could see the stripes on your arm when you stopped and felt the seat, and I can make out your face by looking closely, but someday it'll disappear entirely."

"While it lasts, you're lucky," said Larry. "Any is better than none at all."

"Sometimes I wonder," said Diamond. "I'm a little tired of looking at things I know I'm going to miss someday. My eyes are all right, but the works are gone. I got a chunk of shrapnel in my brain."

"I didn't meet you at Valley Forge."

"I guess I was in another ward," said Diamond. "I've had about five operations during the past nine months. I have a plate set in my head. I was a jeweler. Now I'm silver-plated for life."

"Oh!" said Larry, expressing a lot in the single word.

Diamond laughed. "Funny, isn't it? There have been three generations of Diamonds in the jewelry business in Boston. I graduated from Harvard and then went into the business because my father was in it before me. I doubt if I'll ever take it up again. What are you going to do, Sergeant?"

"Nothing," said Larry. "A sniper got me. One of my eyes is out, and the optic nerve in the other's dead. So why the hell should I worry?"

"No. Why should you?" Diamond agreed. "Did you go to college?"

"Two years at the University of Florida."

"It might be interesting," said Diamond, "to go again. You get a lot out of college."

"I didn't get much," said Larry, "and what I got I wish right now I didn't have. It's done nothing but cause a turmoil in my brain."

"Turmoil isn't as bad as shrapnel," said Diamond. "The turmoil may come out with time, but what they've taken out of me they'll never put back again. The turmoil only causes temporary pain."

Sergeant Kelley came and announced their lunch. The singing stopped at the end of the car.

"Hook on," said Diamond, "and I'll take you in."

They went through doors and into the diner together. Diamond put him in a seat by the window and after a while a waiter came. They didn't order, but food was put down in front of them—meat loaf, mashed potatoes, and a vegetable that was easy to handle. Then came ice cream and coffee.

Adams, Larry's detachment escort, sat across the table with a fellow named Emil Brancato. Diamond was silent during the meal, but Brancato kept laughing and joking. He hadn't much education, but he was full of fun.

"Now, ain't that somethin'!" Larry heard him say. "Look at that there airplane. That's the biggest thing I ever seen—flying right over the train!"

"And that's the oldest trick in the world," said Adams. "And

damned if I don't fall for it every time one of you blind guys
leans forward and looks out a window! I always nearly break
my neck trying to see what you're looking at, and I suppose
I'll do it again."

They finished a second cigarette and Adams said, "We'd
better move. They gave us the diner all to ourselves and there
are other people waiting."

Back in the coach, Larry sat by Diamond again.

"Brancato has guts," Diamond said. "His right arm's gone
and I understand his left hand's paralyzed. That would worry
me like hell, if I couldn't read Braille."

"There are Talking Books," said Larry.

"But they're not the same thing. Have you learned Braille?"

"I started," said Larry, "but the going's tough."

"Everything's tough," said Diamond, "except sitting on your
tail. And you'll find that gets a little tiring too."

"Maybe I'm tired of everything," said Larry. "I spent my
whole life learning to read, and now I can't see. So I'll listen.
There're Gray Ladies and Talking Books, and a radio and
phonographs, and people to play music for me. I should wear
my fingers down, scraping them over Braille!"

"Yes, it is rather silly, isn't it?" said Diamond. "I just thought
maybe you wanted to read. Lots of people do, you know. Or
maybe not so many. But some do. I know one blind man
without any hands who's learned to read with the stump of
his wrist. There's another one without any arms who's learned
to read with the tip of his tongue. You see, it's not the same
thing as listening. A reader may put different interpretations
in his voice from the ones you'd give the words yourself. And
then you feel a little foolish if someone's reading to you and
you have to ask him to read something over again. I've read
one book through four times since I've been at Valley Forge."

"It must have been some book," said Larry. "What was
the name of it?"

Diamond didn't answer. Down at the other end of the car,
the boys started singing again. Jack Moses, a colored boy, had

brought a banjo, and he played it well. Larry decided Diamond hadn't heard him. "I said that must have been some book for you to read it four times in Braille. What do you call it?" He spoke loudly against the banjo and the rattling of the train.

"Did you ever go to college?" asked Diamond.

"Yes," said Larry. "Two years at the University of Florida. I thought I told you."

"Yes. Maybe you did," said Diamond. "Do you get tired riding on a train?"

"I guess I do," said Larry.

"It beats against your head," said Diamond. "It's like natives in the jungle playing on a drum. I spent four years in Harvard. My family was in the jewelry business. Diamonds in the diamond business. People used to make jokes about it. Now they've silver-plated my brain. I think when I get out of the Army, I'll go through Harvard again."

"We were talking about the book," said Larry.

"What book?"

"The one you read at Valley Forge four times in Braille."

"Oh, yes," said Diamond. "It's one of the best books I ever read. Maybe I've only read it twice."

The song at the end of the car grew ribald.

Larry made another try. "What's the name of it?"

"Sometimes the drum beats get awfully loud," said Diamond. "They beat and beat, and they hurt like hell. And I don't know where I'm going or where I've been. And people think it's funny. Then everything comes back clear for a while, and I find I'm lost."

"Well, you're not lost now," said Larry. "You're right on a train. We're talking about that book you read. I still want to know the name of it."

"So do I," said Diamond. "That's why I've read it four times. It's always new, and always just as interesting. I learn a lot every time I read it. I learned a lot in Harvard. That's why I think I'll go again. Now I think I'll sleep awhile. Your name's Nevin, isn't it?"

"Yes," said Larry. "Larry Nevin."

"I'm Arthur Diamond. I like you, Sergeant. You were hit in France by a sniper, and one eye's gone and the optic nerve's dead in the other. You won't be mad if the next time we talk I seem not to know you?"

"No," said Larry. "Go to sleep. When you wake up, if you want to talk some more, just holler. I think I'll go down and add my fruity tenor to the singing."

"I like to sing too," said Diamond, "but the words are hard to remember. Stick to your Braille, Sergeant; you'll find you need it. And keep on using your brain. You'll find you need that too." He gave a laugh that was very gentle. "It would be funny as hell if I went through Harvard a second time and suddenly remembered the whole damned thing. I might come out with four degrees. The doctors say I may someday. Come back and see me again."

"I will," said Larry. "Just holler."

Diamond called when he was three seats down the train: "Sergeant!"

There was a pleading note in the single word that brought him back to Diamond's seat. He stood in the aisle bending over. "I thought you were going to take a snooze."

"You think I'm nuts, don't you?" asked Diamond.

"No more than anyone else," said Larry. "What's bothering you now?"

"I just wanted to let you know that I'm not, or they wouldn't have let me out of Valley Forge, I can assure you. It's just that at times it's awfully hard to think. I remembered part of the book I read. I thought if I told you, you wouldn't think I was crazy. It says, 'Love thy neighbour as thyself,' and something about 'Thou shalt not kill.' "

"That's the Bible," said Larry.

"Oh, sure," said Diamond. "The Bible. It's cram-chock-full of things like that. I suppose that's why I keep reading it over.

Thank you, Sergeant. It's funny as hell how I keep forgetting that name."

They stopped in New York for fifteen minutes, and then moved on. Adams told him he hadn't missed anything, for the train came in in the tunnel and stayed underground in the station. Larry felt pressure in his ears again and found it difficult to swallow, as the train moved out, tunneling under the river. Adams described the Hell Gate bridge and the boats below, tiny craft cluttered about City Island.

There was talk with Grebe about unions, and singing and sleep, and an hour spent describing from memory the typewriter keys to Corporal Bill Letter.

They were late in New Haven, but the railroad, consistent with its marvelous policy toward the blind boys, had held the Hartford train. They crossed the platform and got into a crowded coach where seats were saved. When the train moved out, a couple of the boys wanted to know if anything could be seen of Yale.

The end of the journey was near, and for close to an hour, excitement grew. The day had turned warm and sunny and spirits had risen with it. Kelley had them in line and ready for alighting ten minutes before they stopped in Hartford.

Larry found he couldn't forget Arthur Diamond. He was being a coward with darkness in his eyes. Diamond was bravely fighting a blacker darkness, a darkness of the eyes and mind. He sought out Diamond as the train pulled into the station. "Well, I guess this is it."

"Yes," said Diamond. "Let's get off together. I'm glad you came back again. I've been in Hartford. It's a lovely city. Full of big trees and beautiful buildings. If you want to sit by me on the ride out to Avon, I think I can even tell you the things we're passing."

"Swell," said Larry.

The train slowed and stopped. Outside he could hear a hearty voice, full of assuring greeting.

"Welcome to Hartford, fellows. I'm Lieutenant Brisbane

from Old Farms. Hello, Glatter. Hello, Grebe—I haven't seen you since Valley Forge."

No pity here, no Army; just cordial good will and a welcome to a group of expected, important guests.

"Brancato?"

"Yes, sir."

"Welcome to Hartford. And Silberger, and Letter. Jack Moses! Gosh, Jack, they fixed you up! You're blacker than ever."

"Yes, sir, Mr. Brisbane."

"You're Ivan Stern?"

"Yes, sir."

"Welcome to Hartford. Alf Campanella too."

Larry held fast to Diamond's arm as they went down the steps, the last ones off the train.

"You're Sergeant Nevin?"

"Yes, sir."

"Welcome to Hartford. It's good to see you."

A strong, friendly hand clasped Larry's.

"And you too, Colonel. I thought we'd lost you. Swell to see you again."

Larry put his hand back on Diamond's arm as they started forward. "Who the hell's the colonel?"

"I was," said Diamond. "Forget it. It's gone with a lot of other things I can't remember."

Larry had learned something more: All colonels didn't die in bed. Some of them lived with shrapnel in the brain.


## 23. "LOOK AWAY! LOOK AWAY!"

LARRY sat in the back seat of the Longjohn between Grebe and Colonel Diamond. The Longjohn was confusing, an Army conveyance like an overgrown station wagon with seats across, and many doors. He had difficulty getting in. Once in, he found the seat was very comfortable, but the leg space was cramped. He sat rigid, knees spread for room, his hands clasped on his cane.

Lieutenant Brisbane was full of energy, bustling about efficiently. The officer had a voice you couldn't mistake once you heard it. It wasn't exactly deep, but the tone was penetrating in a lower scale. He talked as though life was very wonderful and full of hurry instead of worry. The words came fast and with impact. Larry pictured a voice on silent roller skates, a voice which gazed frankly into his sightless eyes whether it spoke from front or rear.

The swiftness with which it moved about was a trifle disconcerting, almost startling. One second the voice would be bidding good-by to Sergeant Kelley some distance away; an instant later it would be asking, "You fellows in the back seat comfortable? We're about to start." And the words would come from a point close to Larry's head.

Larry wondered if the lieutenant ever walked around at a normal pace. Brisbane's enthusiastic energy was creeping contagiously into the Longjohn and inoculating Larry and the others too.

Grebe said, "What the hell are we waiting for?"

Someone up ahead remarked, "Let's go!"

From behind the Longjohn, Brisbane's voice was giving last instructions about loading luggage into a truck.

A headiness seized Larry, a desire to move and do things. It might be very stimulating to jump out onto the sidewalk and pirouette around his cane.

"Well, fellows, we're off. This is Sergeant Terroni driving. We'll be there soon." The winning point of Brisbane's voice was that every word was sincere.

Larry was sure they'd be there soon.

The Longjohn went through second and into high as smooth as oil, and turned a corner like a bat out of hell. Larry knew something of handling oversize vehicles. He imagined himself behind the wheel. Sergeant Terroni, whoever he was, knew his business. The sensation was swell.

The Longjohn spurted and went into second. Brisbane said, "Are there any questions? Anything you want to ask about leave, or furlough, or pay? Speak right up!"

Colonel Diamond said in Larry's ear, "We're going up the Asylum Street hill. A little farther along we take a left-hand street at a fork and go out Farmington Avenue all the way. The right-hand street at the fork is Asylum Avenue."

Someone asked the lieutenant, "How about passes to town?"

"That's easy. Any of you can get passes into Hartford to-night, or any night you want to. The last bus back leaves at five past midnight from the station where you just came in."

"How do we get in?"

"There's a bus from Old Farms at six forty-five every evening."

"How long does it take?"

"About half an hour."

Colonel Diamond said softly, "We're passing the Aetna Life Insurance building on the left—the largest example of Colonial architecture in the world."

Larry said, "You haven't forgotten much about Hartford, sir."

Diamond said, "I wish you'd forget the 'sir.' My rank's the same as yours now, Larry. We're in this thing together, sink or swim. I'm feeling better since we're off the train."

"I think I am too."

The Longjohn paused. Larry heard traffic cross and guessed a stop signal. The Longjohn speeded up again.

"How about liquor, Lieutenant?" That sounded like Brancato. "Can we bring it on the post?"

"Be sure it's inside of you, and not too much."

Everyone laughed.

"That's our one really very strict rule," Brisbane continued when the laugh died down. "You can do about as you want to at Old Farms so long as you attend your classes and behave yourselves. The routine's easy, for most of you are almost ready to leave the Army."

"Thank God!" said someone, and got another chortle.

"We're strict about A.W.O.L. Passes are easy to get if you see your C.Q."

"Hell, I can't see anything!" That was Bill Letter, trying to sound rueful.

"Then talk to the N.C.O. in charge of quarters. You'll find him on your dormitory floor. Get passes and get back on time. No liquor on the post. Stick to that and there'll be no trouble."

"How about dames?"

Brisbane laughed. "That's one thing that the Army leaves up to you, Sergeant Stern. From what I've heard there isn't any shortage in Hartford."

"They started rationing them in Phoenixville," said Letter. "You need tickets with Ivan Stern in town."

Colonel Diamond told Larry, "We just passed Mark Twain's old home on the left. It's a tremendous house of red brick that's been turned into a memorial museum and library. He had the kitchen built toward the street so the servants could have something to look at, according to Mr. Clemens."

"Can you see that?" asked Larry.

"Not very well. In fact, not at all. I just know about where we are, and I've seen it many times before."

Jack Moses got another laugh by asking about dice that were marked in Braille.

"I'll probably be able to get those for you, too," the lieutenant told him. "We get darn near anything at Old Farms that we try for—and we try for anything you boys want. That's our business."

" 'Tain't much use, nohow, Mr. Brisbane," Jack said sadly. "Ain' nobody in Memphis goin' to let me use 'um, nohow, when Ah gits home."

The lieutenant gave a capsule description of West Hartford as they went through. "—All of you fellows will get to know it better when you come down here for orientation."

Larry said, "The streets can't be any tougher to navigate than Phoenixville. I hope there's no snow."

"Larry's from Florida," said Ivan Stern.

"We had plenty of snow all winter, but it's all gone now," Brisbane told them. "The trees are actually starting to bloom."

The Longjohn increased its speed and started uphill on a smooth-riding highway. Larry couldn't help thinking that everything possible was being done by the Army to pave his way with smoothness. God knows it had been rugged enough since he was first inducted. It was a shade ironic to realize that none of the boys could see to appreciate such service: private cars and exclusive Pullman diners; instantaneous seats in the train that was held twenty minutes in New Haven, the traveling public firmly shunted out of the way.

How long would it last once he was back in civilian clothes? Until the war was over and victory won? Hell, the public's memory was short as an inchworm! Strip him of ribbons and uniform, and he'd be reminded that he was a nuisance the very first day.

The lieutenant spoke of Farmington.

"It's beautiful here," said Diamond.

The Longjohn took a rolling curve and spurted along. The boys were silent, the silence Larry was beginning to feel before the end of every journey, the silence of travelers speeding along a lonely road, devoid of signposts, with the destination unknown.

The road turned sharp left and dipped to a bridge which gave a hollow echo.

"We're on the school grounds now," announced Brisbane. "We just crossed the Farmington River."

Larry made an attempt to picture the country, judging that it was rolling from the road that dipped and rose again. There might be hills in the distance, hills that were starting to bud in green. The houses would be old and white, with shingled roofs and well-kept lawns, typical of a movie New England.

The sound of the Longjohn's tires changed as it turned

sharp right on another curve. It swung left again and stopped abruptly.

Brisbane said, "Welcome to Avon Old Farms, fellows. You just passed the flagpole. All out now. We're there."

Larry climbed out slowly. There were voices all around, fellows milling about him. Diamond and Grebe had disappeared somewhere. He listened hard, but couldn't locate Ivan Stern.

"Sergeant Nevin?"

"Yes."

A hand clasped his. "I'm Tony Gaskell, P.F.C. I've been assigned to you as orientor. It will be my job for the next few days to show you how to get around."

Tony's voice sounded really glad to see him, and was touched with some of Brisbane's energy. Larry was reminded of Flagg as he touched his fingers to Tony's arm.

They went up a step and through a door. Flagstones sounded underfoot.

"The C.Q.'s office is on your left," said Tony. "Here. You can feel the door. This is building Number One. Your room's upstairs in this building. Is there anyone you'd like to have in the dormitory with you?"

Larry started to say Colonel Diamond, but didn't. The colonel might think him presumptuous. Instead he asked, "What about Ivan Stern?"

"I'll fix it," Tony promised. "Do you want to go upstairs and wash up now? There's coffee in the Red Cross social room."

"I can wait," said Larry. "Where's the coffee? I think I can do with some."

"Come along. Easy now. There's one step down. We're going through another door."

"That building isn't very big."

"You're in a quadrangle now. Paths cross in the center and another runs all around. You're entirely hemmed in by buildings. All the buildings look the same, much like the one you just came through."

"I'll say I'm hemmed in," said Larry. "This is a hell of a place."

"You'll get on to it quick. It's a simple quadrangle," Tony assured him. "The boys get out a paper called the *Quadrangle Review*."

"I'll be glad when they get me out," said Larry. "What are we coming to now?"

Suddenly fellows were all around.

"Nevin! Hey!"

"Who is it?"

"Masterson, you lug! How are you?"

"Fine. Who's that with you?"

"Oscar Hamilton. My God! Have you forgotten everybody in Ward One?"

"Who could forget a mouth as big as yours?"

"Did Stern come up with you?"

"Sure—and a colonel."

"Diamond. That's good. He's a real guy."

"Gee, this is great! What about a party tonight in Hartford, Larry? The four of us—you and Stern and Masterson and me."

"Okay by me, if I can get a pass. What about it, Tony?"

Tony Gaskell said, "It's practically done. Come on, fellows. We're having coffee in the social room."

The rest was pretty much of a blur: Red Cross girls, soft-voiced and soft-handed, passing out coffee, homemade cake and doughnuts. A piano playing boogie-woogie, and good, although the instrument had seen better days. A juke box blaring out and drowning the piano. *Don't Fence Me In*, remindful of a bar in Phoenixville.

The Registrar—everywhere you went in the Army they asked the same thing. It seemed like they might get to know you after a time.

The dormitory—winding stairs of stone—a tiny cubicle, third on the left—a table, a chair, a typewriter, and a comfortable built-in bunk. Drawers beneath the built-in bunk, and nothing as yet to put in them.

The latrine way down at the end of the hall—two cans without doors and a shower. Who could see you anyhow?

Then to the mess hall—he'd starve to death before he ever found it alone—and you stood in line and carried a tray cafeteria-style, then had to find a table. The place was nuts, completely nuts! A hundred blind guys chattering, laughing, and eating in a mess hall big as a roller rink.

"Larry! I thought I heard you—"

He was cold inside, and the mess hall chilly, as though the sun had disappeared behind a cloud, robbing all heat from the day. He stood stock-still clutching his dinner tray.

"Who is it?" he demanded, realizing that the question was silly enough to brand him an utter fool. He knew damned well who it was. Never in his life again could he mistake that Southern drawl. It would always bring back the first black days of Valley Forge when the world stretched ahead so drearily and the corridors seemed so hopeless and so long.

That voice was the first bright light of friendship to shine through the walls of the dungeon to which fate had everlastingly condemned him. That voice was a beacon blasting a path through ignorance to beckon him out and on. It had started him thinking, jolted him into reasoning; thinking and reasoning—rafts spelling safety when the ship was sunk and gone.

"It's Joe—Joe Morgan. There's a seat over here, Larry. Man, I'm glad you finally got here. Touch my arm and trail along."

Somewhere down South, Larry's father was speaking: "You have power now, Larry. You say you like him, then go around with him. Get other white blind boys to do it too. There's nobody in the country will ever dare to raise a voice against you."

Damn it to hell, he was cold inside because he was yellow! What the hell would Masterson think, and Hamilton? Officers were watching him, detachment men, and Tony Gaskell. What would they say if he ate his first meal at Old Farms sitting down with a Negro?

He wasn't afraid of Ivan, but Ivan was Jewish. Somehow that made him different. Ivan would say, "There's only one Jew that I can't fool, and his name is Ivan Stern."

But *his* name was Larry Nevin. Could his mother, Chris, Dr. Bannerman, Mr. Paterson, and fifty million others be entirely wrong?

He needed someone to turn to, and time to consider, but you played it alone in blindness. This was his first great crisis. God above, he was lonely now, but his loneliness might double if he made his own decision and found that *he* was wrong.

Nigger-lover Nevin! He could only think of a single one in the whole wide world who might help him, and she'd been in love with a crazy boy. Well, another crazy boy needed her now. He'd never written Judy. Where the hell had she gone?

"Larry!" Joe had left and returned again. "I thought you were with me. Touch my arm and come along."

"I'm eating with Masterson and Hamilton, Joe. They're saving a seat at their table. Isn't that right, Tony?"

"There's a couple of seats," said Gaskell slowly. "Joe can eat with us there. Everybody up here likes Joe, Larry. We'll be glad to have him."

"I'm sorry, Larry." The sadness of ages was in Joe's voice. "I think I'll run along."

The mess hall was full of clatter and chatter. Larry touched the back of his hand to Gaskell's arm.

"Where are you from, Sergeant?" Gaskell asked as they walked toward the table.

"Florida."

"Oh," said Gaskell. "They've repealed the Jim Crow laws at Old Farms, Sergeant, except for a few of the fellows from your part of the country."

"I didn't mean—"

"You didn't? Then watch the tone of your voice, Sergeant. A kid as sensitive as Joe might sometime get you wrong." He started whistling between his teeth.

"Look away! Look away! Look away, Dixieland!" Larry cursed himself for following the words of Gaskell's whistled song.

## 24. THE ROOM

THE room in Dormitory One was small and lined with wide oak planks that felt very ancient. Somehow it reminded Larry of a stateroom on shipboard, except for the fact that the ship was still.

He stood for a time in the doorway, listening to the fellows breathing; water running in the latrine, and a murmur of conversation somewhere down the hall. Then he went inside and shut the door.

The door was heavy, with huge cast-iron hinges and a sliding wood latch which he quickly pushed into the socket, bolting himself in. There had been no doors in the hospital at Valley Forge. His hands stayed long on the wooden latch, as if it might be a symbol, bolting a door that shut out the world. Somewhere in the past he had heard that the students at Oxford called it "sporting your oak"—shutting themselves in like that when they didn't want to be disturbed.

He was grateful for the door and its latch. It was the first time he had known real privacy since the beginning of the war. He touched his Braille watch and found it nearly one. He felt exhausted but not sleepy.

Before he undressed, he started in systematically to braille the room. There was a closet in one corner. He opened the door and felt inside, touching wooden pegs instead of metal clothes hooks which he rather expected. A mirror and a wooden towel rack were fastened to the back of the closet door.

He shut the door and felt along. The projecting corner closet formed the foot of the built-in bunk. Beside the bunk, at the head, was a casement window. Below the window a radiator was covered with an elaborately carved wooden grille. There was a heavy oak chair of the one-arm, lunchroom type near a small wooden pullman table which projected out from the wall. Curious, he stood on the chair and felt overhead, touching solid hand-hewn beams. He got down and sat wearily on the edge of the chair. It wouldn't take long to learn the layout. The room was very small.

It was strange, but shut off in the room with the world outside, the universe seemed contracted into a ball. He had taken everything into the bedroom with him: his childhood, his school, his family, the Army, his blindness, Valley Forge, and his furlough. It was all together now, rolled into the shape of a pill which could be readily swallowed.

Digesting life was growing to be a habit. Events were too great, too noisy and too exciting to assimilate at the time they happened. Without his eyes, he was beginning to drift through normal happenings: listening to people, talking to them, answering questions. Not until they were over did the events take shape.

His furlough, for instance. It hadn't been anything at all. Neither had Valley Forge and his training. Neither had Judy, nor Joe, nor the evening he had just spent with Masterson, Hamilton and Ivan Stern going around Hartford on a tour of the bars.

All his vaunted explorations into brand-new lines of thinking were nothing but bravado. He was kidding himself. Maybe he was a neuro-psychiatric. Maybe Colonel Diamond was better off than any of them, compensated by an ability to forget.

The smartest thing that Ivan Stern had ever said was, "There's only one Jew that I can't fool, and his name is Ivan Stern." Well, tonight, with everything shut in his room, there was one G.I. that Larry couldn't fool. Ever since the sniper picked him off in France he had been reading a book—and writing it too. The trouble was, he understood nothing of what he had read or written. He just was not prepared to face his ordeal. As well give a volume of Kant or Hegel to a child in the sixth grade of school.

Maybe he was nuts.

Take Joe: He had thought the whole problem out, talked it over with his father, wrestled it out with himself, and found the solution simple. He couldn't tell if Joe Morgan was white or black, but he had built a picture of Joe with red hair. That was a cinch. If he wanted to be friends with Joe Morgan, he'd be friends with him. If he wanted to go downtown to Hartford or any place else with him, he'd go. Yet he just couldn't do that, and he didn't know why.

It was easy until he faced it.

When he faced it in the mess hall, he'd yelled "Nigger!" at the top of his voice, without saying a word. If Tony Gaskell got it, then Joe must have gotten it ten times worse. And Tony had clicked without a doubt, just as Larry had clicked to the tune that Tony was whistling.

Larry Nevin might be blind, but he wasn't dumb. There were plenty of things that you didn't need words to tell people about. There were ways and means of letting them know.

Jack Moses let you know he was a Negro. He talked like one. Larry never did picture Jack with red hair. He was true to type, a character right out of a minstrel show. And if he wouldn't go downtown with Jack Moses, why should he go down with Joe?

It was all too confusing. He'd probably never understand. Yet, if he didn't understand, nobody would—except, maybe, his father. There was a bond there of some kind, and the old man probably knew about blood and lice and cold and hunger and death and dismemberment. He probably understood about monotony, and sleepless nights; the soaking clothes and rain and snow, and frozen fingers, and guys such as Jimsey being blasted to hell. The old man might even think that Dr. Bannerman's boss might not be so hot; that anybody with all that miraculous power would have pulled a few strings if he had even half of a G.I.'s I.Q.

The old man might even know about dames.

Well, he'd thrown down Joe, and tossed Chris over, and had let down his father too.

Maybe he'd better write to Judy.

He took the lid off the typewriter, but put it back again. He'd flop with Judy too.

He had to quit going through things, and not living them until after they were gone. He had to quit talking to people and not having any idea what he was saying until after the people had gone. He had to quit going places and not being there until two weeks later.

If he could build such pretty bodies for people, why couldn't he build something attractive about things that were going on?

He was facing a chance to learn—eighteen weeks of it. All his instructors could be supermen, if he wanted them to. Every woman in Hartford could be a goddess, if he wanted her to.

He'd been living like a zombie.

He undressed and got into bed, then got up quickly and opened the door.

The hell with the room! He wasn't going to shut things up in it any more. He was just as smart as any guy at Old Farms, and just as blind. He would live things while they happened, and absorb them while he heard them from now on. He went to sleep quite peacefully, and had not forgotten when the rising siren blew at dawn.

Apparently Old Farms wasn't strict about anything. Ten boys had told him that much. Civilian life was close at hand— eighteen weeks away. The C.O. and the officers took that into account, and much of the Army red tape and tightness was relaxed.

Larry could feel it in the atmosphere—the early morning chatter of fellows dressing, the patter of a shower, accompanied by a burst of song. It brought back memories of the dormitory in college. Only maybe the fellows in college weren't so cheerful. Maybe the guys at Old Farms were trying to prove something. His mother had always told him, "Laugh before breakfast, cry before dinner." Maybe so damn much cheerfulness was forced, and indicated something was wrong.

Tony Gaskell picked him up for breakfast, and Larry was

glad of it. Old Farms was full of booby traps—angles, curves, low doorways and double doors in unexpected places. If he ever needed a cane, he'd need it in that man-made puzzle. The corridors of Valley Forge loomed easy by comparison. At least when you got in a corridor you kept on walking, with a wall on each side, and you couldn't very well go wrong.

Yet, strangely, the mess hall was a shade more familiar and not quite so complicated as it had been on his first visit the night before. Maybe, given proper time—say, two or three years —he could learn to pick up a tray as the others seemed to be doing. Meanwhile, he stuck close to Tony, trailing after him with utter confidence.

Tony was full of cheer, and made no mention of his sarcastic rendition of *Dixie*. Instead, he kept up a running patter of explanations—the stairs, the hall, the door, the quadrangle, plots of grass and dangerous trees. He mentioned the lounge as they passed through a building which he called Number Three; the social room, the Training Division, the Post Office, the Public Relations office, and then the mess hall.

Larry thought it all out as he picked up a tray and felt other fellows pressing in back. "Jesus, it's tough," he said out loud.

"Knives, forks and spoons are right here in a box," Tony explained. "And here's your cup. Feel for yourself."

"I don't mean this," said Larry. "I'm talking about getting around."

"Sure, it's tough," Tony agreed, as the line moved up. "I damned near knocked my brains out."

Larry stopped short, and a fellow pushed him gently from behind and said, "Sorry!"

"Don't try to tell me you're blind too!" Larry remarked, with utter disbelief in his voice.

"No, thank God," said Tony, "but I was when I learned my way around. They taped up my eyes so I couldn't see. I was worse than any of you guys, I'll tell you. I banged my nose into every door in Avon. You seem to have some obstacle perception, whatever that is. But me—oh, boy! When I was taking my trainer's course, I was black and blue from every door I found." He got back to the business on hand. "French toast and bacon?"

"Right," said Larry.

"Pick up your tray and hold the back of your hand against my arm. We turn left here, and turn again. There's a rubber mat underneath your feet. Do you feel it?"

"Yes."

"Okay. You get milk, butter, and rolls here, and cereal in a package. Stay on the mat and you can't go wrong. The door sets off to the left a little, so watch yourself or you'll bang your tray. There's a sighted man at most every table, and if he sees you hesitating he'll tell you where to sit down."

Larry met new boys at breakfast, and while he was eating tried to hook up voice with name. When the meal was finished, Tony took him back out to another room and showed him how to clear his tray, dumping garbage in one container and milk tops and paper in another. Then, back over to Building One again, for Personal Orientation.

Damn it, you'd think he had eyes—dusting his room with a limp wet rag, sweeping it out with a broom, hanging his clothes in a closet, putting his toilet articles in place, making a bed in regulation fashion. Everything down to where to hang his tie. Then, out for an eight-thirty meeting which he must attend or take a day's restriction—no visit into town that night.

That was in the lounge room. Tony found him a chair, and Larry sensed fellows all around him—sitting and waiting. More men came in and brushed by his knees. Masterson sat down beside him.

Suddenly, a band began to play. The music was good, and cheered him up. The band stopped and roll was called. Larry asked Johnny Masterson, "What goes on? A show or something?"

"It's the gripe session," Johnny told him. "It's held here

every morning at eight-thirty. If you don't like anything, just holler. This is your chance to say what you have to say."

Lieutenant Brisbane's voice took over, as assuring as the day before. "We have ten new men here with us this morning from Valley Forge. A lot of you fellows know them." He named the lot, and from parts of the room voices yelled a greeting.

Somebody read the menus for the day: meatballs and gravy, French fried potatoes, string beans and escarole, with chocolate pudding for dessert for lunch; roast pork and applesauce, potatoes, two vegetables and mince pie for dinner. There weren't any comments.

From the back of the room somebody yelled, "What the hell are they doing about our laundry?"

Larry sat, stilled by amazement. If this was the Army, he'd never heard anything quite like it before. The fellows certainly said what they had to say.

Lieutenant Brisbane promised that the laundry service would be corrected. Then dry cleaning came up, and was disposed of with a dozen sizzling comments. Someone had failed to receive a telephone call, and the sighted men in charge of quarters—one to each dormitory floor—were given a thorough raking.

Sergeant Lefty Moffat was introduced. Lefty was a trainee with partial vision which, in time, might narrow down to almost nothing. For the present, he was in charge of the social life of Old Farms. There had been parties in the past where the fellows had been bored beyond belief, so the Red Cross had been put on the carpet. The problem was solved by Lefty being appointed as social arbiter to put the matter up to the boys before a party was arranged. Everyone had admitted the embarrassment to hard-working Red Cross representatives in arranging a party where the guests stayed away in a body.

Lefty announced that ten fellows were invited to dinner and dancing in Avon. Someone yelled, "Any beer?" "Plenty," Lefty said, "and the girls are nice. I've met them all." "You would," said somebody else. The party was quickly filled by ten volunteers.

Masterson whispered to Larry, "They've all been good parties since Lefty took things over."

Lieutenant Brisbane told of tickets available for a concert at Bushnell Memorial, in Hartford; announced a speaker from the American Foundation for the Blind for the following Wednesday, and dismissed the meeting at nine o'clock.

Once again the band began to play. Tony Gaskell spoke in Larry's ear. "You're scheduled for an interview with Lieutenant Brisbane and Dr. Seldin. Come along."

Masterson said, "See you later, Larry. Take it easy. I think you'll like it here."

"Maybe I will," said Larry.

He got up and hooked onto Tony's arm. Last night his room had seemed very black. Now he decided to paint it white. He'd paint the whole of Avon white—have everything in it bright and sunny—have the buildings all glistening, and the people all kindly and thoughtful—and it was something to be able to manufacture sunshine; to be able to flood your room with it at midnight of the darkest night, or at noon of the darkest day.


## 25. ANIMAL CRACKERS

THE door to Lieutenant Brisbane's office was tricky. Once inside, Larry sensed that the room was small. The lieutenant's voice came from straight ahead.

"Come right in, Sergeant, and sit down. This is Dr. Seldin. Sergeant Larry Nevin. Dr. Seldin's the psychologist."

"Good morning, Sergeant." The doctor took his hand and shook it. "There's a sofa over here by the window. You'll be more comfortable."

The sofa was leather, and creaked when Larry sat down.

"Your first week here will be pretty busy, Sergeant," Lieutenant Brisbane was saying. "We want you to be happy and comfortable. The first thing you have to do at Old Farms is to learn to find your way around. You're used to a cane, aren't you?"

"Yes, sir."

"Well, we want you to get used to getting around without one." The lieutenant's voice was still assuring, but it had fallen into a more businesslike tone.

The telephone rang.

Dr. Seldin moved up beside Larry and sat down. "You've been to college, haven't you, Larry?"

The doctor's voice was smooth, and not too forcefully inquiring, but Larry was distrustful.

"Two years, sir." He spoke abruptly, as though the conversation might end right there. Psychologist or psychiatrist or what have you, it was his brain, and the only one he had, and for weeks now he had been thinking it was utterly inadequate. Well, he had a choice of spilling his guts or keeping silent. Maybe, if he talked too much, Dr. Seldin would find out how confused he really was. His brain might be a poor and feeble thing, but he didn't want it taken out and flattened on the ground.

"What did you study?" the doctor inquired.

"Not much," said Larry.

The lieutenant finished his telephone conversation, and papers rustled. "Now let me see, Sergeant Nevin. As I was saying, most of your first week here will be spent learning your way around. How did you and Tony Gaskell get along?"

"Fine, sir."

"Well, that's okay."

Sure, it was swell, thought Larry. Gaskell had eyes. He could see the steps in the stinking place, and the doors and windows, and the paths and the trees, and he'd been blindfolded too, and butted his nose. Everything in Old Farms was on a different level. One step. Two steps. Three steps. Doors like those in dungeons. Yeah, he and Gaskell got along fine. Especially when they were going up or down.

"At ten o'clock you'll meet the representative of the Veterans' Administration, and at ten-thirty you'll see the sergeant about your clothing. At eleven there's an orientation clinic. Gaskell will let you go over the model of the hospital and explain it to you. You used a wire board at Valley Forge, I believe."

"Yes, sir," said Larry, and wished he was back in the corridors again. There they had a minimum of steps, and ramps that took you up and down.

"After lunch, you'll have an eye examination by Colonel Maitland."

The telephone rang again.

Dr. Seldin said, "There's nearly anything here you want to do, Larry. Movies, golf, roller-skating, dancing. This was a very fine boys' school."

"Yes, sir," said Larry. "I've heard about it."

"We have horseback riding, and fishing in the Farmington River and Beaver Dam. The main thing is for you to tell us what you'd like to do."

The lieutenant finished his conversation, and the office was silent. Larry could hear the doctor breathing beside him. Every time he breathed, the leather cushions creaked and moved up and down. Everything in Avon moved up and down.

"I don't know what I want to do," said Larry.

That was a lie, and he knew it, but he had decided not to tell them. He was going to keep his life to himself. He wanted to marry and raise a lot of children and be a big shot in something. He wanted his eyes. He wanted to see the colonel at one and have them stuck back in again—good eyes that could look at the world, and look at a woman. Eyes that could read. Eyes that blinked in the sunlight. Eyes that could stare out clearly at color and food, and Gaskell, and the unseen doctor and the lieutenant with his businesslike voice. Eyes that could watch the smoke drift up when he lit himself a cigarette. He knew damn well what he wanted to do, but he wasn't going to tell them. A psychologist would think he was crazy.

"We have nearly any course you want to take here," the lieutenant went on. "Industrial skills in hand and power. You can learn about gas engines and printing. We have a hobby shop where you can learn woodwork and bookbinding. You've had some typing, haven't you?"

"Yes, sir," said Larry. So long as he just said "Yes, sir," he couldn't go wrong.

"Well, I'm sure you'll want to continue that here."

"Yes, sir."

"In academic work, you can follow up in English if you want to, and there's a course in creative writing. Then there's Braille —which you'll want, of course."

"Yes, sir," said Larry. The lieutenant was optimistic. What the hell did he want with Braille? There were Talking Books, and Gray Ladies to do his reading. He wasn't going to wear his fingers down to the bone.

"There's music," said Dr. Seldin.

"Yes, sir," said Larry. Christ, maybe they thought he'd learn to play a horn! Or he could push a piano around the street on rollers, and sit at the corners and sing hymns. Or maybe he could be a one-man band. He remembered one in Jacksonville —a guy with cymbals tied to his feet, and a mouth organ on a metal brace, and an accordion, and a drumstick tied to one arm. There were a lot of things a blind man could do, but he wasn't going to tell them. Let them both find out for themselves. There was music on the radio, plenty of it to get along.

"We have many courses in business too," the lieutenant added. "Maybe you'd like to run a stand."

"Yes, sir," said Larry. Sure, he'd love to run a stand. There was one in Jacksonville, where you could bet on the races. It always had a bunch of drugstore cowboys hanging around, spitting on the sidewalk and high-signing the babes. That would be an ideal life, when you couldn't see them. You could pass out Chesterfields for Camels, and ten-dollar bills for ones and fives, and never know the difference. And people could squint at your plastic eye.

Yessir, Yessir, Yessir.

He wanted to be an executive—a banker, a lawyer, a doctor. How the hell could he put it across? He wanted to tell them of shattered hopes and blasting guns that snuffed out life, and babies crying in Italy. He wanted to live and laugh and love. The doctor wanted to look at his brain. The lieutenant wanted to give him a stand. So he'd shut his mouth like a bloody fool and answer nothing but "Yes, sir." And, after he left, the doctor would laugh and the busy lieutenant would mark him dumb. He wanted to go to his little room that he had painted so white with sunlight, shut the door and turn on the blackness, and die.

So this was Old Farms. Well, he'd promised to paint the damned place white and think of the lovely people. God knows he wasn't doing it; he was being a droop.

Yet he listened, later, to the man in the Veterans' Administration without even thinking, and drew his clothing, still acting like something that moved on strings.

When Gaskell took him to the orientation clinic at eleven, he asked solicitously, "Are you feeling all right today, Larry?"

"Sure. I'm feeling swell."

"You'd never know it," said Gaskell. "Things will be better when you learn your way around here."

"Well," said Larry, "I'll try."

The model of Old Farms caught his interest. It was built on a table the height of his waist. The buildings were wood, and green turkish toweling marked the grass. Strips of sandpaper served for roads, and smoother Braille paper for navigable paths. The trees were marked by shot-topped tacks.

Larry started at the flagpole with Gaskell directing his fingers, and traveled inside. It was most peculiar. The entrance that had seemed so strange began to take shape. The quadrangle, entirely surrounded by buildings, became a kind of village square. He had the sensation that the end of his finger had turned into an eye.

Gaskell took his hand on a trip from his room to the mess

hall and back; on a trip from his room to the lounge, where the morning meeting was held; on a trip from his room to Lieutenant Brisbane's office. Then they began to stop en route. From Building One to Building Two. From Two to Three, and Three to Four, and back to One, completing the circle. Then they went another way, and he had a picture of Old Farms.

"Now you take over," said Gaskell. "Point out where we are right now."

"Here," said Larry.

"Where's the mess hall?"

"Here," said Larry.

"Good!" said Gaskell. "Now follow a path from here to your room."

Larry traced it.

"Okay," said Gaskell, "we'll walk it. And you try to lead the way. Can you do it?"

"At least," said Larry, "I can try."

Outside it wasn't so easy. The picture faded away again and Old Farms was once more a mass of paths.

Gaskell followed behind, touching Larry's arm, and warned him off of a wall and a tree. They got through doors, missed the flagged path, and struck onto grass.

Larry stopped. "I don't know where I am."

"You just came through Building Three," said Gaskell. "Building One is straight ahead. Try following the edge of the grass with your foot—and keep to the right."

They finally got there and Larry said, "I'd never have made it without your help. I'm hopeless."

Gaskell laughed. "It took me two solid hours to do not as well as you've done in twenty minutes. I'll make you a bet."

"What?" asked Larry.

"A dinner in town, that after eight hours of trying, you'll be able to walk this place and find any room as fast as I can."

"You mean all alone?"

"Absolutely alone," said Gaskell, "and without a cane. A hundred other guys here can do it, and you can."

"You mean there are a hundred blind boys in here right now that know this place without a cane?"

"Up and down, and inside and out," said Gaskell. "And put the whole hundred together and you won't find a single eye. Not only that, they know every bar in Hartford—and most of the stores."

"If a hundred fellows can do it," said Larry grimly, "so can I."

They went back to the orientation room. Gaskell found him a chair by a long wood table.

"Now let's get your hands to work. There's something I want you to try. What does this feel like to you?" He put an object in Larry's hand.

"It's a circular pyramid of some kind," said Larry. "It feels like a lot of wooden discs set on a peg about the size of a pencil. They're different sizes, and the biggest is at the bottom. There are seven."

Larry moved his hands. "The peg's fastened into the bottom one, but the other six come off."

"Good," said Gaskell. "Now listen carefully. I want you to take off those six, mix them up on the table, find them again and put them back on the peg in the fastest possible way. '

It sounded simple. Larry picked off the discs in a single group, spread them on the table and searched around for the largest, which he put on first. On the second, he wasn't quite sure. It might not be the next in size. He hunted until he found a smaller one, then finally found the remaining three and stacked them all together. Once he had them in a pile, he slipped them back in rotation.

"Good," said Gaskell. "Except for one thing. You didn't listen to what I said."

"You mean I was slow?"

"No," said Gaskell. "As a matter of fact, you were faster

than average, but you might have done it faster. Do you remember what I told you?"

"Sure," said Larry. "You told me to put them back on in the fastest possible way."

"And you put them back in rotation," said Gaskell. "The biggest at the bottom, the smallest at the top. And you had to stop to do it. You're blind, Larry, and the object of this test is to teach you not to always believe your ears. You have to think. You should have picked up any disc your hand encountered and pushed it on the peg, regardless of size. I didn't care if you mixed them up. I told you to get them back on the peg in the fastest possible way. Keep that in mind. Sometime somebody may tell you to jump. They won't say whether it's jump to the right or the left, or front or back. Just jump, toots, and don't stop to figure in which direction. That little lesson may save your life someday."

They moved a little farther along the table.

"Now, what's this?" Gaskell asked him.

Larry closed his hand around an irregular object, then brailled it. It had eight sharp points, three at one end and one at the other, and four on one side. He started to say a dog, and changed his mind. A dog's mouth didn't go straight down beneath its ears.

"A goat," he said.

"Swell," Gaskell commended. "Most of the fellows miss that. The beard underneath is as stiff as the horns. I suppose in the model it has to be that way. Take a try at this one now."

"An egg beater," said Larry, without delay.

"And this?"

"That's easy. It's a stopper on a chain for a wash basin."

He went through several others quickly. A typewriter eraser with a brush attached won Gaskell's unstinted approval when Larry described the color of the eraser by the feel of its texture, and explained on questioning that a red eraser was always smoother than a gray one.

"Well, try your teeth on this one, wise guy," Gaskell told him.

Larry had never felt anything quite like it before. It was round, with legs in front and back, and oversize hams. The head felt as if it had horns. The back was deepened into a hollow cavity. Larry went over it three or four times before making a guess. Finally he said, "It's some kind of an animal made into an ashtray."

"What kind of an animal?" asked Gaskell. "So far you're okay."

Larry turned it upside down and brailled the stomach. It offered nothing. He tried to picture animals in the zoo, but this one had bony structures beside its head, rather than horns. The fat hams had him puzzled, and the blunt, fat head.

"I'll give you a hint," said Gaskell, after a time. "That one's awfully tough. Most of the fellows miss it. Think of something that lives around the water."

Larry's mind flashed back to natural history. "A hippo?"

Gaskell laughed. "You're forty miles away. Did you ever see a hippo sit on a lily pad?"

"Hell," said Larry, "a frog! Take the thing away!"

"Now we'll try the wiggly block," said Gaskell.

"I'm willing to try anything," said Larry, "if you'll tell me what it's for."

"We want you to get used to using your hands and thinking," Gaskell was quick to explain. "Some fellows lack perception in their fingers. We can save them a lot of time if we know it. If you have it, there are lots of things you can do, such as mastering Braille and learning to work a trick machine."

The wiggly block was long and smooth and polished. It came apart like a giant puzzle, separating itself into fluted columns. With Gaskell holding a stop watch, Larry found the pieces and put it together again.

Gaskell sighed. "I think you've hung up a record. Would you mind explaining just how you went about that?"

"I found the middle first," said Larry, "and located the pieces that went around it by feeling the angles on the ends."

"And by using your head," said Gaskell.

They moved along to another table.

"Were you ever in a mystic maze?" Gaskell asked him.

"I went through the one at Hampton Court while I was in England," Larry told him. "And now I've been through Old Farms."

"Well, I'll give you one for your fingers," said Gaskell. He placed Larry's fingers on a board full of ridges. "Start in here and see how quick you can trace your way into the center and out again. And don't jump any walls, because I'm watching."

The finger maze was full of blind alleys, and Larry found he had to think. Finally, by sheer concentration, he learned to keep out of ridges which he had been in before. It took some time, but he made it—in and out again.

"We eat," said Gaskell.

Larry hooked to his arm and started off for the mess hall. Outside of the orientation room he stopped. The sun was strong against his face. The Connecticut air was warm with spring.

"What's the matter?" asked Gaskell.

"Damn it all," said Larry, "I forgot something."

"What?"

"I forgot I was blind. It must have been fooling around with those animal crackers. Sometime, let's go back in there. I think I'd like to play with those things again."

## 26. "A MAN FROM OUR TOWN"

"DEAR LARRY:

"You certainly haven't written much since you went back North, but I guess I have no kick to make. I'm pretty bad myself and I guess it's even more difficult for you to get down to a typewriter than it is for me. But two little short notes telling us nothing since we saw you off on the train! And your mother says she hasn't heard much more! After all, darling, your month in Palatka after all the time you've been away didn't seem very long.

"I don't have much time for anything after teaching school all day. Father's been having more trouble at the barrel plant. He really needs someone in there to help him. What are you studying at Avon? You never write and say. I hope you've gotten over that silly idea about settling up there someplace. It's foolish if you consider—"

The Gray Lady reading Chris's letter had a musical voice and read with a lot of sympathy. It was Monday night and the Red Cross lounge was full of girls. A dancing class was going on. Over the words of the letter Larry was listening to the teacher's chant, following the shuffle of unskilled feet, and trying to anticipate the next piece the pianist would play.

The adjoining lounge was large enough for a nice-size dance floor. The room he was in was smaller. He'd already discovered that the size of a room affected voices. That is, he could tell if the room was large or small. He might develop greater accuracy later.

"One—two—slide! One—two—slide!"

*"What are you studying at Avon? You never write and say."*

If you put the two together you could make a little song:

> One—two slide! One two slide!
> What are you studying at Avon?
> You never write and say!
> There was a man from our town,
> And he was wondrous wise.
> He fell into a bramblebush
> And scratched out both his eyes!
> And when he found his eyes were gone,
> He cried with might and main,
> And fell into a bramblebush
> And scratched 'em in again!

He wasn't studying anything at Avon. He was an overstuffed mummy whose ears were better than average. He could braille a lot of china animals and never feel the nipples on a woman's breasts rise up under his fingers.

The room was full of perfumed girls. He could hear them and smell them. They were like the blind—untouchables! They were just like Chris—a bunch of hostesses who would shrink away in horror if he reached out and caught one.

The music stopped for the dancing teacher to give some verbal instructions.

The Gray Lady was finishing Chris's letter:

"—so even if you don't write me, Larry, try to find time to write your mother more often—and good luck, Larry—
As ever,                                                             CHRIS."

"Thank you, Mrs. Allen."

"You're welcome, Larry. Any time. Are you going to dance?"

"Not tonight. I'll try to get off a letter."

"That's a good idea." She got up from beside him. "Whenever you need me, I'm here on Monday, Wednesday and Friday evenings. I'll be glad to read for you." She was lost in the crowd.

"As ever, Chris." As ever, hell! He was too damn busy to write to anyone—busy having his eyes scratched in again. He'd heard that rhyme since childhood—"There was a man from our town." It would be a joke if the dope who wrote it had really meant something. Maybe he was blind himself—maybe he knew the second bramblebush you fell into when you tried to live again.

Chris, Christ, and Christopher Columbus! The Army must have read that rhyme. First they spent a year or two sticking you full of brambles so you could lose your peepers, then they spent another year sticking you full of brambles to adjust you to your unfortunate condition.

"*As ever, Chris.*" Well, she wasn't as ever. He wasn't as ever. And in spite of all that Old Farms could do, nothing was as ever.

He wanted to rape a girl—any girl. He wanted to quit being a yellow-bellied turncoat bastard and to make friends with

a nigger. He wanted to be liked and admired by Joe. Was that
as ever? Hell, no!

The Army was throwing its dough away on Larry Nevin.
He'd tell Dr. Seldin in the morning. With every step of training he was getting worse. He didn't give a tinker's damn for
their animals, their dancing class, their hobby shop, their
orientation, or their facial vision that was a hell of a sight
worse than nothing. He'd kidded himself and Gaskell and
everyone at Old Farms from Colonel Maitland down to lowly
black Joe.

If he ever told Dr. Seldin the truth the doctor would put
him away in an N.P. ward. He'd be crazy as Larry Nevin was if
he ever let him go.

He'd revised his estimate of Dr. Seldin. The doctor was
really trying to help; trying to find some basic interest that
Larry might work with. Larry felt a bit contrite about his
surliness during the first day's interview.

The trouble was that Larry Nevin had no basic interest.
That's where the doctor went haywire. All that Larry Nevin
could do was wish himself in bed with a nice warm babe.
Jimsey had died with that wish on his lips. Maybe it wasn't
far wrong.

> Fell into a bramblebush
> And scratched 'em in again!

Damn that little song!

Colonel Maitland was regular Army. He didn't beat around
any bramblebush, and yet he was kind. Larry had talked with
him the previous Saturday.

"No hope, Colonel?"

"None. And don't let anyone tell you there is. After you
get out of here you'll hear about fellows recovering their
vision. Some do, but you won't. Recovery of sight makes a
good newspaper story—like 'facial vision'—and like facial
vision it's more than often overwritten to make the story. Lots
of quacks will be ready to milk you boys of your pensions. My
advice is don't throw your money away, Larry."

Yet inside, Larry knew that hope he might see again, some-day, would never die. Maybe when he was thirty, or forty, or sixty, something might develop—something like radar carrying television straight to the brain. His eyes were gone, so what? Fifty years before, anyone would have branded a man as crazy who dared to predict that the world would see pictures and hear voices that were a hundred miles away.

Maybe the man from our town was really wondrous wise! Who in the world was competent to say?

Somewhere in the other room he heard Joe Morgan talking and laughing. Had Joe been dancing with white girls? Or maybe some of the hostesses were colored. Shades of General Robert E. Lee! The girls at the Red Cross dance were the cream of Hartford. Were they asked to mix and dance on the floor with Negro couples? Did they do it without protest merely because the boys were blind? Or had something happened?

He was sitting taut and uncomfortable, full of a strange frustration, when the music started again. He'd been trying to sort out voices—women's voices, to see if some of them registered black. He had to know, yet he couldn't ask.

Damn Judy! "The only blackness, Larry, is blackness of the brain."

Joe came in. Larry knew it was Joe before he felt the gently inquiring touch of Joe's cane.

"Who's that?"

"Larry."

Joe started onward without reply.

"Joe, please sit down. There's a seat right here beside me." He wanted the girls from Hartford to see, and the Red Cross workers, and all the detachment men. He was fighting the toughest fight of his life, battling a dozen ancestors—gray-clad soldiers who'd lost their lives for the Stars and Bars. If his voice showed feeling, as Gaskell had said, then it must have been full of entreaty and blinding pain.

Joe stopped and stood silent, while the teacher in the other room called "One—two—slide! One—two—slide!"

"Joe, I'm sorry. I've been a fool. I'd like to be friends. Please sit down and give me a chance to explain." Gaskell had taught him to walk straight lines while following a buzzer, and then to walk them with no sound at all to guide him. It was helpful now, for he had no time for wavering. He must talk straight lines to Joe Morgan, talk with his shoulders back and head erect; swing out in his stride with courage. If he lost this time, he'd never have a chance again.

The couch beside him sagged, and Joe sat down with a chuckle. "Larry, I'm a Negro born and reared in the South. I've been to a Negro college. I've been in a war and blinded. It's only since I lost my eyes that I ever forget my color as I did when I met you at Valley Forge and the evening you came here to Old Farms. You were reared in the South as I was. I've been the damn fool, Larry. There's nothing for you to explain." He started to rise.

Larry reached out and stayed him. "Joe, I liked you the moment I met you—better than any fellow I've known. I like you now. Don't you see you've taught me something?"

"That a blind man can't tell black from white?" Joe chuckled again. "We hear those things, Larry. I liked you too —liked you so much that I thought you knew I was colored when we went in town to Phoenixville together. I like you now—like you because tonight you've proved you're honest. I like you so much that I won't be friends and make you unhappy." His rich drawl lowered, cutting through the steady piano. "You've taught me something too, Larry—never to trust a Southern white man again."

"Joe!" Larry's voice was desperate. "We're both of us wrong. My father said I had power since I was blinded. He told me if I liked you, to go around with you and get other fellows to do it too. He said that nobody could raise a voice against us. Joe, you've got to help me. I'm up against something I've never even thought about before."

"It's no good, Larry. I've thought about it plenty before. My father's thought about it too. He's a hopeless cripple, Larry—dragged from his Ford and beaten until his back was broken because he picked up a nine-year-old white girl one morning and drove her three miles through a pouring rain to school."

"Even you think I'm crazy, Joe. When I went back home to Palatka, the girl I was going to marry wouldn't even kiss me. She teaches school—teaches kids to hate decent guys like you. She'd never in God's world understand how I could even talk to you."

"Do you know of a white girl who would understand?"

"Yes," said Larry thoughtfully, "I think I do. A girl named Judy Greene. I met her in Phoenixville. She was in love with a kid who went crazy and killed somebody. She told me once that the only blackness was blackness of the brain."

"And who's she in love with now, Larry?"

"How the hell would I know?"

"Doesn't she ever write you?"

"No." He paused. "She knew about Chris—that's the school-teacher in Palatka. She told me she wouldn't write while I was home on furlough. It might embarrass me having to have somebody read me letters from another girl."

"Yeah," said Joe, "that's true, but I suppose you've written her."

"No, I haven't. What's more I don't intend to."

"Why?" asked Joe. "Or maybe it's none of my business. I was thinking that she sounded like a mighty decent sort of a girl."

"She's too damned decent." Larry lit a cigarette and the match flame trembled. "I looked her up when I got back North to Phoenixville, but she'd gone on a vacation or something."

"Why don't you write her now, Larry? There's one thing we need worse than anything else, and that's a woman to love us."

"I don't want anyone to love me," Larry said fiercely.

"Judy's had a hell of a life. Do you think I'm going to hunt her up and prey on her sympathy—maybe finish up by saddling her with *me* for life? Give me a little credit, Joe. She's loved one guy who turned out wrong. Well, I've turned out wrong already. I'm no damned good for anything. You said yourself I couldn't even think straight. There's nothing worth a good goddam about me now except my plastic eye!"

"The gods have always loved lunatics, Larry. Even if one of them has a plastic eye."

"The girls don't love them," said Larry.

"I'll bet they do," said Joe Morgan. "Black and white. Even as you and I!"

## 27. PUBLICANS AND SINNERS

"What you need is a dame, Larry."

"I need a drink, Masterson. A nice long shot with another beer."

"I'll buy, Larry," said Ivan Stern.

"I'll buy, damn it! It's my turn, Ivan."

"I'll get it, Larry."

"This one's mine, Ivan. Nuts to you!" Masterson cut in.

Masterson paid. Masterson always paid if you weren't quick. A good egg, Masterson. All good eggs—Masterson, Hamilton and Ivan too. Ivan paid, if you weren't quick.

"What bar's this, Ivan?" Larry was blind as a bat and drunk as an owl. It was nearly ten, or eleven, or midnight, or daylight, or sunlight or daylight wartime saving time that saved everything but your goddam eyeballs.

"How the hell do I know? It's the sixth we've been in. Isn't that enough?"

No. It wasn't enough. There were lots of bars in Hartford. Lots of bars and lots of babes. He wanted to become familiar with them all. Hear them gabbing all around:

"And I said—"

"And he said—"

"Docked my pay—the bastard did—"

"Eighty-four motors and nine assemblies and then kicking about my overtime—"

"Will we get the last bus, Masterson?"

"The hell with the bus. What you need is a dame. Doesn't he, Ivan?"

"And how, and how. He's wearing me down with his sexual inhibitions. Hark, lads! I hear a couple of familiar voices bearing towards our table."

"I want another drink, Ivan."

"You've had too many now. Hey, waiter!"

"H'lo, Ivan. And Masty, too. This is a surprise."

"Hello, Beth—and I'll bet my glass eyes that's Corinne of the bulging bosoms with you. This is Larry Nevin, girls. Rub right over his eager legs and sit you down."

"D'ya mind, soldier?" Warm lithe legs pressed meaningly against his own—Corinne of the bulging bosoms. How could he miss those contours scraped suggestively along his arm?

"Don't call me 'soldier'!" Larry's voice must have been unnecessarily vicious, for the table silenced.

"Well! You don't need to bite my head off, handsome." She gave a short and nervous laugh. "How did you know that I was Corinne?"

"I'm learning to braille animals," said Larry. "Of course, they're all in miniature form."

Both girls laughed.

"You'll find he's quite a lad, fair ladies," said Ivan Stern. "Don't let his moody mien disturb you. Under those jet black glasses you'll find a heart of gold."

"But not a pot," said Masterson dreamily.

"You boys are nuts," said the girl called Beth. "I never know what you're talking about."

"I'll order another drink," said Larry. "Hey, waiter!" He banged his glass on the table.

"See. I told you he was sweet, didn't I?" Corinne moved closer.

Larry hadn't remembered what she'd told them. Fire was flooding his body again, coursing through him, too much whisky, too much wondering, too much waiting mixed with the supple wriggle of her hip and thigh.

Drinks came and he tossed his down. He wanted to move and couldn't. She crossed her legs and was taunting him, rubbing the warmth of her calf against him.

Future and past merged together. Would everything in his blinded life begin and end drinking whisky in a bar? Judy, Chris, his father, the girl beside him, wooing him for money; they were blurred together into a haze.

That was happening too frequently—that blurring together. Life ceased to have focus and clearness. Perhaps that was why the haze was so pleasant, like a dope fiend dulling his mind with morphine. Life would be so easy if you drank it away in the confines of a bar.

His hand moved down to stroke her leg. The flesh was cool and bare, and he smoothed it gently with burning fingers. He was thinking of Chris on the porch at home—Chris standing mute as he brailled her in the presence of his mother. He was thinking of Judy and that first warm kiss the night he met her in Phoenixville, that kiss that had turned to ice in the freezing air.

Strange that he had no fear at all of taking this stranger beside him. She was younger than either Chris or Judy, probably more beautiful. Suppose he took her home and failed? But he wouldn't fail. He knew it. He could satisfy every spark of longing that was slowly eating his heart away. The miserable nights of torture would vanish into a peaceful day.

He also knew the answer. Whisky was a marvelous thing; it made one think so clearly. He was blind as a bat and drunk as an owl. He could take this little trollop beside him because he could buy her. She had something to sell—her luscious young body. She'd shut her eyes and blank her feeble little mind and give herself to him, blind or not, because he was able to pay.

He moved his hand up higher, tightening his fingers cruelly on the softness of her inner thigh.

She stood up suddenly, freeing herself. "Larry and I are going somewhere where we can dance. What do you say?"

"Count me out," said Masterson. "I'm not as young as I uster be. I don't like dancing anyway."

"And I'm too tight," said Ivan Stern, "to trip the light fantastic toe."

Beth said, "I'll go with them."

"I'm sure, my lovely Beth," said Ivan, "that I want your company much more than Larry. He's a lad of strange moods, and is now under military sentence for breaking the arm of a two-star general who interfered with his dancing the other day. Add to that the fact that your lovely voice can be wearing to a sergeant's ears, that you chew gum loudly, and dance too close to your partner, and that I'm going to break your arm if you move—and I'm sure you'll reconsider your unreasonable decision and have another drink with Masterson and me."

Beth giggled and said, "You guys are nuts. I guess I'd better stay."

Larry was moving in a dream. He reached for bills in his pocket.

Masterson said, "Keep your folding money under cover, Larry. There's nothing to pay."

He'd have caught the warning in Masterson's voice if he hadn't been as drunk as an owl. Afterwards it was like the wall, and the waterfall of lichens—something he'd remember until his dying day.

Corinne led him out with consummate skill. "Too much skill," kept running through his foggy brain. He clung to her arm, and for all his unsteadiness never touched a chair or table. She paused at the door for the one step down, giving him ample time to find it.

He had griped at the world for its clumsy handling of those who were blind. Now he was sulking, thinking how many blind guys had clung to her arm to breed such surety. Inside he knew that nothing Corinne could do would please him. She'd broken him down, but he didn't have to like a slut. He only had to like her body, and that was his, or anyone's who had the money.

They walked a block and waited. The air was warm with a night of too early summer.

"What are we waiting for—a cab?"

"A bus, Larry." She twined his fingers into her own. The back of his hand was against her breast. Once he'd stood with Judy like that and felt the throb of her beating heart.

"I thought we were going dancing." He'd make it as tough as possible for her. She could damn well coax him into bed. Let her earn her pay.

"Do you want to?" Her fingers tightened. "I thought you might like to have a drink at my place. It's just out Farmington Avenue a little way."

"I don't care." He felt very clever. Make her think he didn't want her. Show indifference. Handle things in a businesslike manner.

A bus rolled up. She helped him on and he reached for tokens, but Corinne said, "Pay as you leave, Larry." He always had trouble remembering that with the busses in Hartford. Pay as you leave going out of town. Pay getting in when you went the other direction. What did he do with the girl beside him?

The bus driver laughed and made some crack which Corinne answered. God! She even knew the drivers. She found a seat, sat Larry down, and pressed in close beside him. He hated her worse because he liked it, because he felt so helpless to escape the thrilling contact. The jouncing bus was torture, and still he couldn't move away.

"Where were you wounded, Larry?" Her voice sounded softer, almost the frightened voice of a kid.

"In France." It was none of her business.

"How?"

"By a sniper."

"My brother's in France. With the Ninety-fourth."

"Yeah." She had a nerve to pull that on him. She'd never even seen a brother, nor a father or mother either.

"He's been over there a long time, Larry. I hope he gets back okay."

"He'll get back okay."

He wanted to scream. He was all on fire, flaming and trembling. He wanted to whip her—strip her and lash her for lying—tie her up naked and begging; stripe her lovely body for the mythical boy who was fighting in France; lash her into submission because Larry Nevin had lost his eyes and had to pay her because he couldn't see.

She lapsed into silence.

The bus rolled on and he cursed himself for a bloody fool. Why was he always so involved? Why was he filled with such desires, with terrible thoughts that seared his blood? He must be crazy. Why couldn't he go to bed with this girl, pay her, and forget it? Why in the name of all that was holy couldn't he take things casually?

"We get out at the next stop, Larry."

He started at the sound of her voice. "Okay, baby. Here are tokens."

"I have them all ready, Larry."

He didn't argue. Instead, he reached out beside him and rested his hand on her knee.

They got out at a street that smelled of trees. Larry followed her stumblingly. Half a block from Farmington Avenue they entered a house through a vestibule. Corinne opened the door to the click of a latch key. A radio was playing somewhere. They climbed a flight and stopped while she opened another door which closed behind them.

Larry judged the place to be small, but the room had an air of freshness and of being neat and clean. A light switch snapped. Corinne led him to a seat on a soft divan. When he tried to pull her down beside him she neatly evaded.

"I'll mix a drink."

He heard her move to another room and after a moment water ran and ice cubes clinked in a kitchen sink. His head was swimming so he put it down on his folded hands on top of his cane.

"Here, Larry."

He held out a hand without raising his head. His fingers closed tight around a tall glass so cold that its touch was heaven. He didn't want to drink the contents, he wanted to hold the tumbler, feel it chill the pounding blood in his veins and send the coolness coursing upward through his arm to cool his heart and clear his brain. He wanted to—

"Are you feeling okay, Larry?" She'd been standing watching.

"I'm fine."

She was gone again.

The picture was wrong and cloudy. This was a sordid dive he was in, a bawdy flat of ill repute. Its owner was a harlot preying on soldiers, a chiseler living by selling her body, a girl of ill fame. This was sin. She was young as a baby and old as Eve. Her face was the face of a serpent—a serpent with crimson tempting lips—Corinne of the bulging bosoms. Breasts for sale! She was Chris and Judy stripped naked. This was damnation—the theme of Dr. Bannerman's sermons.

"And I say unto you—she's yours for the taking, the chance you've asked for to prove your manhood, to show that you cannot fail!"

Everything was wrong and cloudy when you had no eyes to see. He liked the wanton little bitch—wanted her as he wanted Judy. He liked her flat of ill repute. He loved her body, God help him! "There is no sex in America, Larry. How can something that doesn't exist be wrong?" Ivan had lied. Judy had lied: "The only blackness, Larry, is blackness of the brain."

She was taking the cold glass gently from his fingers, gently loosening his other hand from its grip on the crook of his cane. Her hands were smooth against his cheeks, her hot moist lips were tight against his own.

He drew her close with fearful strength, roughly searching the curves of her body naked under a dressing gown. She fell back slowly on the divan, breasts pressed close, clinging arms around his neck inexorably pulling him down.

His lips were free for an instant. He had to be fair. "I haven't much money, baby. Something around eleven bucks. Is that okay?"

Her strength was surprising. His cheek received a stinging slap. Slender arms pushed him insanely. He rolled to the floor and, mad and hurt, finally got to his knees and started groping for his glasses, which had fallen somewhere near him.

"Damn you!" he muttered. "I ought to kill you." She was sobbing somewhere across the room. He found his glasses, put them on and started toward her. He really wanted to beat her now, pummel her flesh with clenched-up fists until her skin turned blue and brown.

"Get out, God damn you, Larry! The door's to your right and your cane and cap's at the end of the couch. Don't come near, or I'll brain you. Get out of here! Turn to the left outside the door and you'll find the stairs. I hope to God you kill yourself going down."

Her racking sobs and her desperate tone half sobered him, but his mind was a blank, resolutely refusing to function. He couldn't find his cane and cap. The hell with them then; he'd leave them both. He turned toward the door.

"No, Larry, wait!" Her speech was so broken he scarcely could understand.

"I'm getting the hell out of this dump."

"That's what I want, Larry. I never want to see you again. But for the sake of the other blinded boys coming out of this war you can spare a minute. Don't come near me. A chair's beside you. Just sit down."

He hesitated, found the chair, and perched on the edge.

Horrible silence was holding him, silence made more racking by the break of her endless sobbing. Finally he heard her blow her nose, and the sobs decreased.

"I work every day, Larry, here, at a plant in town. I make over fifty dollars a week. There's lots of girls just like me with fellows and brothers overseas—girls away from home on war work, or maybe their families gone. We're lonesome, yes, but not so lonesome as you boys are."

She stopped a minute. "We see you every night, Larry—searching Hartford with your canes for something, forgetting yourselves with booze in every bar. None of you can buy us, Larry. Pass that on to the others. We have nothing to sell."

She was crying again, weeping softly as Larry had wept when told that his eyes were gone. "If any of you find us easy pickings, it's because we love you—love you for what you've lost for your country, love you all for what you've done and what you are. Now and again we meet one of you who happens to be more attractive than the others—"

"And who turns out to be a goddam fool," said Larry. He got up and found his cap and cane. "I'll tell the fellows there are some things that dough can't buy."

He made his way out, got to the corner and started walking out Farmington Avenue. He was very tired when a police car pulled up beside him and an officer said, "You look like you're lost, Sergeant. It's half-past two. Going far?"

"Sometimes I wonder," said Larry, "just how fast I'm going, and how far."

## 28. WESTERN UNION

"You look as if you were going to run into a horse," said Gaskell. "There aren't any horses in here. Can't you walk erect without holding your head way back? You're not going to hit anything."

"That's what you think." Larry stopped stock-still in the center of the training room.

He'd hit something already. What did wise guy Gaskell know about it? Gaskell could see. What did he know about snags in one's life? What idea could a sighted man form about hopes that could never be?

Larry Nevin was finished, washed up, totally and completely through with everything. Joe Morgan would have none of him, neither would Chris, neither would a cheap little wench in town. Probably a dozen guys had laid Corinne, but she'd thrown big shot Nevin out on his ear.

The hell of it was, he had it coming to him. He was beginning to remind himself of the progress of civilization. Larry Nevin, symbol! The more he was trained scientifically, the less he really knew how to do.

"Sit down, for the love of Pete," said Gaskell.

Larry obeyed automatically, settling himself on the edge of a chair.

Gaskell stayed quiet while cigarettes were lighted, then burst out abruptly, "What the hell's the matter with you?"

"Nothing."

"Quit relaxing your facial muscles, and don't stare into space," said Gaskell. "It gives you a deadpan expression and looks as if you aren't listening to what people are saying."

"I'm not," said Larry. "I don't give a damn about what people say."

"That explains what's the matter with you. You have to care what people say. It makes you take care of yourself—makes you keep your clothes neat, shave carefully with your electric razor, shine your shoes as I've taught you, clean your teeth, and comb and brush your hair."

"People talk plenty about me now. What difference does it make if they talk some more? I'll quit going anywhere."

"Umm," said Gaskell. "A recluse. Hermit Nevin." He put a hand on Larry's knee. "Listen, Larry. Has anybody ever loosened up and really told you the truth about your eyes?"

"Christ almighty—!" Larry broke off, unable to think of anything to add. The truth about his eyes! He was learning to throw darts at sound, and shoot at a target with a buzzer bull's-eye. He was mastering Dr. McCloy's technique for paratroopers on "How to Fall." Maybe dumb cluck Gaskell thought Sergeant Nevin was off to war again!

His ears were growing to elephant size from being trained to recognize voices: Colonel Maitland, Lieutenant Brisbane, Dr. Seldin, Sergeant Bart Carey, the colored editor of the *Quadrangle Review,* all on a record speaking separately— "This is Colonel Maitland. How are you boys?"—then all of them scrambled together. Maybe nitwit Gaskell thought Sergeant Nevin had nothing else to listen to!

"Don't get ratty, Larry. I asked you a question."

"I heard you," said Larry. "I talked to Colonel Green at Valley Forge and Colonel Maitland here. There's nothing anybody can do."

"For a guy with your intelligence," said Gaskell, "there are streaks in you that are just plain dumb. I've been through Valley Forge myself—in fact, I was a patient there with a chest wound. Now I'm stationed at Old Farms helping to train a hundred G.I.'s who are just as blind as you. I know damned well your vision's gone. I want to know if you know how your eyes look after that plastic job done by Colonel Waters."

"They look like hell," said Larry grimly. "I don't need to hear it from you."

"Can you take it?" asked Gaskell. "I may spoil a lot of your pretty pictures if I give you the lowdown. Do you want me to?"

"What pretty pictures?"

"Don't you have pictures?" Gaskell sounded surprised. "Pictures of all the sexy babes who look just like you want them to look; pictures of all the people around staring at nothing but you; pictures of all the guys you know with the hair and bodies you gave them. Pictures of Old Farms and lots of places you've been to, but never seen."

"So what?" asked Larry. Gaskell was digging into stuff that

was none of his business. The probing brought back Larry's
train trip South, the bearded girl with horns on her head, the
pig-like baby. He didn't want Ivan's yellow hair displaced.
He didn't want to disturb his thoughts of lanky redheaded
Joe.

"If you don't have pictures you're not like the rest, Larry.
Most of the fellows do."

"And what's that got to do with my eyes?"

"Before I tell you, are you willing to admit something—
providing you think it's true?"

"Sure." Larry was getting impatient. His cigarette burned
his fingers, smoked too far down. He stepped it out on the
concrete floor.

"Will you admit," asked Gaskell slowly, "that some of your
pictures may actually be wrong?"

"They're okay to me," said Larry. Nobody living was going
to tell him his picture of Judy might be wrong.

"I mean wrong to people with eyes," said Gaskell. "Will
you admit your picture of me, say, and a picture of me taken
by a kodak may be entirely different, even though your own
idea of how I look is right to you?"

"Sure," said Larry after a time. The admission wouldn't
change his pictures, right or wrong.

"Okay," said Gaskell. "Now take off the cheaters and I'll
give you the lowdown."

Larry cautiously removed his black glasses and held them
by the frame, swinging them between thumb and finger.

Gaskell said, "Your eyes look swell. I can't tell the plastic
from the real one, so don't tell me. There's a small red scar
near the end of your right eyebrow and the eye's a little drawn.
You might have been in a motor crash. If anything, it gives
you a slightly rakish look that would draw the gals like flies
to honey, if you'd shed those glasses."

"I don't believe it," said Larry.

"I know you don't," Gaskell told him. "That's the main
thing that's eating you. You're in danger, Larry. You're a

swell-looking guy—dark-haired, brown-eyed, a straight nose and fine teeth. Your face lights up like a movie actor when you laugh or even smile."

He paused, and Larry said nothing. He was thinking of the morning when he stood before the mirror at Valley Forge—a mirror he'd never see—and wondered what he looked like. He was thinking of the night he first kissed Judy when the shutter opened and showed him the horrible picture, the picture of a guy with a twisted face and a plastic eye.

"The danger is," Gaskell continued, "that you're going to lose every friend you have, and possibly every girl."

Larry's lips moved numbly. "I haven't any friends to lose."

"Nuts," said Gaskell. "The trouble is you're too damn good at beating your blindness. You've built too damn much faith in yourself and not enough in others. But your belief in yourself doesn't take in enough. It skips your fine appearance.

"You'll believe me in a second when I tell you you're about to hit a door. You know that I can see the door, and that I wouldn't lie. You'll believe me when I tell you that your hair's okay, or when I help you to adjust your necktie.

"So you're losing your friends by being a grouch, and seldom laughing, and drinking too much. You're losing your life by refusing to believe that any girl could love you. I can't see the pictures, Larry, that you've built in your mind about others, but I can see you. The picture you have of yourself is wrong. I don't know where you got it, but it's wrong. For the love of God, Larry, throw away those movie star glasses and let the world take a look at Nevin! You're worrying about nothing when you worry about the looks of that plastic eye."

Gaskell gently plucked the glasses from between Larry's thumb and finger. "Can I keep these for you?"

Larry grinned. "What the hell will I wear, Tony, when I feel like I want to cry?"

"Black crepe," said Gaskell. "And I'll give you a sponge to mop that plastic eye."

Larry heard him get up, go out, and close the door.

With the closing of the door Larry found himself possessed of a strange elation, pleasant and not a little frightening. Once he had sat in a dentist's chair and taken gas. At some point of the administration he had seemed to be God. A vast understanding was given him, an ability to look at himself as an object suspended in a globe of timeless space. Events surrounded him clearly, everything that would sometime come, everything that had gone before.

He had much the same feeling of utter depersonalization, when Gaskell closed the door. He could see himself sitting detached and looking very handsome—understanding himself and his crying need.

Maybe Judy wanted *him*. Maybe she saw him with Gaskell's eyes. Maybe she'd come—God in heaven, what was he waiting for?

There was money in his bedroom, tucked away in a wallet in the drawer. He got there somehow, missing the path a dozen times and banging into a door.

Coming down the stairs again, he moved more calmly. The stone stairs curved in a spiral. Larry stuck close to the right-hand side where the stairs were broad by the wall.

He had to send a telegram. Judy had no phone in Phoenix-ville. God, what a dope he was not to have written! How the hell did you telegraph when your eyes were gone? It was part of the training he hadn't yet had, although Gaskell had taught him on the dummy how to dial a phone.

Well, he'd send it somehow, or kill himself trying. This was a message he wouldn't entrust to anyone. It was this constant necessity of thinking about the simplest functions of life that was getting him down. From the moment your feet hit the floor in the morning until you searched for the bed covers to pull them up at night, every tiniest motion, every desire, was a mental chore.

At the bottom of the stairs he turned left, walked a few steps and went through a door into the quadrangle. He kept straight across, following the flagstone path, and found another door which led into a lobby similar to the one he'd just left.

All the four lobbies were similar at Old Farms—so similar that once you lost your bearings, you couldn't tell which of the four you were in.

Across the second lobby was another door. He passed through that, found grass at the right-hand edge of a flagstone path and followed it around.

The way became tricky. A small island of grass and bushes split the path. Larry's hand scraped the bushes and he wished he had his cane.

He bore off to the left and located the door to the mess hall —two doors, really, and tough to get through.

Mothers wondering why their sons didn't write! Sweethearts wondering why the boys didn't send them telegrams! Nothing to it at all.

Inside of the doors he kept on past the place where he picked up his tray at mealtimes; straight through the kitchen —one step up—and watch it too! He stopped a second, becoming stubborn, trying hard to picture it all.

He had it again. On through the room where you dumped your garbage and cleaned your tray after eating, then through another doorway and turn left in a hall.

Somewhere there were wooden steps—a booby trap. He remembered them keenly. The first time he'd tried them, he'd taken a nasty fall. He felt his way cautiously along the right-hand wall.

The steps turned sharp to the left when two-thirds down, but he made them safely. He was in a hall which turned sharp right a little farther on.

That was easy. He made the turn and walked with unhesitating confidence to the end of the hall. The PX was there, and off to the right a model newsstand where later on he'd have to work for training. Right now it was quite familiar, for he'd brailled it all.

A girl's voice spoke. "What can I do for you?"

"I want change for a five, please." There were two five-dollar bills in one compartment of his wallet and some ones in another. The fives were folded in a special form. He'd wondered at first why they gave him no special wallet. "They're hard to replace," Gaskell had told him. "Get yourself familiar with using any kind at all."

Larry put down a five and received four bills and some silver, then asked for change for another dollar. There were public telephone booths in the lounge and money had to be deposited for the telegram the same as for a long-distance call.

He sorted out his quarters, dimes, and nickels, then retraced his steps until he reached the lounge. There he skirted several rows of vacant chairs and found a booth at the back. He went inside, sat down, and carefully closed the door. He deposited a nickel, dialed the operator and before she could answer him hung up the phone. The nickel came back.

His mind had gone blank.

What was he doing? It struck him full force that this wire might mean marriage. Certainly it meant that he was deserting Chris forever—turning directly for company to another girl. Would Chris come North if he wired? She would like hell! Judy liked to kiss him and hold him close. Judy liked to—what? He hadn't written. He hadn't done anything. He'd sat around like a silly dope letting loneliness eat at his soul. He'd never know what Judy liked if he didn't put his money in the telephone.

For the first time he wished he knew more Braille. You could punch out a message in no time with a stylus, and at least read it over. Well, now his heart must write the wire instead of his head.

He deposited the nickel and asked the operator for Western Union.

"I want to send a telegram, please—Miss Judy Greene, 196 Gay St., Phoenixville, Pennsylvania.

"May I come to see you my next week-end pass? I feel terribly alone."

He hesitated just a second, then added "Love" and signed it, "Larry."

All afternoon he walked on air. He'd done the right thing and nothing could affect him now. They'd do up Hartford together—they'd do up the world together. He'd make a million and build her the world's most beautiful home.

At four o'clock he was summoned to the telephone and dashed crazily into the lounge to bark his shins on a chair.

"Are you Sergeant Larry Nevin?"

"Yes."

"Did you send a message to—"

"Miss Judy Greene, 196 Gay St., Phoenixville, Pennsylvania. Yes. What's the answer?"

"Your message wasn't delivered, sir. The party has moved."

"Did you forward the message?"

"The party left no address, sir. She has quit her job in Phoenixville. She's no longer there."

At five o'clock the news of Franklin D. Roosevelt's death came in over the air.


## 29. THE TERROR BY NIGHT

IN A LIFE of perpetual blackness there was no logical reason why night should be different from day. Yet Larry knew that doubts and fears always crystallized with the approach of bedtime, growing in proportion as midnight came, and lingering to haunt him through the smaller hours of morning until sleep finally drove them away.

Subconsciously, although he had never discussed it, he realized that the other fellows felt the same. Many of them deliberately sat up half the night writing letters, listening to the radio or Talking Books, or practicing softly on various musical instruments they were learning to play. Those who went into Hartford for the evening seldom returned before the last bus out from town.

To Larry, as to most of the boys, Old Farms Convalescent Hospital was an entity endowed with life. Unable to see it, it assumed a personality full of definite reactions. Living and breathing in tune with its trainees, its heartbeats, pulsebeats and spirits rose and fell with their own.

On the night of President Roosevelt's death the spirit of Old Farms was very low. Unaware politically, the fellows since their blindness had unconsciously found a strong measure of protection in the only President any of them had really ever known. He had become a timeless symbol. He had taken care of their families in adversity, banished fear, and fathered them through the bloodiest of conflicts until victory was close at hand.

What matter if, blind, they'd never see him? His kindly tired face, deep with humor and understanding, was engraved on every blind boy's memory. He was *there*. Sooner or later he'd visit them again, sit down with them personally to discuss the nation's problems. He could be summoned like a genii by twisting the knob on a radio. When he said "My friends!" he meant my friends. You could stretch out a hand through the blackness and touch him in every Old Farms room.

Then he was gone. Death in the afternoon. More than death, for with his passing an era had passed on.

Larry was tired of playing soldier. He was sick to death of being brave, of facing life with sightless eyes and smiling face. He was fed to the teeth with training to be useful and to carry on.

Judy had vanished; the President was dead. Larry wanted to bury his face in his mother's apron and cry. He'd fought to the death and now he was beaten.

He was blind. He didn't know what was coming and had no one to cling to and no one to love him. He was going to be independent, by God, and the only way a blind man could be independent was to die.

You could learn things up to a point and then you were cooked. You could sugar your coffee, but somebody had to find you the sugar. The sugar was love—"I'll tell the fellows there are some things that dough can't buy!"

The road was very clear now. He could walk it again without an error—now that it was too damned late for a second try. The answer was that you had to have a woman with you—a woman who loved and didn't fear you.

She'd have to love you, for you needed a hell of a lot of attention. She'd have to have brains and a steady hand, for it would always be her job to drive the car. The world was reversed. You needed more than a mother. You needed a woman with love so great and such strength of heart she could be both wife and husband and never let you know it. You needed Judy.

He was blind and lost for the very first time. He'd traveled alone and couldn't return. He'd gone too fast and too far.

Now the whole stinking business was whirling in a burst of red dots as the world had spun after he was hit in France. Nothing was clear, except the fact that he understood everything in the way he'd understood while under gas in the dentist's chair.

He was drunk without being drunk. His brain was in a turmoil with the stimulation of realization, cloudy with the deadly methyl alcohol of hopelessness.

And Christ almighty, he was trying to rationalize, trying to sum up his perceptions of nothing! Jimsey—Judy—Chris—his father and mother—Joe Morgan—Ivan Stern—they were nothing because he couldn't see them.

Masterson was a Dartmouth graduate—nothing. Hamilton was—what? Hamilton never said anything, just sat quietly listening. Hamilton hadn't the life of Roosevelt—and the President was dead. But the President's voice had been alive on the air. Damn it all, you couldn't sit quietly around blind men and say nothing. If you did you became nothing. Unless you moved they didn't know you were there.

Yet that's exactly what Larry Nevin was doing right now—sitting in the small black cubicle of his room and saying nothing. Well, he felt like nothing—so what the hell did he care?

There were others in the room—others who persisted in jumbling together—Joe Morgan, sitting beside him and contaminating white men; Jack Moses, blacker by far than Joe Morgan, who after all had red hair. By looking hard it was easy to see Joe's bright red thatch flaming like a stop light against the wall.

On the bed, Colonel Diamond was remembering—remembering better than Larry. For the life of him, Larry couldn't remember how many times the colonel had read the Bible. Was it four, or forty, or two?

The colonel kept quoting things, as though that was going to help anybody. His voice blended in with a radio that was intoning down the hall—

"He shall cover thee with his feathers, and under his wings shalt thou trust: his truth shall be thy shield and buckler." That was either the radio or the colonel, or maybe both.

Well, damned if Larry Nevin wanted to be covered with a lot of feathers or with a shield and buckler either. He wanted Judy, and that was all.

"Thou shalt not be afraid for the terror by night; nor for the arrow that flieth by day; nor for the pestilence that walketh in darkness; nor for the destruction that wasteth at noonday." That was definitely Colonel Diamond speaking.

"That's a nice deal, Colonel—particularly when everything scares the ass off of me. I'm extra fond of the pestilence that walketh in darkness," said the voice of Ivan Stern.

Larry kept forgetting Ivan was there—and Grebe, and Masterson, and Hamilton. How the hell could you pack them all in the camera box? Or maybe they were sitting in his room.

The answer was quite apparent if you gave it thought. You were nothing; the world was nothing. So none of this crazy foolishness was happening at all.

"A thousand shall fall at thy side, and ten thousand at thy right hand—

(Fell into a bramblebush
And scratched 'em in again!)
but it shall not come nigh thee."

"That's a fine lot of horse manure," said Hamilton unexpectedly, answering either God, the colonel, or the radio.
"We're the unlucky bastards included in the thousand that
shall fall."

God, the radio, or Colonel Diamond answered him back:
"Only with thine eyes shalt thou behold and—"

"Turn that goddam stinking thing off—before I throw it
out of the window and you with it!" The voice that yelled
came from outside and was high with hysterical anger.

The dormitory was silent except for the tick of a clock somewhere.

The colonel whispered, "Only with thine eyes shalt thou behold and see the reward of the wicked."

"The Bible's plum' full o' eyes, ain't it?" remarked Jack
Moses. "Mine eyes also shall see mah desires on mah enemies—"

"Not this year, bud," said Masterson, "and neither shall I lift
mine up to the hills, because they're up on a hill already."

Larry Nevin and a colonel were entertaining Negroes in
Larry Nevin's room. Or maybe they were sitting in a camera
box. Of course they couldn't be there either, for Larry Nevin
was blind and for the rest of his life must wander in darkness
alone.

The doors were thin between buildings. Larry could hear
the muffled sound of soft chords strummed on a guitar. The
player started to whistle.

Larry thought of Corporal Bruce back in Valley Forge.
"He doesn't hear you, Sergeant. He's deaf and blind and
minus an arm. When he's feeling tops, he whistles. None of
us mind."

That was long ago. It was white of the nurse not to mind
the corporal's whistling. The corporal probably had a girl
somewhere. So he'd lost his eyes, his ears and his arm. What
the hell was the difference! His girl liked what was left of

him. Nothing made any difference if you found someone to care.

Grebe said, "I always went for machinery. I've worked all my life. My old man, too. I stuck my neck into this on my own, feelin' it was the right thing to do. I don't know nothin' about Russia or nothin', but I had a hunch—"

Everybody waited, but Grebe didn't go on.

"I have a silver plate in my head," said Colonel Diamond. "A Diamond plated with silver."

Old Farms was listening—a guitar, a radio, a Talking Book— meaningless sounds seeping through perpetual night.

How could you live without anyone to love you? How could you find a girl who was hopelessly gone? "Dear Mr. Greene— Winchendon, Toy Town, Massachusetts— Where's your daughter who loved the crazy boy named Paul? I have a good match for her now—a brainy G.I. whose eyes are gone."

"—a billion, three hundred million ounces of silver all in bars," Colonel Diamond was saying. "Isn't that a lot of silver? We could have used that metal instead of tin back in 'forty-two, but the Senators kept the price up. It was nice of the Senators to protect the price of silver. The Diamonds have always been in the jewelry business—"

Words whirled around you when a girl was gone. The only thing you needed to fear was fear.

"We had to get tin from Bolivia," the colonel was saying, "then ship it to England for refining, then back here for plating, then over to England again. We couldn't use silver for metal parts in tanks and ships and trucks and bombs. Silver's expensive like this plate in my head. What would people say? Can you picture the rage and ranting at the man who died today? My son was on a tin ship—"

"So the price of silver stayed up," said Ivan Stern softly.

"Yes," said the colonel, "the price stayed up, but my only son went down one day."

It must be close to morning, for Old Farms was very still. People came into your life and talked and all that you knew about them was from what you heard them say. This one was black and that one was white, this one old and that one young, this one had children and that one none. This one was blind and that one could see.

"Thou shalt not be afraid for the terror by night; nor for the arrow that flieth by day." Larry added a verse of his own— "Thou shalt only fear the people who insist that everything be made to pay."

Jack Moses said suddenly, "Ah'm glad I'se blind, and glad that you is too, Joe Morgan. Ah'm glad every nigger that's blind is blind. All we's got is pensions—but we's that many less niggers left for the whites to screw."

Larry got up and left the room. The wall of the stairs felt very damp as he cautiously followed it down. Out in the quadrangle the air was chill with the touch of dawn. He walked slowly to the center where the flagstone paths crossed at right angles.

There, he stopped.

Strange that he had never thought about Old Farms being an expensive prep school for boys. The former students were pressing about him now, shadows walking through him, busy with ghostly work and play.

Larry was suddenly all of them put together—Larry Nevin, symbol again—all of the former students and all of the blind alumni. He was all the boys of a thousand schools wondering what the schools had failed to teach them.

Was the science too thorough? Was the economy too rigid? Were the social graces helpful when you bumped ground in an L.S.T.?

Was there ever a course in any school called "There, but for the grace of God, go I"?

He was blind, alone, and without much knowledge to help him. Straight and erect he stood in the center of Old Farms feeling like a flagpole—a naked flagpole towering up in the dawn. The banners of learning and education should be flying, but none were there. Larry Nevin, flagpole—after the flag was down.

## 30.  BLIND DATE

"HI, LARRY!" Ivan Stern was calling from the hall.

"What?"

"Let's go! Hamilton and Masterson are waiting. A bus pulls out at six-fifteen."

"I'm not going."

"The hell you're not! Put your clothes on."

"They're not off."

"Well, put 'em on anyway. Make yourself decent. We've got a girl lined up for you in town."

"That's why I'm not going." Larry pushed the bolt, locking his bedroom door, and turned to his Talking Book machine.

It had become quite possible to live in a shell. In fact, he had developed a rare ability to turn himself into many different things almost at will—symbols, flagpoles, and various types of shells and vessels for the world to pour knowledge in.

Since the night he learned Judy was gone, he had been a shell. Inside, he was a hermit crab, carrying his sightless body around from place to place with swiftly increasing skill.

A hermit crab had a very simplified nervous system and required little food and a minimum of sex life to sustain it. The outside world was scarcely, if ever, interested in its heartbreaks and love affairs. Let anyone attempt to approach it, and it immediately retired within its house, neatly sealing itself in. A hermit crab never acted the part of an ignorant fool, trying to buy breasts and love when both were freely offered. A hermit crab . . .

There was a banging on the door. "Look! You're going, if we have to carry you. I'll get Masterson and we'll break the door down, or beat on it all evening. We're damned sick of you sitting around all night listening to that Talking Book machine."

"It's more interesting than you and your gals." The talking record wasn't making sense above Ivan's disturbance. Larry was thinking of Corinne. He certainly wasn't going through any such experience again. The humiliation was too much to take.

Footsteps sounded in the hall. There was a conference in whispers. Masterson's voice said, "Larry, let me in."

"No. God, you guys are persistent! Why don't you let me alone?"

"Because we know what's good for you."

"You think you do. I met one of your girls."

Masterson groaned. "Okay. You'll sit alone for the rest of your life. Corinne told me you didn't like her. So what? There are others. We'll skip the dames if you don't want to meet them, but let's have a drink together."

Larry reached out and shut off the Talking Book machine. So Corinne had told the fellows he didn't like her—taken all the blame herself. He was unbelievably stupid, picturing her spreading the story of what had happened in her apartment. Not satisfied with misjudging her once, he'd done it again.

He had quit wearing his glasses at Gaskell's suggestion. That was helpful as hell, if he sat in his room all the time. Judy was gone. The letters from Chris were getting fewer and colder.

"Are you coming?" asked Ivan.

"Yes," said Larry. He unbolted the door and opened it. "Come on in."

"We'll wait out here. Hurry up. The bus leaves at six-fifteen."

Larry found a shirt and put it on, then tied his tie, brushed his hair, and got into his jacket. It felt stiff and confining, reminding him of the Army again. You could forget the Army at Old Farms and at least wear comfortable clothes all day, as long as you kept yourself clean.

"Coming?"

"Nearly ready." Larry found his cane. That was something, at any rate. You could take your cane when you went downtown.

He went out into the hall and stopped a moment at the C.Q.'s desk so the detachment man could look him over. "Okay?"

"God!" the C.Q. exclaimed ecstatically. "You're beautiful!"

"At least," said Larry with a grin, "I don't have to look at you. I'm on my way."

Hamilton and Masterson were waiting in the downstairs hall when Larry and Ivan came down. Outside, the bus rolled up with its usual swoosh on the packed dirt road. The four of them slipped into the press of fellows moving forward to board the bus.

Larry got in easily, finding the steps with his cane. He might be a hermit crab, but he was turning into a wonderful machine with arms and legs that felt around like tentacles.

Busses were becoming as familiar as his bedroom. There was a model set of bus steps set up in the orientation clinic, and Gaskell had taken particular delight in training him to use them. His leg muscles had fallen into a pattern until he knew without thinking exactly how high a bus step was from the ground.

Once in, he located an empty seat just by knowing nobody was sitting in it. His ability to do that was still a mystery, even to himself.

Only that morning, in the testing clinic, he had sat in front of a movable screen set on tracks thirty feet long, and pulled the screen slowly toward him by turning a wheel. A metronome was ticking in the corner. Suddenly, he was conscious of the same sensation he felt in the handball court at Valley Forge—the falling of a shadow across his face, the blackening of something already black.

He had released the wheel and told Dr. Seldin, "I think I can feel the screen."

"About how far?" the doctor asked.

Larry had thought a moment, trying to picture a six-foot man lying between the tracks stretched out before him. "It feels as though the screen had stopped exactly seventeen feet away."

"Are you guessing?"

"No, sir, I don't think I am. Somehow the whole track seems clear to me. Maybe I can never do it again, but I'll stake my life that screen has stopped at seventeen."

"You have extraordinary hearing, Larry," the doctor had told him. "The screen's exactly at seventeen."

Masterson called from the back of the bus, "Where are you, Larry?"

"On the left side four seats in."

"Where's Ivan?"

"Here beside Larry," said Stern.

"Where are you going?"

"Bond Hotel first." Ivan paused. "Some girls are meeting us there."

"Then what?"

"Bowling, maybe. What about it, Larry?"

"I don't care. Anything suits me." Loneliness had gripped him again, sullenly tightening a vise about him.

"Pliable, isn't he?" Oscar Hamilton's voice put in. "How did you blast him out of his shell, Ivan?"

"He's woman-crazy," said Ivan. "He really couldn't stand the idea that I'd lined up something luscious for him. What about it, Larry?"

Larry said, "I'd rather bowl. You sex-starved guys get me down."

"A man can't live by brain alone," said Ivan. "Talking Books have their place, but it isn't in a bedroom. I like something that wriggles when I braille it. A Talking Book record just keeps going round and round."

The bus doors closed and the bus moved on.

Ivan got up. "Don't let anybody grab my seat. I'll be back in a minute."

The bus slowed and stopped at the entrance to Old Farms, then started again, swinging in a ponderous left-hand turn and heading toward town.

Larry Nevin was certainly a clever fellow. He had adjusted his life in no time at all. He had lost his eyes, but, God, what a marvelous hunk of man had been left to him! He walked like Mussolini: arms swinging free, chest stuck out, and chin set firm. He knew when a screen stopped seventeen feet away.

In the future, that rare ability was bound to be helpful as hell. He'd be a big insurance executive. . . . At least, he was trying hard to learn, studying like the devil to answer a million questions. Anyhow, he'd have a private office and ring the bell. Miss Price would come in, or possibly Miss Matthews. The names sounded very efficient. . . .

*"Come in, Miss Price. Would you mind sitting down? There's a chair exactly seventeen feet from the desk here. Would you pour me a drink of water? My thermos bottle is seventeen feet from the desk, by the wall."* Or, *"I wish you wouldn't cross your legs, Miss Matthews. It gets them slightly out of focus. Take a letter, please. Messrs. Price and Matthews, 17 East 17th Street. We are shipping you on the 17th seventeen life insurance policies for seventeen dollars each. These run for seventeen years."*

He'd certainly never get involved with a woman if he kept them all seventeen feet away. Maybe if he lived long enough, he'd grow an arm seventeen feet long. He could reach out with it and pat a fanny.

The bus picked up speed, and someone sat down beside him. A woman had taken Ivan's seat.

Larry said nothing.

It was fun to sit there in silence and build a body for her, a creation of his own. She was young and very beautiful and had smooth dark hair. He knew a lot of other things about her too, intimate details much better kept to himself. She'd be quite embarrassed if he burst out suddenly with a description of the color and texture of her underwear. Nor could he tell her about her slender throat and the way it sloped, cascading down into beautiful curves that were soft and firm.

So he'd had his chance and muffed it. There was only one girl who looked like that, a girl who had once loved a crazy guy. He'd known her in Phoenixville, and let her slip through his fingers. That was before he became a hermit crab, carting around his empty shell.

The bus slowed down for Farmington and made a stop. More people got in. Larry took out a cigarette and the girl beside him struck a match and lit it.

"Thanks," he said. She had a nerve. As a matter of fact, she was damned officious. He was quite capable of doing things for himself without anyone helping. He could tell a china goat just by feeling it. He knew how to serve himself and eat his dinner. He'd even brailled a railroad—counted the seats, felt the baggage racks, and discovered how to tell the men's room from the ladies'.

The girl beside him had no right to wear that particular perfume. Or was she actually wearing it? Its odor was always with him, and would be for life. It had followed him from Phoenixville to Florida, and back again to Old Farms, building pictures as it permeated the air.

The world lay open before him. The hell with the perfume! He could run a chicken farm if he wanted to. Wetnurse ten thousand lousy hens and listen to their cackling troubles. He was learning Braille, speeding up his typing. He could be a top mechanic—tear down engines and accurately diagnose motor trouble by touch and sound. He could own a garage and run one.

He liked Lieutenant Brisbane, but at times the officer was terribly dumb. Of course, the lieutenant couldn't know about the wall and Jimsey. "You've a good mechanical background, Larry. You have great manual dexterity. Why don't you follow up our course in gasoline engines, industrial skills and power machinery?"

"I'm afraid I prefer insurance, sir."

The tires on the bus were singing.

*The tires on the truck were singing. It was slewing sideways, jolting him to pieces. "I've made this haul so many times, I can drive it blindfold."*

"Like hell," said Jimsey. "There we go again."

*The lichens descended in ripples and rills; and next to the lichens, the wall had been shot away.*

"Can you sit up, Jimsey?"

*"I'm in bed now with a nice warm babe."*

Lieutenant Brisbane wanted him to work on trucks. The lieutenant couldn't possibly know there was a truck locked up in Larry Nevin's screwy brain. He never wanted to touch a truck again.

He never wanted to touch a woman again, not unless she was seventeen feet away. There was a woman locked up in his screwy brain, and all his life every woman would be just like her.

Take this one beside him now. She thought she'd tricked him. Ivan, Masterson, and Hamilton thought they were smart as hell. They'd brought her out from Hartford, set her down beside him and thought he'd fall for that perfume in her hair. Well, he didn't even intend to speak. He'd trick them all by changing her into the only woman he wanted there.

The perfume was strong and wonderful as heaven. And he was so goddam lonesome he thought he'd die. So, let her sit beside him in silence, and for a time he'd know she was Judy. Once he got into Hartford, he'd fill himself up with whisky and wouldn't care.

Whisky was unquestionably the thing. Blindness ran you into pockets, let you in for the same illusions that the Army wished on you—even when you had eyes that could see. Illusions weren't good, and lots of whisky brought you back to sanity again. Your senses became properly dulled, and over-keen senses did nothing but let you in for trouble.

Full of whisky, you would never kid yourself, never allow yourself to love anyone to a point of madness. Drunk, you didn't give a damn about people who sat beside you in a crowded bus. You quit building bodies, ceased entirely the fruitless pastime of endowing women with personalities other than their own. When he was drunk every girl in the world wasn't Judy.

Yet he wasn't drunk and he knew damn well that Judy was there. An inner peace and comfort had filled him as soon as she sat down. He could ride beside Judy in silence; ride beside her forever. The restlessness, that had grown steadily worse with every passing day, was missing.

This was no hallucination. This was no happy dream to be brushed away by a dawn he couldn't see. Somehow she'd found him. Through some great miracle she'd sensed his need and come to take her place beside him. The fellows might do lots of things, but they'd never try to fool him about Judy. There were some things that they understood too well. He didn't need eyes to know she was there. He didn't need the smell of perfume. Her presence had transformed the world from turbulence to calm.

Yet not until he heard her voice was he freed from the crushing fear that he might be wrong.

"Hello, soldier. Why so glum?"

"It had to be you, Judy." His throat was tight and the words came in a whisper. He said them again, afraid she couldn't hear.

"I missed you in Phoenixville when you came back from your furlough."

"Yes," said Larry. "I tried to find you. You weren't there."

"You never wrote me, soldier."

"I wired, but the wire came back. You weren't there."

"By that time, Larry, I was on my way up here." She took

his hand. His fingers tightened crushingly. If he ever let go, he'd find she wasn't there.

"What are you doing in Hartford, Judy?"

She was silent for a second. "I know quite a lot about insurance. Isn't Hartford the logical place? I have a job up here."

"Is that the only reason?" He tried to keep it from sounding like a desperate plea.

"No," said Judy. "I know a stubborn idiot at Old Farms who keeps things locked so tight in himself that one of his friends who's not so blind as he is had to write me."

"Stern mixes into everything," said Larry.

"It wasn't Ivan," said Judy. "The letter that brought me up here came from a guy named Joe."

## 31. LIGHTS OUT

THE tunnel stretched from Hartford to New York, from Connecticut to New York and on to all points in every direction, world without end. It was the longest tunnel in the world.

Riding with Judy in the chair car, the tunnel had windows. She could open the windows by merely speaking and painting little pictures with words—the station platform at Wallingford, the troop train waiting beside you at New Haven, the kid on crutches who looked so thin.

The tunnel held no terrors with Judy in the Pullman chair beside you. Reach out your hand and touch her arm, make sure she was there, and one of the friendly windows would open, dispelling the blackness by letting sunshine in.

There wasn't any smoke in the tunnel. The air was clean and touched with perfume. The train moved through the tunnel smoothly, taking its time like a lazy boat carrying you through the tunnel of love where lovers held hands forever and nobody seemed to care.

"Judy."

"What is it, soldier?" She hadn't gone and she wasn't asleep.

"I just wanted to make quite sure that you were still there."

"I'll always be beside you, darling."

"Judy."

"What now, soldier?"

"Did we really get married this morning?"

"That's what they tell me, Sergeant Nevin. Weren't you there?"

"Yes, but I didn't see much of it. You're sure that minister wasn't a phony?"

"He came highly recommended, darling. He certainly looked real enough. He was wearing a surplice, and had nice white hair." Paper crackled, and she put a parchment-like sheet into Larry's hand, then took one of his fingers and moved it along a line. "In case you don't believe it, Mr. Nevin, it says, 'Mrs. Larry Nevin' right *there.*"

"I hope it's decorated with a couple of bare angels to make it official, Mrs. Nevin." He returned the marriage certificate. "Take good care of it, Judy."

"Just try to get away, Mr. Nevin."

"I don't want to get away." The sun was bright through the windows in the tunnel. "Judy, darling, what made you care?"

"It couldn't possibly have been you, could it, Larry? That grin of yours at the moment when I think the world looks blackest to you? Or maybe the touch of your hand, or the tiny wave in your hair?"

He was silent for a while, then, "Do I remind you of Paul?"

"No, no, Larry." Her denial was fierce. "It's because you're so different, so damned independent in your own sweet way. You take things in, Larry—digest them, ask questions, try to find out what makes the world move on. Paul was mentally unbalanced. You'll never be unbalanced, Larry. I love you because you have a brain."

"I hope so, darling. Anyhow, I adore you. Just stick around, and life will never be dark to me again."

He leaned his head against the chair back, closed his sightless eyes, and listened to the noise of the speeding train.

With the coming of Judy to Hartford, his training had suddenly ceased to be training and had taken on form. All he had learned at Valley Forge and at Old Farms had fused together, assuming a new relationship. Each painful step became, in itself, of relatively small importance. The concrete whole was all that mattered.

The first fearful steps at Valley Forge were forgotten, his furlough home, the trip to Hartford. The stumbling, groping efforts to orient at Old Farms had become no more than unpleasant items, partly erased from memory.

Left to him now, on his wedding day, were surety of travel; confidence when eating; obstacle perception, which might be bettered by diligent practice, but which really only worked under diligent concentration; ease in dressing and handling his personal grooming; poise in social contacts; and a primary knowledge of insurance, a business at which he hoped someday to make his living.

This was his Ph.D. in blindness, the diploma he would carry soon from Old Farms. It seemed like a damned slim dowry to bring to a girl who loved him for his brain!

Everything had been made so easy. The Station Master at Hartford had personally seen to their baggage and escorted them to the Pullman. Captain Welch at Old Farms had made their reservations. Lieutenant Robinson had secured the minister. Every officer from Colonel Maitland down had wished them luck and happiness.

Yet the very fact that he wasn't fooled was an indication of dawning perception, an added pointer to the fact that Larry Nevin was forming new standards of value, standards that would mature and become more accurate during the coming years.

The attentions given to him and Judy, that unostentatious

easing of marriage and honeymoon, were not for Mr. and
Mrs. Larry Nevin, members of the general public. The attentions were for Sergeant Larry Nevin, blinded in action.
He was riding for the present, his way made smooth, on the
well-inflated tires of war emotion. He and Judy were recipients
of partial remuneration from a staggering debt that the nation
was trying in vain to pay.

Strange that a single thought in an instant had swept away
twenty-three years of his life. Suddenly, sitting in the chair
car with Judy, he found himself one with every Negro and
every Jew, one with every sensitive soul who had ever been
buried in the hell of a lost minority.

Understanding of a hundred happenings since he had lost
his eyes flooded through him—the party in Palatka; the break-
up with Chris; his friendship with Ivan Stern; his liking for,
and his stilted unsatisfactory attempt to get anywhere with,
Joe.

Yet Joe had understood enough to write to Judy when
Larry was about to let her slip from his life forever. That
wasn't the understanding of black for white. It was the understanding of one blind man for another.

Damn it to hell! With Judy's help, he'd break down Joe.
He'd wipe from Joe's mind the color of skin and the false
traditions that stood between them. Maybe he could even
teach Joe to think that Larry Nevin was black, as he had
learned to picture Joe with bright red hair.

Joe had come to their wedding that morning at Judy's in-
vitation. Larry had forgotten his color completely. Afterward
they'd lunched together—Hamilton, Masterson, Colonel Diamond, Joe Morgan, and Ivan Stern.

Blindness was power. You could do the things you knew
were right, and the world dared not gainsay you. Hell, Larry
didn't know how the minister looked, or what he wore. None
of the boys at the wedding knew. None of them knew if a man
was well dressed, or a woman well groomed and pretty. None

of them knew a black from a white, a rich man from a laborer, a Catholic from a Protestant, a Gentile from a Jew.

But all of them knew the ones who loved them, all of them knew selfishness from stinginess, all of them knew the right from the wrong. All of them knew that the world refused to think of, or understand, blindness just as it equally refused to think of, or understand, a Negro or a Jew.

As a matter of fact, there were a hell of a lot of important things that any blind man knew.

He reached out and Judy took his hand. It was heaven to cling to her hand and not to care if passengers were watching. He'd bought her an orchid. He leaned over closer and let his fingers brush it and toy with the ribbon.

"Happy, soldier?"

"What do *you* think?"

"Come, come. Speak up, man! Say something sweet. I've had a permanent and you've never even mentioned it. Blistering myself under a hot machine for you, darling, all day yesterday. Be complimentary!"

He touched her hair. "It's lovely!" He moved his hand very gently. The halo which crowned her was cloudy gold, caressing his fingers. Roughness might dispel it. "I love you, Judy."

"And I you, soldier."

She'd always call him soldier. Even when his uniform was packed away.

They had reservations at the Commodore Hotel. He'd never been in New York before, and the station seemed quiet. He'd expected bustle and confusion. Judy told him of the cathedral size, where sound was lost. He could feel it too. They walked an endless distance, with nothing but the swish of feet and muted voices around him.

After a while she guided him through a revolving door. His feet sank in carpets as they walked upstairs.

"Do we take a taxi?"

Judy laughed. "Idiot. We're in the Commodore lobby. Our baggage is already here."

He stayed close by her, touching her hand. There was perfume in the lobby, and lots of women. When they looked at Judy, how envious they and their men must feel. None of the women smelled so nice as Mrs. Nevin. None of them wore a halo in her hair.

Their room was waiting. An elevator shot them skyward endlessly. His hand closed tight on Judy's arm. He put his lips very close to her ear and whispered, "This is a hell of a big hotel."

Once in the room he was happy to feel he could find it again, or retrace his steps through the station to the train. He might be wrong, but the satisfying confidence was there.

The bellboy left and Judy took him around the room and bathroom and let him braille. He tried to stop his hands from trembling, and wondered if she noticed.

"What about cocktails in the lobby, soldier?" She smacked her lips. "Mr. and Mrs. Nevin might celebrate with a vurra sma' drap o' good champagne distributed in a number of cocktails."

"That's a strange combination of Scotch and French if you ask me, darling, but I like the idea. Is this a radio?"

"A surprise," said Judy, "from the fellows at Old Farms."

It warmed him inside. He washed with care, combed his hair into smoothness, and they returned to the lobby.

A waiter seated them back of palms which brushed Larry's face in passing.

Judy said, "I've a lot to learn, soldier. That won't happen a second time."

"You're better than Gaskill," he told her. "Anyhow, I like you better." He told the waiter, "Champagne cocktails, and *imported* champagne."

They went to "21" for dinner, and moved on to the Stork Club for dancing. New York seemed filled with a hectic excitement that seeped into his blood stream. Tonight he wanted to see it all. It was headier than the champagne. He knew, once more, that his blindness was getting attention; easing them through to tables; bringing them faster service.

Somehow he didn't seem to care. He'd take the favors while they came. It might never happen again.

They were asked to leave at midnight. There was a curfew law, the waiter took care to explain.

In the taxi the music lingered, and the friendly voice of a columnist, and a startling pop of flashlight bulbs. He held on tight to Judy's hand, thinking that the intimate touch might help him. Instead, it hindered. By the time they reached the hotel room he was close to a chill, worried sick about the shutter in his brain.

He stumbled to the writing desk and switched on the radio—

"—rumors that the Nazis have unconditionally surrendered have been denied by President Truman. Himmler's offer to surrender to the Americans and British was refused. No surrender will be accepted unless the three Allied powers—"

It left him even colder. He switched it off again. After you'd seen enough of slaughter it wasn't even exciting to be in at the kill.

How did you watch a woman undress from a plastic eye? She was moving about, opening and closing bureau drawers. She was his to take, providing he could take her. She was his to make the mother of his children—and he couldn't undress. All he could do was shiver and think that in France guns would flash for another night and another day, and maybe longer. And more kids like Jimsey would fertilize the soil; and other kids would walk through life remembering a wall.

"You going to sit up all night, soldier?"

"I'm not very tired—." Merciful God, that sounded feeble! He waited for the light switch to click. In the dark he could undress himself and grope around. Maybe, at last, she'd fall asleep.

"How about my reading some? I brought some books along."

"That would be swell."

"Well, come here and help me. I've finished unpacking. Husbands have some duties, you know—getting wives out of difficult dresses and helping them put things on."

She took his hand and pulled him slowly to his feet. "Try to get this over my head without ruining my permanent, darling. Otherwise, I'll have to sleep with it on."

His hand touched flesh. He ripped at cloth, tearing restraining folds away; holding her close against him; covering her face, her arms, her neck with kisses.

She was life, and love, and everything: the clashing of all the guns in France, the brilliance of flaming rockets. Her tears were salt against his lips, falling like the waterfall of lichens on the ancient wall.

She kissed his eyes, the dark one and the plastic one, and with her kiss the shutter closed forever. She could see his eyes and still she loved them.

The lights were still on.

Later, he lay quiet, thinking, and listening to her gentle breathing beside him.

She'd have a son, a dark-eyed boy with wishful eyes and lots of dreams. Another Larry Nevin to look on life and see the glistening sun.

Once his father, who'd never see him, could do that too. What should his father teach him? What should his father learn, to save his sighted son?

God wasn't money. God was work, and play, and things that grew. God was the woman beside you!

Larry Nevin had been to Dr. Bannerman's Sunday school, but a hell of a lot of good it had done.

He was tough, and hard, and trained to kill. With nearly every word he spoke, he swore. He'd never used his mind at all. Now he was blind as a bat at twenty-three.

What a hell of a way to learn that God wasn't the money your country worshiped—that God was merely loving everyone, black or white or yellow or brown, of every nation!

He felt the bedlight overhead. The bulb was hot. He turned

it out. The room wasn't any blacker. He leaned over gently and pressed a kiss on Judy's lips—the mother of his unseen children, the wife he'd never see.

"Thank you, darling," he whispered, "for having Joe at our wedding."

She murmured something and kissed him. The halo shone around her hair.

Overhead he heard a plane. Maybe the war with Germany was over.

The tunnel stretched from now 'til death. It was the longest tunnel in the world. It led one way with no return, and in it, if your mind worked straight, you saw only things worth seeing. If you peopled it only with beauty and truth, then beauty and truth would remain. If you peopled it with falseness, you traveled for life with intolerance and your journey was long and racked with pain.

You had to fight to show the world that a man or a woman possessed a soul, regardless of creed or color. You had to strive to prove to others that the only blackness was not of the eyes, but blackness of the brain.

You could see a lot from your plastic eye since you'd learned that God wasn't silver—"*The price stayed up,*" said *Diamond. "My only son went down.*"

It was as simple as that.

Larry lay back down on his pillow, and suddenly sat up again. The room was filled with brilliant light, brighter than he'd ever known, brighter than the shells in France, brighter than the halo on Judy's hair.

He'd learned the answer to teach his son: "Love thy neighbour as thyself!" It didn't mean maybe. It meant that your neighbor was everyone.

The light that was flaming would never die. It would grow ever brighter. He couldn't be blind with such a light. It must be that the world was blind—or maybe a hundred and thirty million Americans, too God-damned dumb to see!

THE END